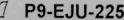

P9-EJU-225

VICTORIA DAHL

REAL MEN Will

HQN™

Recycling programs
for this product may
not exist in your area.

ISBN-13: 978-0-373-77609-2

REAL MEN WILL

Copyright © 2011 by Victoria Dahl

This edition published by arrangement with Harlequin Books S.A.

For questions and comments about the quality of this book
please contact us at Customer_eCare@Harlequin.ca.

® and TM are trademarks of the publisher. Trademarks indicated with
® are registered in the United States Patent and Trademark Office, the
Canadian Trade Marks Office and in other countries.

www.Harlequin.com

Printed in U.S.A.

For my husband.

ACKNOWLEDGMENTS

All the credit for this book goes to my family and friends. The romance community is notoriously supportive, and I felt that support in full this year. I can't possibly name all the friends who helped push me forward, but I'll have to do my very best. Thank you, Lauren, Jami, Courtney, Tessa, Carrie, Julie, Barb, Jeri, Louisa, Zoe, Meljean, Rosemary, Viv, Ann, Megan, RaeAnne, Anne and Carolyn. Jodi, Carrie P. and Lara, thank you too! Whew. It takes a village!

And to Jennifer Echols—
friend, therapist and critique partner extraordinaire—thank you for making me laugh in good times and bad. You're the best.

Thank you to Amy, Tara and Leonore for all your hard work and patience. And thank you to all my wonderful readers!

But most of all, thank you to my amazing husband and the best two boys in the world. I'm so glad we're in this together.

REAL
MEN
Will

CHAPTER ONE

BETH CANTRELL HADN'T thought about him in almost six months.

Well, that wasn't *exactly* true.

Beth cleared her throat and shifted, glancing around as if everyone in the brewery could feel the lie she was telling herself.

The truth was that she'd thought about Jamie Donovan plenty of times. She'd remembered the hour or two they'd shared, she'd fantasized about what might've happened if she'd stayed the whole night in that hotel room.

But in the past six months, she'd never once let herself think about seeing him again. She hadn't considered calling him or making contact in any way. That had been their agreement, after all. One night. One time. No strings attached and no expectations. She'd had to abide by that, because she would never have let herself meet him in that hotel room otherwise.

He wasn't her type. He wasn't part of her social circle. And she definitely wasn't part of his. Beth Cantrell managed the White Orchid, the premiere erotic boutique in Boulder. Her friends were her employees: women she loved like sisters. They were bold and powerful and sexually progressive. And they dated people like themselves: tattooed, pierced, educated and cool.

Absolutely cool, even when they'd only reached the pinnacle of cool by being so incredibly nerdy that they actually circled around to cool again.

Beth, on the other hand, wasn't cool. She was just… Beth. But that was okay, because she was their manager and they loved her, and they did their best to pull her into their sphere. They fixed her up with guys. Friends of theirs. Men they knew and liked. Men who were cool and hip and progressive. And not one of those guys had ever pushed her buttons the way Jamie had.

She still flushed when she thought about him in his tidy polo shirt and khaki pants. His wide white smile and broad shoulders. He'd looked even better in a business suit. The perfect vision of middle-class preppy beauty. And Beth had wanted him so much it hurt.

They'd been strangers, despite this small town. But in that hotel room, with the promise that it would happen only once…the isolation of the act had made it safe. Yet she couldn't stop thinking about him.

And right in the middle of the first good date she'd had in years.

"Hey," her date said as he waved a hand in front of her face. "You okay?" He smiled, taking any sting from the words.

"Sorry." Before she'd started thinking about Jamie, her date had been talking about…something. She racked her brain. Something artsy and important about Robert Mapplethorpe's early career.

"I'm really sorry," she finally said. "I didn't realize how tired I was until the glass of beer hit me. I'm not usually so rude."

He smiled in a way that told her he hadn't taken offense. "I'm glad you didn't mind coming to the party with me. Faron and I have been friends for years. I didn't want to miss it. And I figured you knew her, too."

"Yes, we have mutual friends." The party wasn't the problem. Or the guest of honor. The problem was that Beth had had no idea the party would be at Donovan Brothers Brewery. Not until her date had pulled into the parking lot, and Beth's heart had sunk to her toes.

It wasn't his fault that the party he'd decided to take her to just happened to be at Donovan Brothers.

She'd spent the forty-five minutes since scanning the line of customers and servers at the bar, but Jamie wasn't there. It was pure luck on her part. Jamie Donovan was an owner of the brewery, but he was also a notoriously friendly bartender. Or so she'd heard. When she'd spent time with him, he'd struck her as serious and intense.

She didn't want to see him again like this. Didn't want him to think she'd bring another man to his brewery. She kept expecting Jamie to walk by at any moment, and she couldn't think past the torture of that.

"I'm going to run to the restroom," she blurted out. She watched as her date took a beer from the waitress, giving her a warm, open smile as he said thank-you.

"Do you want me to order you another beer while you're gone?" he asked Beth.

"No, thank you. ..." Her mouth hung open for a moment. Oh, God, she'd forgotten his name. Yes, it was their first date, but he'd been so nice. "No, thank you," she repeated, grabbing her clutch purse and sliding out of her chair so quickly that she nearly stumbled. "I'll be right back."

Unfortunately, she had to walk past the bar to get to the restroom, and her knees felt as if they wanted to buckle under her weight. She scanned the bar, noting that the guy behind the tap was the same slender young man she'd spotted before. Then her eyes raced over the whole room again, her heart drumming a terrified beat.

He wasn't here, thank God. When she reached the short hallway that led to the bathrooms, she nearly broke into a run. She pushed open the door, said a quick prayer of thanks that the bathroom was empty and pressed her hand over her eyes.

"He's not even here," she told herself.

Once her heart had stopped its mad gallop, she set her purse on the counter and washed her hands in cold water. The icy shock made her feel better. "It's going to be fine," she whispered, trying to convince herself that she was ready to go back out. But when Beth met her own wide eyes in the mirror and saw just how pale her face was, she knew she'd need a few more minutes.

She put her hands on the sink and leaned closer. "It's going to be fine," she repeated.

Two minutes, and then she'd walk out with her head high and her heart back in the right place. And she wouldn't think about Jamie Donovan again tonight.

GOD SAVE HIM FROM THE sexually liberated.

Eric Donovan crossed his arms and frowned at his shoes, trying to process what he'd just heard from his brewmaster. "Wallace, I don't understand. Faron is here with her husband. Her *husband*. How can you be upset about that? She's married to the man."

"He's a philandering scoundrel!" Wallace yelled, shaking his fist toward the front room of the brewery as his face flooded red with rage.

A *scoundrel?* Eric ran a hand through his hair. "I'm

sorry. I don't understand. They have an open marriage. As a matter of fact, you're *dating* Faron, so how can her husband be cheating on her?"

Wallace Hood, a bearded giant of a man who looked like he went home to a log cabin every night, gave Eric a look of prim horror. "I'm not dating her, man. I'm in love with her. And of course her husband can cheat on her. Don't be an idiot."

Eric probably should've felt irritated at being called an idiot, but he was too confused by the conversation. He glanced around the tank room of the brewery as if someone else could help. But they were alone amongst the brewing tanks and mash tuns. Eric shrugged and shook his head. "I'm sorry. I don't get it."

The brewmaster sighed and ran an impatient hand over his thick beard. "There are ground rules in open marriages, and her bastard of a husband has stopped even pretending to follow them. He cheats on her. He lies about it. And then he vetoes all the men she wants to see, claiming that he doesn't like them. That's what he did to me, despite that I've known them both for years. And then tonight he brought her here on *purpose*."

"Why?" Eric asked carefully.

"He's taunting me, because he knows I see him for what he is. I tried to tell her a few months ago. Faron is a queen, and he's not worthy to even kiss her feet. But she's loyal and sees the best in people. She wants to give him a chance."

"She seems really sweet." And she had, the one time that Eric had met her. In fact, he'd been startled by her quiet voice and shy smile. The tiny girl with gentle brown eyes hadn't fit Eric's assumptions about that lifestyle at all.

"She is sweet." Wallace sighed. "And she was falling for me. And now that bastard is taking her away to California, and he purposefully arranged this farewell party for her friends at *my* brewery."

Technically, it was Eric's brewery, but Wallace was as possessive and passionate as any owner, so Eric just rolled his eyes. "You can't leave right now, Wallace. I need—"

"Well, I can't stay here, can I?"

What was Eric supposed to say to that? He gazed into the kitchen through the glass wall of the tank room. Despite the late hour, there were still workmen out there, laboring overtime to cut a ventilation hole in his wall. Eric grimaced.

"She's right there, man," Wallace grumbled. "I know it's a bad time, but…she's right there."

It was a bad time. The bottling line was acting up for the third time this month, they were behind on branding for the winter brews, and the kitchen had been invaded by outsiders. Granted, the outsiders had been brought in by Eric's brother and sister, but still… These changes to the brewery weren't Eric's idea, even if he'd approved them, and he wanted nothing to do with them. "I really need you here tonight. You promised to stay late and transfer that small batch of amber to the new oak barrels."

Wallace looked so heartbroken at Eric's words that he wished he could take them back. "But…" Eric finally conceded. "I guess it's just a few hours."

"I'll be in early tomorrow. I swear."

Eric sighed. "Maybe it's a good thing she's moving to California."

"She's a good woman," Wallace said, his voice suspiciously raspy. "She wants to trust the man, and she won't walk away until she feels it's really over. But he's going to break her heart."

Eric still couldn't understand what marriage meant to someone who dated at the same time, but he'd never really understood Wallace's lifestyle. Despite the man's intimidating mountain-man looks, Wallace dated men, women and some people who seemed to skate between genders. But this was the first time Eric had seen Wallace in anything other than complete control. Love had hit him hard, it seemed.

Eric stole another look around the tank room, trying not to feel a sense of greedy anticipation. "All right. I'll take care of the barrels. You—"

"Oh, I don't know if I want you to—"

"Wallace," Eric snapped. "We're already off schedule."

Wallace narrowed his eyes. The man was protective of his beer. Almost obsessively so. But it was Eric's beer, too, and he'd lost enough control over his life this year. He wasn't going to let Wallace think he could snatch a little more.

"Fine," the brewmaster finally said. "Just don't screw it up." Wallace tossed his work gloves on the table and stalked out, slamming the door behind him. He paused for a moment, his eyes locked like lasers on the double doors that led to the front room and Faron, but then he shook his head and stalked out the back door.

"Jesus," Eric muttered. Everyone around him seemed to be controlled by love and sex these days. His brother and sister were both in serious relationships, and now Wallace, a man who treated dating like a professional sport, was miserably in love with a married woman. Eric felt like the only person untouched by the craziness.

Not that he didn't have any experience with it. He'd had his brush with it a few months ago, and even that brief encounter had left him shaken. He couldn't imagine being faced with that kind of emotional intensity every day. Maybe he could forgive the fact that his siblings seemed to have lost their minds.

Eric rolled his shoulders, trying to dislodge the weariness that had settled in. He was always tense at work. But the stress usually didn't bother him, if only because he couldn't imagine life without it. He ran a business; of course he was stressed. What he didn't like was the gnawing uncertainty that had taken him over in the last couple of months.

It had been one nightmare situation after another. Lost deals, theft and fraud, and now this mess in the kitchen. His brother, Jamie, was turning the family brewery into a pizza-serving brewpub, and Eric felt as though he'd lost complete control.

Grimacing, he watched masonry dust puff from the kitchen wall like a tiny cloud. Eric would much rather stay hidden in the peace of the tank room, but unfortunately, the casks would have to wait a couple of hours.

When Eric stepped into the kitchen his scowl faded away despite the roar of the masonry saw. The place might be chaotic and dusty, but Jamie stood watching it all with a grin on his face. This wasn't Eric's dream, but it was Jamie's, and Eric would do everything he could to make sure it happened.

Jamie glanced over with a quick smile. Things had been easier between them for the past few months. Thank God. It still felt tenuous, but Eric was relieved as all hell that their years of fighting seemed to be behind them.

He walked over and slapped Jamie on the shoulder. "How's it going?"

"Great!" Jamie shouted.

Eric turned to watch the progress with his brother for a few seconds, but he knew nothing about ovens or restaurant equipment, so he eventually slapped Jamie's back again. "I'll go check on the front, make sure everything is running smoothly."

Laughter roared from the front room as he drew close. Eric glanced toward the crowd as he pushed through the doors, keeping a close eye out for Faron and her scoundrel of a husband. Before the doors had swung closed behind him, someone crashed into Eric's shoulder. He grabbed for the woman, trying to steady her before she stumbled. She reached out, too, and her hand slid along his side just as she looked up.

Her face was so close to his that, for a moment, Eric thought he was imagining things. He smiled even as the nerves of his fingertips seemed to activate one by one. The wash of stark feeling progressed slowly up his fingers, his hands, his arms. By the time she pushed away with a gasp, his whole body felt as if an electrical shock was running through it.

Beth. His hands were on Beth Cantrell. His brain flickered through panicked thoughts.

Holy shit. His hands were on Beth Cantrell in his *brewery.*

He felt her trying to step away, but somehow his hands tightened on her shoulders as he glanced at the doors behind him. Jamie was still in the kitchen. As

long as he didn't head out to the front room, everything
would be fine. No harm, no foul. No reason to panic.

Except, what the hell was she doing at the brewery?
Had she come to see him?

"Beth," he started, just as she slipped away from his
hold. The tingling in his fingertips faded slowly, but
now it had progressed to his brain.

If Jamie walked into the front room, Beth would be
awfully surprised to meet him. Emphasis on awful.

When she backed a few feet away, Eric followed,
hoping they'd be unnoticeable in the hallway.

"Hi," she whispered.

"Is everything okay?"

"Yes. Absolutely." She was just as stunning as she
had been six months before. Just as gorgeous and sophisticated. Her dark hair wasn't pinned up tonight, and
it fell over her shoulders in soft waves. Her body, all
long legs and generous hips, had mesmerized him the
first time he'd laid eyes on her, and it was no different
now. He drank in the sight of her curves until her dark
gaze slipped past him.

He looked behind himself again, but no one was
there. If Jamie walked in, if someone said his name...

God, maybe he should just tell her. Maybe it wouldn't
be that big of a deal. *Funny thing, when you called me
Jamie at the business expo...I should've corrected you.
My name's actually Eric. Crazy, huh?* And then she'd
laugh and shake her head and tell him it didn't really
matter because it had just been a one-night stand.

Yeah. Sure. He'd be lucky if she didn't murder him
right there with one of her stiletto heels.

Beyond the adrenaline pushing through his veins,
Eric's skin still prickled at the idea of being close to

her again. Because he could still picture that night perfectly. Her body naked. Her lips parted on a moan. Her ass plump and firm, the muscles flexing as he fucked her from behind. Heat washed over him.

"What are you doing here?" he asked.

Heat seemed to wash over her, too. Her cheeks turned pink. Had she come to see him? As anxious as he was, Eric felt a sudden, ferocious hope. He wanted to touch her again. Wanted to feel those sparks. The lust. The need.

He shifted closer, close enough to touch. When Beth closed her eyes, he clenched his hands to fists and stopped himself while he still could.

BETH ALMOST CONVINCED herself she was just imagining him. He smelled the same. And he looked exactly the same: dark-haired and tall, his brow furrowed in worry, as if he never set his thoughts aside, no matter what month or week or time it was.

"Beth?" he said again, and she suddenly felt as if she'd swallowed a heart that was way too big for her chest. She wanted him to touch her so she could turn to him. At the same time she wanted to edge around him and run away.

She shook her head and opened her eyes.

He stole another quick glance over his shoulder before turning back to her. "How are you?"

"Good," she managed to say. "Great. I'm actually here with a party."

"Oh." He shoved his hands in his pockets. "You know Faron?"

"Yes! I…" She shifted her purse to the other hand, then back again. "Exactly. I know Faron." It wasn't quite a lie. They had friends in common. They'd been introduced a couple of times over the years.

The hallway was too small, despite being five feet across. His shoulders were so wide, and her memories too big, and the space just kept getting tighter and tighter. He cleared his throat, and she saw that he was just as uncomfortable as she was.

"I'm sorry," Beth said. "I didn't realize the party was here when I agreed to come. I honestly didn't mean to…"

"Of course not," he said quickly. "Come by anytime." But his gray-blue eyes darted nervously down the hall again. Maybe he had a girlfriend now. Maybe she was one of the servers.

Beth wished the floor would open up and swallow her and her sickly thumping heart.

"I was just leaving," she finally said.

Jamie stepped back. "Great. I mean, sure. Of course. That's good. Have a nice night."

Mortified, she edged past him and hurried back to the party. "Welcome back!" her date said when she found him and hovered a foot away.

"Thanks."

"Are you okay?"

"I'm fine!" She smiled and he handed her the beer she'd left behind. When she saw the way her hand was shaking, Beth took a seat at the nearest table and carefully set the beer down.

When he joined her, she hid a cringe. Was Jamie watching? She took a sip of beer to try to wet her parched mouth.

Beth glanced toward the bar, but didn't spy Jamie

anywhere. "I'm sorry," she managed to say, then hesitated over his name again. "I…"

Davis! That was his name. Not David, but Davis, after Miles Davis, because this man had been cool since the day his parents had named him.

Beth felt guilty for her snarky thought, but her guilt vanished in an instant when she heard a girl cry out, "Hi, Jamie!"

Beth's head snapped up so quickly that Davis's voice cut off as if she'd sliced his words with a knife.

"Beth? Are you sure everything is okay?"

Definitely not. She scanned the crowded area near the bar, but she didn't see him. While she watched, a cute blond guy in a brewery T-shirt waved toward someone. A girl broke free of the group and gave him a big hug.

"Listen, maybe a going-away party packed with people you don't know isn't an ideal first date."

"No, it's not that." She tried to think of something witty to say. Tried to concentrate on this man. Yes, he was hip and overeducated, but he was also a nice guy. And his smile could melt butter on a cold day. In fact, the moment she'd met him, she'd thought she might actually enjoy herself on this date. That she might actually look forward to touching this man, to kissing him.

For the first time in six months, Beth had thought maybe she'd finally found another man who could turn her on. And like an evil genie summoned by the thought, Jamie Donovan had popped back into her life, reminding her what it had been like with him.

Yeah, she hadn't had to *wonder* about whether sex with Jamie would be good. He'd turned her on just by feeding her dessert. The way he'd watched her, his gaze glued to her mouth as her lips parted. She'd wished—

Davis put his hand over hers for a brief moment. "I'll say goodbye to Faron, and then we'll go."

"No. I'm sorry! I don't want to cut the party short for you."

"No big deal. Come on. Let's find Faron."

Davis took her hand again and led her through the packed room to the tiny woman standing at the edge of a large group of people. Beth wondered how tall she was without the perfectly round Afro, because even with it, she wasn't bigger than five foot two. A skinny guy with long hair had his arm draped over her shoulder, a proprietary smile on his face. Faron wasn't smiling when they walked up, but her sweet face broke into a grin when she saw Davis.

She hugged Davis and then Beth before they said their goodbyes. Faron's husband had taken a job in Santa Barbara, but no one wanted to see her go. Nobody seemed that broken up about her husband, though.

"Ready?" Davis asked.

"Yes," Beth answered, realizing it was the most honest thing she'd said all night. As she walked through the door, she dared one look back, but Jamie was nowhere to be seen.

The sharp cold of raindrops on her face startled her from her thoughts.

"Run!" Davis said, tugging her along. Beth ran, and by the time they reached his car, she was laughing so hard with relief that she couldn't draw a breath. Davis reached to open the door, then shut it behind her before dashing around to the other side.

"My feet are soaked!" she gasped, stomping her heels

against the carpet. "I think one of those puddles was more like a pond."

"Your everything is soaked," he corrected. He touched her cheek, sliding a wet strand of hair toward her temple. A drop of icy water trickled down to her jaw, and then he leaned close and kissed her.

Beth inhaled sharply and felt him smile against her mouth. When his lips brushed hers again, Beth told herself to relax, to enjoy it.

And there was no reason she shouldn't. He smelled good. His lips parted just enough to encourage hers to part, as well. And his hand was a sweet touch on her jaw. Beth sighed and refused to think about Jamie Donovan. He hadn't wanted to see her any more than she had him.

But then Davis pulled back and the kiss was over before she'd had a chance to make herself enjoy it.

"I'm really glad Cairo introduced us," he said softly.

"Me, too." And she was. When she wasn't thinking about Jamie, she could imagine this man being her lover. She knew from experience that a first kiss said a lot about how a man would perform in bed. For example, that guy two years ago who'd immediately thrust his tongue down her throat…that had been his level of restraint and subtlety during sex, as well. Foreplay had been something along the lines of "Brace yourself, I'm coming in!"

But Davis…he might be quite lovely.

"I admit, though…" He started the car and glanced at her. "You weren't quite what I was expecting."

Her warm thoughts froze. "What do you mean?"

"Well, with the store and the advice column, and… you know. Cairo and the rest of her friends are…"

Beth knew exactly where this was going. She smoothed a hand down her skirt and hid a resigned smile.

"I just haven't dated a woman with no tattoos in quite a while. You're kind of a rarity here in Boulder."

She managed a genuine laugh at that. He was straightforward, at least. She turned her gaze on him and let it slide over his body. He was older than most of Cairo's friends, and a little alternative without being sloppy. Dark jeans and an expensive-looking T-shirt under a tailored leather jacket. And though she could see the edges of a few tattoos peaking past his clothing, not even his ears were pierced. Though there were always hidden spots.

"I get that a lot," she finally said, offering him the same honesty he'd given her. "I'm not what anyone expects, I guess." Even though she said it with a flirtatious smile, the words still squeezed her heart with a painful grip.

"I don't mind being surprised," Davis answered.

It was the right answer, and she liked him, but as he pulled away from the parking lot of the bar and turned toward Beth's part of town, her heart sank. She wasn't what he'd expected. She never was. And she could already see how this would end. He liked her well enough. He was intrigued by her. After all, she was the manager of the White Orchid, a high-end erotic boutique. She might look like any other professional businesswoman, but she spent her days selling sex toys and expensive lingerie. And she spent her evenings giving sex education classes and writing a new advice column as a sex expert.

On the surface, she was fascinating. But underneath it all…

Beth wrapped her hands tight around her purse and tried not to think. She always thought too much. The only time she'd ever been able to turn her brain off had been with…him.

It had been easy to dismiss her thoughts of him on previous dates. She hadn't been attracted to any of those men, so naturally, she'd thought of Jamie. But now he was haunting her good dates, too, and she was beginning to feel a little hopeless.

"I'm glad I didn't pick you up on the bike tonight," Davis said. "Running through the rain is one thing, but it can be brutal on a bike."

She pictured Davis in his leather coat, leaning close against a motorcycle, her arms wrapped around his waist. The picture should leave her shivery. It would any other red-blooded woman.

Davis pulled into her driveway and shut off the car to come around and open her door. He might have been raised by hipster Boulderites, but he had been taught the niceties of dating. There was nothing wrong with this man. And there was definitely nothing wrong with the way he kissed her once they were safe beneath the shelter of her patio. "You're all wet again," he murmured, his mouth sliding against the rain on her lips. Maybe she could be, if she let herself give in. So when his mouth urged hers to open, Beth touched her tongue to his. And what a nice tongue it was. Warm and slow against hers.

Beth kissed him and thought of inviting him in. He tasted so good. He was tall and cute and, as far as she could tell, he'd look great naked. His hand touched her hip, his fingers spreading along her curves as he deepened the kiss.

Yes, she could let him touch her. She'd enjoy it. And probably he'd enjoy it, too. But she wasn't a girl with tattoos. And she had no hidden piercings. And despite what she wrote in her columns, the things she liked to do in bed were just as vanilla as everything else about her.

So he'd enjoy it, but he'd also be secretly puzzled. They all were. Wasn't the manager of an erotic boutique supposed to be…erotic? Wasn't she supposed to be a little freaky in bed? Or even better…a *lot* freaky? Shouldn't she be better than other women?

Beth clenched her eyes shut and tried to turn off her brain, but it didn't work. It never did. She was too aware. Aware of the way his fingers tightened a bit on her hip. He was getting into this. Getting aroused. And she was just…thinking. Again.

She broke the kiss and drew in a deep breath. "Thank you, Davis. I really had a nice time."

His hand stayed on her hip. "Me, too." He waited one heartbeat, then two, giving her a chance to invite him in.

She couldn't do it. Not tonight, with the thought of Jamie so close at hand. There was no doubt how it would turn out. She'd be thinking the whole time, comparing him to Jamie, comparing herself to who she'd been that night six months ago.

She had to find that again, but it wasn't going to happen tonight. Not with Davis. "Thanks," she said again.

His hand finally slid away and Davis stepped back, looking only slightly disappointed. "I'll call you. Maybe we'll dare more next time. Dinner?"

"Maybe," she said coyly, offering a quick kiss on his cheek before she escaped into her apartment.

Beth set her purse on the table, then hung up her coat in the hall closet. Her apartment was so quiet and so palpably solitary, that she was already regretting sending Davis away as she walked to the kitchen to pour a glass of wine. She'd lied to him about that. One glass of beer hadn't been enough. She should have had three, and then maybe she would have been brave enough to let him in. She could've tried to lose herself. It wasn't impossible.

It was in her somewhere, and it couldn't just be about one man. Beth wouldn't let it be.

CHAPTER TWO

BY THE NEXT DAY, BETH WAS thoroughly pissed at herself. One minute with him, one glimpse, one touch, and she couldn't get the man out of her mind. And the worst part was, it was becoming more and more obvious to her that he'd been desperate to get her out of there. First, he'd edged her farther down the hall, then he'd jumped at the chance to say goodbye as quickly as possible.

He was in a relationship. Which was fine. But what if he was married? What if he'd been married *then?*

Her heart thumped so hard at the thought that she had to press her palm to her chest. That would explain everything, wouldn't it?

She tried to put it from her mind as she walked into the shop and waved to Cairo. She tried not to think about it as she unboxed the newest toys and put them on display. But as she unboxed the high-tech vibrator and showed Cairo how it plugged into an MP3 player to thump in time to one's favorite music, Beth couldn't stop the thoughts swarming through her head.

"Cairo?"

Cairo was busy scrolling through songs on her phone, trying to find something with just the right beat. "Yeah?"

"I was at Donovan Brothers last night and—"

"Oh!" Cairo looked up with a big smile on her face. "I forgot to ask how your date went."

"My date?"

"With Davis!"

"Oh. Great!" Beth nodded with too much enthusiasm. "Yeah, it was wonderful!"

Cairo's brown eyes lit up. "*Wonderful?* Oh, yeah? Do I detect a little dirty morning-after tone to those words?"

"You do not. But Davis was really nice."

"And hot, right?" Cairo pressed, smiling as if Beth was hiding something. "How'd you like that dragon tattoo on his stomach?"

Beth raised an eyebrow. "I didn't see his stomach, Cairo."

The girl laughed, her glossy black bob swinging forward to frame her pretty face. "I know. I already talked to him this morning."

"He called you?"

"No, I saw him at yoga. Which is how I know about the dragon tattoo, and why I fixed you two up in the first place. If I didn't have two men already, I'd hit that so hard he'd never recover."

Beth rolled her eyes. "It was a nice date. Though I'm not sure about a man who'd tell you whether he spent the night or not."

"He didn't say anything about that, but I figured a guy wouldn't need to show up for an 8:00 a.m. yoga class if he'd spent the night in your bed. Good sex is way more relaxing."

Well, that would be an interesting test of Beth's abilities. Let Davis spend the night, then see if he went to yoga the next day.

"By the way…" Cairo said with a familiar twinkle in her eye. "You really, really want to see that tattoo. It's done by the best artist in Colorado. And it follows the muscles in his abdomen all the way past his waistband. His very low waistband. I'm pretty sure he waxes. Everything."

Beth must have winced.

"What?" Cairo said. "Don't tell me you've never been with a man who's waxed?"

She tried to keep her face neutral. She really, really did. But she obviously couldn't hide her horror.

"Oh, Beth!" Cairo gushed. "I swear, it's the best. All that smooth flesh. Nothing between your mouth and his skin.… And with a guy like Davis, you want to get as close as possible, don't you?"

"I…I…." She couldn't imagine the process. Did he have to put his feet in stirrups for the waxer? "I'm sure it's lovely."

"Well, maybe you'll find out for yourself."

"So…" Beth tried to set the image away and couldn't. "Harrison and Rex are waxed?" She'd met both of Cairo's boyfriends on many occasions.

"Oh, Harrison has always kept it nice and smooth. Rex wasn't interested, but he got jealous of all the attention I was giving Harrison, so, yeah…" Cairo's smile seemed to stretch all the way from one ear to the other. "Now they're both clean as a whistle."

Oh, God. She shouldn't have asked. She was going to faint from all the blushing she would do the next time Harrison or Rex came into the store. But that wasn't the correct reaction for a sophisticated professional in this business, so Beth tried her best not to cover her face in embarrassment. "You're a lucky woman," she said instead. "And if I had a dollar for every time I said those words to you…"

"We'll talk about it later, if you keep seeing Davis." She hit Play on the phone and they both looked down at the pulsing head of the vibrator. LED lights blinked and twinkled. Cairo bumped her shoulder into Beth's. "*Are* you going to keep seeing Davis?"

"We'll see." She stared at the dancing lights and tried not to picture Davis without body hair.

"You're off at seven, right?" Cairo asked. "If you want to leave now, I'll cover for you. Maybe you should give him a call." Cairo was Beth's best employee, always friendly, cheerful and just as busy as Beth. In fact, Beth had just made her assistant manager. "I'm good, but thanks."

"So, what were you going to say about Donovan Brothers?"

"What?" Beth asked a little too loudly.

"The brewery. You said you were there last night."

"Oh, right. Yeah. Um, my friend wanted to know if Jamie Donovan is married. You've mentioned him before, right?"

"Oh, God, he's definitely not married."

"Okay. Good. I'll pass that on to—"

"But he was in here last week with his girlfriend, so he's not available, as far as I know. Maybe they date around, though."

Beth was nodding before the words really hit her. "What?" she said breathily.

"I know, I know. No gossiping about the customers. Sorry. I'll get back to work."

Cairo left the unboxed model out as a sample, then headed back to the cash register to finish cleaning the glass. Beth just stood there for a moment, as a pulse in her head started to beat hard. He'd come *here?* With his *girlfriend?*

No, that couldn't be right, could it? He wouldn't do that. He wouldn't bring his girlfriend to Beth's workplace, knowing that they sold sex toys and lingerie and cute, sexy gifts. That would be too cruel.

Cairo must be wrong.

Beth nodded, trying to convince herself, but she didn't feel even a hint of reassurance. Because…why wouldn't he come here?

This was the twenty-first century. Beth was a modern woman with obviously modern beliefs. They'd hooked up one time, no emotions involved. No strings attached. Certainly, plenty of Cairo's ex-boyfriends came into the shop, with friendly hugs all around. Maybe it hadn't even occurred to Jamie that Beth would be hurt if he came by with another girl.

They'd specifically agreed that their night together would mean nothing. Just because Beth wasn't so good at holding up her end of the bargain didn't mean that Jamie had any problem with his end.

She pressed her hands tight together and told herself that she wasn't hurt. Still…thank God she hadn't been here. There would've been no denying the pain of watching him wander through her store with another woman, holding her hand, picking out items to use together later in the bedroom.

Beth drew a sharp breath at the thought of it. Had it not even occurred to him? In the brief hours she'd spent with him, he'd seemed considerate and kind. Or hell, maybe he was just more sexually evolved than she was.

But last night, he'd looked downright sneaky. It didn't make any sense.

She retreated to her office and shut the door. And suddenly she was pissed. She'd felt guilty as hell being at his brewery with another man. And he'd dared to bring someone here? What kind of an asshole was he? And when exactly had he acquired this girlfriend? All the sneaking around that had seemed so exciting at the expo suddenly took on a new, sinister light.

"That bastard," she growled.

She should drop it. Leave it alone. Now, six months later, it hardly mattered anymore, but Beth found herself overwhelmed with the urge to confront him. She turned on her phone, but that was hopeless. She'd deleted his number from her phone two weeks after she'd met him. She'd had to delete him from her life because the memory of that encounter had become its own aphrodisiac, and she'd known she would get to this point sometime. She'd known the temptation would rise up and swallow her.

"Damn it," she muttered.

Maybe it would be easier for her to contact him through the brewery anyway. Less privacy, less intimacy. And no memory of the night her phone had rung and he'd said two simple words. "Room 421."

The hair on her arms prickled as electricity zinged through her body.

Beth cleared her throat and shook her head. She shouldn't call him. She knew that.

But maybe she could find out the truth another way. Between Facebook and Twitter and everything else on the web, people's private lives were no longer private.

"It doesn't matter," she told herself. If he was some

sort of creepy two-timing cheat, that wasn't Beth's fault. But she gave in to the weakness and searched his name on Google anyway. Thousands of hits appeared, all of them seemingly about beer and awards and the brewery. Looking for something more personal, she clicked on a link to Twitter. The account said Jamie Donovan of Donovan Brothers Brewery, but the picture was wrong.

Frowning, she clicked on the photo to enlarge it. The guy definitely wasn't Jamie. As a matter of fact, he looked a lot like the blond man she'd seen tending bar at the brewery the night before. "What the hell?"

Thoroughly confused, Beth clicked back to Google and hit the Images tab. The first picture was the young blond guy again. She clicked back to the results page. *Most* of the pictures were of the blond guy. The only ones she saw with Jamie were group shots. Clicking on the largest of the group shots, she looked at the caption. Wallace Hood, Eric Donovan, Tessa Donovan, Jamie Donovan, Chester Smith.

This didn't make any sense. She clicked through to the next page of images, but they were mostly Donovan Brothers logos and pictures of mugs of beer.

Then she noticed there were two video hits and clicked on that tab, light-headed with anticipation.

The first video linked to a local news channel. Beth pulled it up and waited, holding her breath.

The news theme song played, and then the camera focused in on a tight shot of a perfectly coiffed blonde reporter smiling widely. "Today we've got big news from an iconic local establishment! I'm coming to you live from Donovan Brothers Brewery in Boulder, Colorado, and I've been joined by one of the actual Donovan brothers." The camera pulled slowly back, revealing first an arm, then a shoulder, then the man with the dark blond hair whom she'd seen in the bar. Beth frowned.

The reporter beamed up at him. "This is Jamie Donovan, one of the famous brothers." He winked at the reporter while Beth's mind reeled.

Jamie Donovan. Jamie. But not the man she'd slept with.

This made no sense. The man and the reporter were still talking, their words jangling around in her head like broken glass scraping against her skull. Jamie. But not Jamie. She stared at the name that hovered beneath the man as he spoke: Jamie Donovan of Donovan Brothers Brewery.

Her hand shook as she reached for the mouse and clicked the pause icon.

A weight grew in her throat. Not tears or illness or emotion. It felt as if her actual flesh was swelling up and pressing her throat into a smaller and smaller space. She tried to swallow and couldn't.

The man worked for Donovan Brothers. He'd been at the brewery. He was in the pictures. But he wasn't Jamie.

Beth clicked frantically back through the pages until she pulled up that group picture again. She opened another window and tried querying every name, but she didn't get any good image results. Just picture after picture of the Donovan Brothers' green logo and photos of the awards and labels of the various beers they sold.

Who was he? Was he Wallace or Chester or Eric?

Beth stood up so quickly that she banged her thigh hard into the desk, but the pain barely registered. She stumbled out from behind her desk and into the cheerful brightness of the shop.

"Cairo?"

Cairo popped up from behind the cash register. "Yes?"

"What does Jamie Donovan look like?"

Cairo shrugged. "I don't know. He's cute. Pretty preppy-looking. Straitlaced, but he's got a sweet smile."

"Dark hair?" Beth made herself ask, even though her throat tried to close over the words.

"No, not dark. Sort of gold. Not super blond. Why?"

"Just… We…" All that blood pounding in her brain was doing her no good at all. She couldn't think. She couldn't even feel. Her body had gone numb. "No reason," she managed.

"Are you okay, Beth?" Cairo started to reach for her, but Beth backed away.

"I'm fine. I just…I'm not feeling well. Are you still willing to cover for me for an hour? I think I'd better head home."

"Of course, but…"

Beth rushed back into her office to grab her purse and her phone. She shut down her computer and cleared the history, not quite sure why—all she knew was that she felt ashamed. Ashamed because she'd been tricked. Made a fool of. And, my God, that was an awful, familiar feeling she hadn't had to deal with in years.

She started hearing the words in her head that she'd absorbed over years of studying sexuality and women's history. *Someone else can't bring you shame. Shame means you did something wrong. You did nothing wrong.* But how else was she supposed to feel after being tricked and lied to?

Tears sprang to her eyes, but she growled her frustration as she blinked them back.

She wasn't seventeen this time. She didn't have to simply sit quietly and take it. This time, she'd confront it head-on, and give the shame to the one who deserved it.

When she stalked out of the office, Cairo was helping a customer, dusting a sample of honey body powder on the woman's arm, but she looked up with concern in her eyes as Beth passed. Beth watched the customer bring her arm up and tentatively touch her tongue to her wrist. The sight would have made Beth smile on any other day, but today she simply watched in blank confusion.

Her body was still numb, her head still beating like a pulse. It occurred to her that she probably shouldn't drive, but she pushed through the doors and headed straight to her new cherry-red Nissan 370Z. The engine roared to life with the barest turn of the key. She'd purchased it for herself five months before, because she'd wanted it, and she was trying to train herself to take what she wanted. Though right now all she wanted to do was kill someone. Someone whose name she didn't even know.

The shock of it hit her again, and she gasped in a breath to try to stop the dizziness. She was in a car on a public street. She couldn't indulge the black spots dancing at the edge of her vision. She took another breath, and another. And even though her whole skull still thumped with every beat of her pulse, her vision cleared, and the closer she got to the brewery, the calmer she felt. Not less furious, but more. Angry in a focused way.

When she pulled into the brewery lot, she shut off the engine, got out of the car and quietly shut the door.

Her heels ground sand against asphalt as she walked. She watched her own hand curl around the door handle as she opened it, as if her fingers had nothing to do with her.

She stepped into a cheerful scene. Fiddle music fell from speakers. Laughter erupted from a table nearby. Beth walked through the laughter as if she were in one of those dreams where nothing made any sense, but she just kept moving.

The man behind the bar turned around, and she felt her heart brace itself, but he was no one she knew. A stranger. Though they were all strangers, really.

She waited until he looked at her. "Is Jamie Donovan here?" Her skin burned with regret as she spoke the name.

The man—a boy, really—leaned forward. "I'm sorry? I didn't catch that."

The music had seemed quiet when she'd walked in, but now it swelled in her ears, along with the noise of the early Friday crowd. "Jamie Donovan?" she said more loudly. "Is he available?"

"He's not working the bar tonight. Is there something I can help you with?" He said it as if the request was a common one. As if women walked in here all the time looking for a man named Jamie who'd lied his way into sex. A scalding wash of shame crashed through her. She'd been laughed at before, and she couldn't do it again. She couldn't. So she nodded and started to back away.

A door opened to her left, and she jumped in horror, thinking it could be *him*. But it was just a customer coming out of the bathroom.

When Beth realized that she'd felt genuine fear, she

smashed it down and turned it into anger, like pressure turning coal into diamonds.

She stood straight and met the gaze of the bartender again. "I need to see him. It's personal."

The boy's eyebrows rose, but after a wary moment, he shrugged. "I'll see if he's in the back. What's your name?"

"My name is Beth Cantrell. Tell him that and see if he'll come out." She put a hand on the bar, not to steady herself but to give her fingers something to squeeze, because the anger was eating her up.

And then she waited to find out exactly who she'd had sex with six months before.

ERIC PICKED UP A HALF-FULL bottle of pilsner and squeezed the neck tight in his hand. He wouldn't throw it against the wall. He wouldn't. But this damn bottling machine was supposed to have been fixed last week, and now it was doing an even worse job, jostling the bottles so much that half the beer foamed out before it reached the capping station.

"Shut it down!" he yelled at Wallace.

Wallace scowled and shut down the line, and when the roar of machinery died down, Wallace's stream of creatively foul curses pealed through the cement-walled room.

Wallace didn't care about bottling or distribution or profit margins. His only concern was the beer, and a lot of it was slowly crawling its way toward the drain in the floor.

Eric cursed. "I'm going to have that mechanic's head on a platter."

"Not until I've torn it off his neck," Wallace yelled.

Eric glanced down at the tubing that snaked across the floor. "Goddamn it. You know what needs to be done. There's no way we're getting this back on line today. Maybe not even tomorrow."

Wallace bit back what sounded suspiciously like a sob, but it was hard to read his emotions behind the thick beard that covered his whole lower face. His giant shoulders sunk, bringing his height down from about six-six to six-five. "It's a damn tragedy," he wheezed before turning to stomp toward the door that led to the tank room. A moment later he was back, the valve having been locked, and he mournfully unhooked the hose from the bottler and moved it over to the drain. He thumbed the valve and pilsner poured from the tube directly into the screened hole in the floor.

"I'll kill him," he muttered.

"We probably shouldn't."

"That batch was fucking stellar."

"And there's plenty of it left." Eric put a reassuring hand on Wallace's shoulder and they shared a moment of silence over the beer as it spiraled down into the sewer system.

Wallace sniffed, but Eric was afraid to look and see if there were tears wetting his beard. "I've got to make a phone call about this."

"Rake him over the fucking coals," Wallace insisted.

Eric strode through the silence of the tank room and emerged into the chaos of the...well, it was a kitchen now, though it never had been before. In fact, two men were currently wrestling a gigantic pizza oven into place against the far wall.

Months of prep work had led to this very event, and Eric wished he felt more than just happiness for Jamie.

He wished he felt excited instead of nervous. But Jamie was grinning as he turned away from the stove and headed toward the doors to the front room, Henry hot on his heels.

"Henry," Eric called before the boy could disappear. "Are you working cleanup tonight?"

Henry jerked to a stop, his hand already on one of the doors. His freckles stood out against his pale skin, as if Eric had frightened him.

"I am, but…Jamie has me filling in at the bar so he can supervise the installation."

"Great. But when you're done I need you in the bottling room. Dump all the beer and put the bottles into recycling, then mop the floor."

"Got it."

Henry disappeared and Eric retreated to his office. He wanted to spend time helping Jamie, but he had his own work to do, boring as it was. His muscles tightened to stone as he shut the door and called the mechanic.

He felt a little better after yelling at the guy and demanding that he get his ass to the brewery at 9:00 a.m. tomorrow, Saturday or not. Eric hung up with a little less tension in his shoulders. Still, there was no silencing the laughter from the other room. It reminded him of his brother, and how different they were.

Eric tried to make himself smile at the sound of it. He wanted Jamie to be happy. Without a doubt. But Eric couldn't help the feeling that his own happiness was slipping away. Melodramatic, maybe, but still true.

This place was his whole life. This brewery. This office. This role he had here.

Eric dug his fingers into the back of his neck and

took a deep breath. There was no point sitting around brooding. He had work to do.

A minute later, someone knocked on the door. Eric looked up, expecting to see Jamie, but it was Henry. "Hey, did you get to the bottling room yet?"

"No. Um…some woman is pissed at Jamie and he asked me to come get you."

"If she's pissed at Jamie, then it's Jamie's problem, not mine."

Henry's face creased with embarrassment, but he just stood there with his fingers wrapped around the door.

"Fine." Eric sighed. "I'll be there in a second." What the hell was this? A year ago, Eric wouldn't have been surprised by anything involving Jamie and a woman, but now…Jamie had a girlfriend. A really nice girlfriend. If he was screwing around on her, Eric didn't want to know. It would put a whole lot of strain into their newly easy relationship.

Still, he felt a little surge of satisfaction. This was like the old days, when Jamie had needed him. In fact, if Jamie's girlfriend hadn't been a consideration, Eric would've smiled as he stood up and headed for the barroom, off to make sense of Jamie's screwup again.

The workmen stood in the doorway, holding the doors slightly open as they peered out. Their eyes widened when they saw Eric coming, but he ignored that and tipped his head in the direction of the oven. They shifted toward it as if they were only pretending to go back to work, but Eric held his tongue. He didn't want to step on Jamie's toes.

He pushed through the doors. "Jamie," he said when he spotted his brother standing at the end of the bar with his arms crossed. "What's the problem?"

And then Jamie shifted to the side, and Eric's world split apart as if an earthquake had just torn through the ground beneath his feet.

For a long moment, Eric could only look at her. *Her.* He should have anticipated this, after last night. But his relief had made him stupid. And now here she was, standing next to Jamie.

Reality hit him then, with all the subtlety of a two-by-four across the face. Eric's eyes shifted to Jamie, who was also staring at him, though his eyebrows were raised in incredulity. "Eric," he said, and Eric caught the way Beth blinked in shock.

Oh, shit. This was bad. Worse than bad.

Jamie cocked his head. "Eric, this is Beth Cantrell. There seems to be some confusion about something that happened at the business expo earlier this year."

Something that happened. Okay. Maybe he could still salvage some part of this. If Beth hadn't said anything to Jamie yet... "Beth—" he started, but she stalked toward him like a vengeful goddess.

"Eric?" she sneered. *"Eric?"*

His eyes darted to Jamie. "I can explain."

One of her elegant fingers poked him in the chest. "You can explain? Explain why you told me your name was Jamie?"

"I didn't actually—"

"Explain that you lied to me?"

"Beth, if you'll just—"

"Explain," she yelled, her finger digging a hole in his sternum, "that you let me think you were someone else when you had sex with me?"

"What?" Jamie yelled.

That was it. This was an official disaster. The solemn silence that had fallen over the barroom seemed to confirm the horror of the situation.

"I can explain," Eric said again, weakly. He thought the low growl was coming from Beth, but he couldn't be sure, because at that moment Jamie surged forward, grabbed Eric by his shirtfront and twisted.

"Henry!" Jamie shouted, as if Henry wasn't standing right there, wide-eyed. "Cover the bar. You…" His green eyes burned into Eric. "Into the back. Right. Now."

Oh, this was a new experience, being the one who'd done something wrong. Something hot and scalding slid into his veins. Shame. Eric didn't like it one bit.

He pulled away from Jamie's grasp and kept his eyes on Beth. "Beth, let's talk about this. Alone."

She moved toward the doors with a jerky nod, and Eric held his hand up to stop Jamie from following. "I'll talk to you later."

"You'll fucking talk to me *now*," Jamie countered.

As Beth pushed through the double doors, Eric spared a look around the room. Every eye was on them, and it was a Friday evening, so there were a lot of eyes. "Let me talk to Beth alone. She doesn't deserve to be in the middle of us."

"Seems like she's already right in the middle of us. Or did I misunderstand something?" But Jamie had fallen back on his heels, and his jaw jumped with frustration instead of aggression, so Eric turned and followed Beth into the back.

She was pacing across the kitchen area, her movement followed by the workmen's fascinated eyes. She wore the same kind of hip-hugging skirt he'd seen her in last night, but this time her stiletto heels were dark purple instead of black.

Eric swallowed hard. "My office is this way." He gestured toward the hallway and she glared at his hand as if she wanted to snap it off.

"We might want to stay out here. Whoever you are, you're less likely to end up dead if there are witnesses."

One of the men made a noise that was somewhere between a bark and a laugh, but when Eric shot them a glare, both men pressed their mouths into straight lines.

When he didn't respond, Beth passed by him with a sneer and stalked down the hallway. He gestured toward his office and the chairs in front of his desk, but she didn't sit down. Instead she paced to one corner and then spun around to glare at him.

"You came back," he said quietly as he shut the door.

"Yes, I came back. Is that your big concern right now? How about, who the hell are you? How about we start with *that*?"

"Of course," he said, his face flaming with embarrassment. This was no longer a gorgeous secret they shared. It wasn't a quiet whisper he could offer into her ear to make her smile. There was no more titillation in this for her; it was all betrayal.

Her eyes looked furious and frightened.

"I'm sorry, Beth," he said. "I can't… Listen. When we met, you thought I was my brother because of the name tag on the table. He was supposed to have been working the booth that day."

"Well, that explains the first fifteen seconds of our relationship," she snapped.

"I know. I mean, I knew at the time that it wasn't right. I did try to correct you—"

"You're kidding, right? Did you try really, really hard, *Eric?*"

"I—"

"This is…this is horrible. You lied to me just to…"

"No, it wasn't like that. I swear." Eric felt sweat prickle along his hairline, and his stomach turned as he registered the hurt on her face. "Beth, I'm so sorry."

"Why would you *do* that? I don't understand."

"I don't know. At the time…at the time you said you'd heard of my brother, you knew his reputation, and maybe that made it easier."

"You pretended to be him because you thought that's who I wanted?" she shouted.

"No. Not that. I knew you wanted me."

Her gaze had been shifting wildly around his office, but her eyes flew to him at those words. "You should have told me. Right at the start. Or later, when we met for wine. Or—" Her voice stopped as if the words had been cut in half. They'd met for wine the first day of the expo, and he'd touched her in that hidden booth, making her come while the rest of the bar moved around them unaware. The memory seemed to flash over her face and turn into shame.

"Who are you?" she growled, her hands clenching to fists.

"I'm Eric. Donovan," he clarified stupidly. "I'm Jamie's brother. I thought it would be easier if…" Hell, what else was there to add? He was the brother of Jamie and Tessa Donovan and he helped run the brewery. There was really nothing more he could think to say. That was all there was. Which was why he'd been able to talk himself into this mess in the first place. Because he hadn't been willing to risk ruining the brief, wild spark that had arced between him and Beth. He'd needed that moment to be someone he'd never been before.

Beth closed her eyes and shook her head. "You thought it would be easier," she whispered. "Easier to get me into bed."

"That's not what I meant. I swear to God, Beth, that wasn't it. We were just… It was all just a fantasy, wasn't it? I didn't want to make it…"

"Real?" she filled in. And yes, that was what he meant, but it sounded cruel now. It sounded horrible.

Tears flashed to life in her eyes, and Eric reached for her, knowing he shouldn't. She stepped back and his hand fell, but she watched it as if it were a snake.

"You made me into a fool."

"I'm so sorry."

"And now—" She swept an arm in the direction of the barroom. "Now I let everyone know you made a fool out of me. Jesus."

He shook his head.

"I did," she insisted. "But that's okay, because I wanted everyone to know that you were the one who should be ashamed. Not me." She pressed a finger to her mouth. Her eyes looked far away. "I didn't want it to be me feeling that."

"You shouldn't. I wasn't trying to trick you. I just didn't know how to stop and say, 'Can we start over? My name's actually Eric.'"

"That's no excuse."

"No, it's not."

"You should have told me then. Or last night. Or anytime in the past six months."

He nodded, and Beth met his gaze again, her dark brown eyes deep with sorrow. "You've ruined it."

"I know." He did. It had been a perfect memory. A perfect moment in his life. Her body and her mouth and her trembling hands. And now it was something sordid.

Beth stood a little straighter and seemed to reset herself. The tears stopped and her chin rose in disdain as she stepped forward and brushed past him. "I just wanted you to know that. That you ruined it. Don't ever call me. Don't get in touch. But I guess that was your plan from the start, right?"

She was right, so he didn't dare touch her arm to stop her. He didn't even apologize again. He just let her slam his office door and disappear from his life as quickly as she'd reappeared.

Eric collapsed into a chair, let his head fall into his hands and called himself every name in the book. And yet there was still that small, stony part of him that didn't regret what he'd done. Not at all. It was that same part that had always been selfish, but lately it seemed to be growing.

CHAPTER THREE

As soon as she'd slammed the door behind her, Beth lost her ability to hold it together. She couldn't draw enough air. She was breathing too hard, too fast, and she worried she might pass out at any moment. That would be the only thing that could make this unbearable situation worse: being found passed out in the back hallway of the brewery as if she were some delicate flower of womanhood, overcome with sexual shock.

So Beth put her hand to the wall and made herself breathe slowly in and slowly out. She bowed her head for one moment, keeping an ear out for the sound of Jamie's—Eric's—door opening behind her.

But he didn't follow her, and Beth calmed down, and when she opened her eyes she was steady enough to walk. There were two men on the far side of the kitchen, and they watched her as if they feared she might snap at them like a mad dog. She ignored them, and was reaching for the double doors when they swung inward.

She stopped short, clasping her hands to her chest. It was him. The man who was really named Jamie. And it was all so obvious in that moment. This man was the Jamie Donovan she'd heard rumors about. He was handsome and roguish-looking, and she could perfectly picture him wearing a kilt and flirting as he delivered beers to customers. Eric, on the other hand, looked like a man who never bothered with flirting. If he wanted you, he wanted you; it was as simple as that. It certainly had been the night they'd met in his room.

"Hey," the real Jamie said, his eyes looking down the hall for a moment before refocusing on her. "Is everything okay?"

She almost laughed. Sure, everything was just great. Except that she'd been betrayed and used and made a fool of. Her cheeks warmed. "I just want to go," she said, hugging her arms to her chest.

"Oh. Sure. I'm just sorry about the..." His eyes darted toward the offices again. "Confusion," he finished weakly.

"Confusion. Right." She wanted to smile, to pretend it was no big deal, but instead she found herself blinking back tears. "Sorry I yelled at you earlier," she said quickly. "I was a little surprised."

She brushed past him and started to push through the doors, but he turned and held out a hand to stop her. "Do you want to go through the back?"

She froze. At this point, she could only pray she didn't know any of the customers who'd so eagerly watched the argument. What if she walked toward the front doors and a friend stopped her for more details? "Thank you. The back door would be perfect."

He walked her to a steel door set into the far wall, but when he opened it to let her out, he kept walking with her. She hid her look of irritation, and simply stared straight ahead. "You don't need to keep me company."

"I just want to be sure you're okay."

"I am," she said, but it was a moot point now. They were already in the parking lot. He looked like he wanted to say more, but there was nothing else she wanted to hear. She never wanted to see any of these people again.

She beeped open the door on her car. "Thank you," she said, then slipped inside. She started the car immediately, but when he simply stood there, she gave an impatient wave.

By the time he walked away, it was all beginning to sink in.

How had she let this happen to herself? It was as if she'd been the butt of some fraternity-boy joke. *I'll pretend to be my brother to get her into bed.*

She meant to pull the car out right away, but her face was so hot she had to press her cool fingers to her cheeks. Her stomach rolled with sickness. She'd been proud of her fling before this. It had been exactly the sort of brave and selfish pleasure she'd wanted for years.

And now it was *nothing.* Less than nothing. It was a scar on her pride. It was humiliation. *Why* had he done that to her?

"It doesn't matter," Beth told herself. "It doesn't."

She didn't believe it, but somehow the words helped her calm down. Or just the sound of her own voice, solid and strong.

Whether it mattered or not, it was done. And she'd never see Eric or Jamie Donovan again, thank God.

ERIC HEARD HIS BROTHER'S footsteps long before Jamie got to his office. And that said a lot about Jamie's mood; these floors were solid concrete.

Pushing to his feet, Eric told himself he was ready for this, but he still ground his teeth together when the door flew open and banged a tall filing cabinet.

"What the *fuck?*" Jamie ground out.

"I know. It looks bad."

"It looks *bad?* It looks like you used my name to get a woman into bed. But you'd never do something that sleazy, would you?"

Eric swallowed and didn't answer the question.

Jamie leaned forward and put his fists on the desk. His eyes blazed with fury. "Would you, Eric?"

"It was a mix-up," he managed to answer, trying to control the fury rising up from his guilt.

"You fucking bastard," Jamie growled.

"Listen, Jamie—"

"I'm not listening to shit. This is… Christ, I wouldn't have expected this from anyone I know, much less *you.*"

Eric clenched his hands and pressed a fist to his forehead. He'd never been in this position before. He was the brother who did the lecturing. Who demanded answers. Who did the right thing for his family. He wasn't the one who had to be ashamed.

Except that now he was, and Eric felt as if he'd explode from the frustration. And the regret. "It wasn't like that," he tried again. "She called me by the wrong name, and I didn't correct her. And then…I'd let it go too long. It seemed like it wouldn't hurt anything to let it stand."

"Jesus, are you *kidding* me? You can't see what it would hurt to have a woman out there who thought she'd slept with me?"

Eric answered honestly, realizing it was a mistake even as he let it happen. "I didn't think it would make much of a difference. You've slept with a lot of women."

Jamie's hand was a blur when it shot out and grabbed Eric's shirt. "First of all, fuck you. Second, that woman is a stranger to me, so don't let yourself think I'm honored she thinks I did her. Third, I have a girlfriend, in case you hadn't noticed. You could have screwed up a lot of things for me."

"It was months ago," Eric said.

Jamie's sneer let him know that wasn't quite the point. "Have you done this before?"

"No!"

Eric sat back in his chair when Jamie let him go. He watched his brother pace the short distance to the door and then back again. "Why would you do this?"

"I didn't use your name to trick her into anything. We...we had a connection. Chemistry. But she thought I was you. A carefree, easygoing bachelor. A guy who could offer no-strings-attached fun. So I used your reputation as...permission."

"That's so damn ironic it hurts." His laugh certainly sounded as if it was jagged with pain.

Eric cringed.

"You've spent your whole life telling me I was doing the wrong things. For years, you've basically said I was a no-good, irresponsible jackass."

Eric pushed to his feet. "That's not true. I—"

"And then you turn around and use my name to fuck around?"

"Jamie..." Eric's thoughts had scattered. He didn't know what to say. It had seemed harmless at the time. A little white lie.

Jamie pointed his finger at Eric as if it was a weapon. "If you ever, *ever* throw my past in my face again, I swear to God, I'll make you sorry."

He already was sorry. "Jamie—" But Jamie just turned and slammed out of the office, leaving Eric standing there, his lips still parted.

Jesus Christ. He lowered himself slowly to his chair, his chest tightening until he couldn't draw a breath.

It had been only six months since that night with Beth, but it felt like a lifetime ago. It felt as if someone else had done those things.

Eric Donovan would never slide his hand between a woman's legs in a public place. He'd never make a woman come after only knowing her for hours. He certainly wouldn't rent a hotel room for the express purpose of one meaningless, animal encounter.

And he would never, ever lie to make that happen.

He wasn't that person.

He looked down at his hands. The hands that had touched Beth Cantrell. The hands that had held her hips as he'd thrust into her. That wildness had been all for him—it had had nothing to do with Jamie's name or reputation.

But Eric had ruined that with his stupidity and now he'd be nothing to her but a mistake.

CHAPTER FOUR

SHE LEFT THE LIGHTS OF THE store turned off when she got in at eight. The shop didn't open for another two hours, and she liked the starkness of the pale sunlight that shone through the front windows. It comforted her. She felt alone, and she needed that for a little while.

She'd tried her best not to think about Eric Donovan last night, but she'd woken at 6:00 a.m., an hour before her alarm, and she hadn't been able to keep her hurt feelings at bay anymore.

Logically, she could tell herself that it didn't make a difference. It was a name. Nothing more. And he was a man she'd had a brief physical connection with. She didn't love him. She didn't know anything about him. Even less than she'd thought, apparently.

But she felt so stupid, and she thought she'd left all that behind. Feeling stupid about sex and her body. Feeling used. She'd built a whole life designed to put her above that. And even if she hadn't been totally successful, she sure as hell hadn't let a man bring her shame. Not until now.

"I have nothing to be ashamed about," she muttered, slicing open a box with a vicious slash. But she immediately regretted her anger. She couldn't sell damaged erotic toys, and she held her breath as she opened the cardboard to inspect the damage. Thankfully, she hadn't even sliced through the plastic packaging. She needed to calm down. She needed to let it go. He was the one who had to live with what he'd done.

So Beth made herself turn on the lights in the back room and focus on what she was doing. After all, she should be paying close attention to the toys. She might be spending a lot of time with vibrators in the near future. It was either that or arrange a date with super-smooth Davis.

Maybe that would be okay. Cairo seemed to think it was…luscious.

Beth bit back a shudder and grabbed the first packages out of the box. Personally, she wasn't interested in a toy with a vibrating appendage shaped like a wolf's head, but werewolves were popular right now. Whatever her personal likes were, Beth didn't judge what got other people off. The dildos with chillable inserts were especially in demand as well, and if people wanted to fantasize about cold vampire sex, that was fine with her. "You go, girl," she murmured as she hung the wolf toys up.

Once the box was empty, she polished the glass cases—nobody wanted to look at intimate toys through fingerprints—and straightened the displays.

By nine o'clock, she felt better. Solid and nearly okay. And then her cell phone rang. She knew without a doubt that it must be Eric Donovan. He had to get in touch, didn't he? He had to apologize again and maybe grovel. So it had to be him.

But it wasn't.

"Hi, Mom," she said, trying to keep the weariness from her voice.

"Hey, sweetie. Where are you?"

"I'm at the store."

"Oh," her mother said, that tiny word conveying so much.

"Mom," she said, sighing. "I wish you'd come see it sometime. It's not what you think it is."

"Oh, Beth, I couldn't. I don't want to see all those... things."

"All those things are in the back room. The front room is all pretty lingerie and fun gifts. It's a place for women, not some sleazy video den."

"But you sell..." Her mom took a deep breath, and Beth heard the muffling sound of a hand cupped over the phone. "Dildos."

"Yes, we do." Beth glanced up at the twelve-inch-long black glass beauty they kept behind the counter. "But that's okay, you know. There's nothing wrong with that."

"No, if your father ever found out I'd gone into a place like that..."

Right. And if he ever found out that Beth ran a place like that... "I still think you should tell him."

"No, ma'am," her mom gasped. "He'd never forgive either of us."

"I'm not sure what he'd blame you for." Granted, he was conservative. Old Argentina conservative, not to mention Roman Catholic conservative. He still complained that women no longer covered their hair in church.

"He'd blame me for all of it!"

Beth rolled her eyes. "Well," she muttered, "I hope he's happy thinking I'm managing a women's undergarment shop."

"Oh, he is! He's very proud of you."

She had no idea what to say to that. Sometimes her mom was a little off. Or a lot. "Is anything going on? Are you both feeling good?"

"We're wonderful, sweetie. We're ready for some cool weather, though. It's been so hot here."

"Turn your air conditioner up, Mom."

"You know your father hates it when I use it in September."

"Tell him you're a delicate Anglo and you can't handle the heat. And September or not, it's still hot as hell."

Her mom giggled, even as she chided Beth for her language. Poor Mom. She'd probably drop dead if she heard her baby talking cock rings and anal plugs with customers. Or maybe she wouldn't even understand what was being discussed.

"I love you, Mom." Beth hung up with the same mix of frustration and comfort she always did. Her parents had provided her with love and a safe home and plenty of emotional support. But they couldn't support the choices she'd made. They just couldn't. There were lines they couldn't cross, and she'd found that out the hard way.

But they still loved her, and that was a hell of a lot more than some of her friends had. So Beth chose to feel a little stronger as she walked into the front room and turned on all the lights.

The room blinked to life and she looked over it with pride. Fuck Eric Donovan. He was lucky she'd remembered his fake name, much less bothered to find out his real one.

She wasn't going to let him make her back into the girl she'd once been. No chance in hell.

ERIC HAD BRIEFLY CONSIDERED calling in sick today. After all, he felt sick. He hadn't gotten one damn hour of sleep the night before.

He'd known better than to lie, but he'd still done it, and look what he'd done to Beth. And to his newly forged relationship with Jamie.

In the spirit of punishing himself, Eric had dragged himself from bed and hauled his ass into work. Jamie had been there to greet Eric with a glare as soon as he'd walked in. Luckily, they'd spent the first half hour in separate areas of the brewery, so Jamie's anger hadn't yet burned a hole in Eric's skull.

But once Eric had the mechanic settled in, he had no excuse to lurk in the bottling room and oversee the work. When he stepped back into the tank room, Wallace grabbed his elbow in one meaty paw.

"The new stout," he said, as if that explained his tight grip on Eric's arm.

"Yeah?"

"It's ready."

Oh, that was why Wallace's eyes glinted with worry. The last batch hadn't worked out, and Wallace had been frustrated, to say the least. Eric had thought he'd been thinking about Faron again, but maybe he was already fully recovered.

"Come on," Wallace growled. "You and Jamie can taste it at the same time."

Eric opened his mouth to say no, but even he couldn't justify that kind of immature answer. He couldn't bring himself to say yes, either, so he just waited for Wallace to grab the glass of stout, and followed him into the kitchen.

Jamie was already there, an uncharacteristic frown

on his face when he glanced up from examining the pizza oven. He jerked his chin up. "Hey, Wallace."

"It's time," Wallace said ominously.

"Time for what?" Jamie asked.

"The chocolate stout."

Jamie stood and wiped his hands on the rag he'd thrown over his shoulder. "The Devil's Cock?"

Eric shook his head. "We haven't decided on that name yet."

Jamie ignored him completely and nodded toward the glass in Wallace's hand. "Let's do it."

Wallace gathered up three small sample glasses and poured. The dark brown brew looked solid and crisp, the head a nice cream color.

"This is the new cocoa, right? The Mexican?"

Wallace grunted as they each took a glass. "Yeah. And the chipotle peppers." There was a reason they were considering the name Devil's Cock. This stout was the darkest of dark, accented with chocolate and a kick of heat. It smelled black and wicked.

"Sláinte," Eric said, and they all tipped the glasses to their lips. Richness filled his mouth, flowing with the bitter hint of dark chocolate, sweetened by the malt. At the very end, smoky pepper touched his tongue.

"Christ, that's smooth," Jamie said.

Wallace didn't smile. "Yeah?"

Eric nodded. "This is it. A one-hundred-percent improvement over the last batch. It's gorgeous."

Wallace's eyes tilted a bit, as if he'd finally dared a small smile. Eric couldn't be sure past the beard.

The brewmaster took another drink and wiped the foam off his facial hair. "I was thinking end of November," he said.

"It'll be perfect for winter," Jamie agreed.

Eric nodded, but he wasn't sure. "Any chance we could do a limited rollout by mid-October? It could be a nice Halloween beer."

"No," Jamie said before Wallace could answer. "We've got the Harvest Ale, not to mention the work on rolling out the restaurant. And we haven't even decided on a name for this one, much less started a logo. It'd never get approved by the liquor board in time."

Wallace's eyes darted from Jamie to Eric as if he were waiting for an argument. His anticipation wasn't unfounded. Eric felt his neck tighten to rock. Jamie's words sounded like thrown fists, they were so hard.

Eric wanted to throw a few hard words back. He was the one who made these decisions, not Jamie. But Jamie was shouldering his way into the decision-making process now. A good thing, Eric assured himself. "Fine. Late November."

"And the name?" Jamie pressed.

"We'll talk about it."

His brother scowled. "It's a good name. Wallace, you like it, right? It was your idea."

Wallace shrugged one massive shoulder. "You two work it out."

"Good work, Wallace," Eric said as Wallace turned to retreat back to his tank room. It was his personal cave, and even though it belonged to the Donovans he growled like an ogre at anyone who entered without his permission.

Just as Wallace disappeared, the back door opened and their sister, Tessa, walked in on a shaft of morning sunlight. She was like a Disney character, bringing happiness and smiles with her. Eric used to joke about seeing bluebirds darting around her head. But after the past few months, he no longer looked for bluebirds. Little Tessa was all grown up now, and she had a man living in her house to prove it.

"What's going on?" she asked, strolling over.

"It's the new chocolate stout." He dipped his head toward the glass.

Tessa poured herself a sample and tried it. "Oh, so much better! It's perfect. I love the kick at the end."

"We're going to roll it out in November. I'll need you to start the logo process. I'll deal with the liquor board."

"Did we decide on the name?"

Jamie smirked. "Everyone still loves Devil's Cock, but Eric's scared."

"I'm not scared. I just don't want to offend anyone."

Tessa tilted her head. "I think it's fine. You know, names and logos are getting more and more edgy. And the logo will be a rooster, right? With devil horns?"

Eric crossed his arms and shifted.

"Jesus Christ," Jamie barked. "You were on board with it a few months ago."

"I only said I'd consider it."

"Hey, I've got an idea," Jamie said, leaning toward him as if he meant to share a secret. "Why don't you try manning up?"

Eric dropped his hands, balling them into fists. "Excuse me?"

"You heard me."

They were right back where they'd been for years, and Eric stepped into the old groove with ease, his decade of anger at Jamie snapping quickly back into place. "Look, little brother. I know your idea of planning is to throw anything and everything out there and hope something sticks, but that's not the way a professional goes through life. I'm responsible for the reputation of this brewery and—"

"Oh, you're kidding me, right? Because that is pure, hilarious irony coming from you. If you think—"

"Hey!" Tessa shouted, and Eric realized they'd both been yelling. "What is going on here? I think I missed something."

Eric's anger fell away like spilled water. He should've kept his mouth shut. Jamie, on the other hand, looked morbidly delighted.

He smiled. "Why don't you ask Eric?"

Eric shook his head. He didn't want to tell Tessa. She was his baby sister. He'd been her hero, once upon a time. "It's just a fight."

Her eyes narrowed. "I heard something about a woman coming in and starting an argument with Eric, but I assumed…" Her gaze slid to Jamie. "Everything's okay with you and Olivia, right?"

"Olivia and I are great, but thanks for the vote of confidence. Ask Mr. Perfect here what that was about. Oh, and watch out for falling pedestals, Tessa."

She rolled her eyes. "What's that supposed to mean?"

"It means the higher you are, the harder you fall. Especially if you've been pretending to be an angel."

"All right." Eric sighed. "That's enough."

"Not by far. But I'll let you explain to our sister. I've got to get to work."

Jamie disappeared into the barroom, and the doors swung silently in his wake, but Eric winced as if a door had slammed. His brain scrambled for a way to explain it all away, but he couldn't think. He was so damn tired. And guilty.

Tessa folded her arms. "*You're* having girl trouble? Is this April Fools' Day?"

"I wish it were."

"Come on. Give me the dirt." She was smiling as if it was a joke, because she couldn't imagine that Eric would ever do something scandal-worthy. He was the responsible one. The steady one. The one who never had time for fun, and didn't miss it for a second.

"It's no big deal," he lied. "Just an argument with a woman."

"Oh, is that all?" She leaned forward. "Seriously, Eric. *What* woman?"

"Someone I saw a few months ago. It was just one date. Nothing serious."

"Then why did she come in here to yell at you last night?"

Oh, that. He held his breath for a few moments, hoping that an earthquake would hit or a tornado siren would begin to sound. Anything to distract his sister from the question. But no natural disasters struck. And Tessa would find out, whether he told her or not. "What did you hear?"

"Come on," she groaned. "Out with it."

Eric took a deep breath, but it didn't make him feel any better. "The woman I went out with thought I was Jamie," he said quickly.

Tessa didn't react with horror. She didn't gasp and press a hand to her forehead. She just snorted. "That's ridiculous. You two don't look anything alike."

"Right. But she saw Jamie's nameplate at the business expo last spring, and she thought I was Jamie. That's all."

"Oh. Well, that's weird. Why would you... Whatever.

As long as you didn't sleep with her." That was when her amusement finally fell away. "You didn't, did you?"

Eric wished they were in his office so he could sit down. His legs didn't feel quite right. He paced to the glass wall that separated them from the tank room and watched Wallace as he polished one of the tanks.

"Eric? I was just joking."

He cleared his throat and made himself turn to face her. "I didn't correct her at first, and then it seemed too weird to bring it up. I didn't know what to say."

"You slept with her and never told her your real name?"

"I wasn't planning on seeing her at all! And then we…then we agreed that it would be a no-strings-attached thing. That we'd never see each other again, so I told myself it didn't matter."

Now she pressed a hand to her forehead. "Oh, no."

"Yeah."

"She found out."

"Yeah."

Her green eyes widened in dismay. "Oh, Eric. That's just…*terrible*."

"I know. I tried to apologize, to explain. But she was pretty pissed."

"Pissed?" Tessa echoed. "She probably feels awful!"

"I wish I could go back and change it, but I can't. At the time, it didn't seem to matter much."

"That's ridiculous. Why didn't you tell her your name? You must've had a reason!"

Yeah, he'd had a reason, but he wasn't going to tell Tessa about it. The first moment he'd seen Beth Cantrell, he'd wanted her. And that was before he'd realized who she was. The manager of a sex store. The curvy, gorgeous, sophisticated manager of an *erotic boutique*. She'd been way outside the boundary of his world. And then…she hadn't been.

She'd liked him. She'd been interested. Part of that interest had been Jamie's reputation as a man who was willing to play the game. And Eric had thought… Hell, Eric had thought he deserved to have the kind of fun his irresponsible brother had every day of the week.

He'd figured his brother's reputation was so wicked that one brief encounter wouldn't matter to anyone. But Jamie now claimed that the majority of his reputation was exaggeration, that he had hardly dated at all in the past few years.

Eric rubbed a hand over the tension in his neck. "I don't know. Every second I waited seemed to make it more significant. Suddenly, instead of a mix-up, it was a cover-up."

Tessa put her hands on her hips and glared. "Then you shouldn't have slept with her."

"Right." But that was the most ridiculous thing he'd ever heard. Beth Cantrell was a fantasy. His fantasy, anyway.

"By the way, since when do you have one-night stands?"

His face flashed to a blush. "I…"

"Is that why you never seem to date? Because you just pick up strangers all the time?"

"No! Good God, Tessa. You should go…wash your mouth out or something. No, I don't sleep with strangers all the time. Which should explain why I screwed it up."

"You need to go talk to her."

"I already apologized."

"I know, but she must feel like an idiot, Eric. Because of you."

He squeezed his eyes shut. "It's not a good idea. We were never supposed to see each other again."

"Well, that sounds a little over the top. Is she the daughter of your sworn enemy or something?"

Eric managed a smile. "It's not like that. She's nice." Actually, he had no idea if Beth was nice. She'd seemed nice during the few times he'd spoken to her. But what they'd done together hadn't been nice. It had been wicked.

And really, really nice. His shoulders slumped. "So I should talk to her?"

Tessa shrugged. "All I know is, I'd be feeling pretty freaked out if it were me. She probably thinks you're a serial killer now."

"So I should hunt her down and surprise her, huh?"

"You know what I mean. Just make her understand it had nothing to do with her. That it wasn't a game."

"I'll think about it," he said.

She shoved him toward the door. "Do it."

"Tessa—"

"Do it! Or I'll think you're a terrible person." She walked away and left him with those awful words. He didn't have a choice now, did he? Tessa was a girl; if she thought Eric needed to apologize again, then he probably needed to apologize again.

But surely Beth didn't want to see him. Hell, she hadn't wanted to see him again even when everything had been good.

Maybe he could just call. He opened the contacts file on his phone, but it was hopeless. He'd purposefully deleted her name and number. It had been distracting to see her there, one little name that seemed to glow brighter than the others. That name had tempted him, and some nights he'd found himself staring at it, trying to convince himself that one more meeting wouldn't hurt anything. Boy, had he been wrong about that.

He glanced up at the clock. Nine-thirty. What time did an erotic boutique open? He could drop by, see if she was there. Beth ran the place, and if she was anything like Eric, that meant she got there early and stayed late.

Shifting, he looked around, hoping some responsibility would drop out of the sky and demand his attention. But his responsibilities were dwindling by the day. Jamie had taken over some and Tessa had assumed others. They didn't need him the way they once had.

He knew where the White Orchid was. In fact, he probably could've driven there with his eyes closed, despite never having set foot in the place. It wasn't that he'd purposefully driven by, but the store was only half a mile from the brewery, and it pulsed like a beacon in his mind.

It *reminded* him. Of Beth and the fact that she was always so near.

Tessa was right. He needed to make amends, and then maybe Beth Cantrell would get out of his head for good.

CHAPTER FIVE

BETH CAUGHT THE METAL flash of a car pulling up, but by the time she looked out the door, the car had driven past and she couldn't see it. Kelly wasn't supposed to be in until eleven, and they didn't open for another twenty minutes.

She grimaced at the prospect of having to send an early customer away. The last time she'd done that, the guy had begged and pleaded, claiming to have some emergency that required massage oil *right away*.

That hadn't convinced her to unlock the door and let him in.

And here was another man. Why was it always men who—?

"Oh, no," she breathed, instinctively taking a step back. This wasn't just a man with an early-morning erotic need. It was *him*.

He—*Eric*, she reminded herself—looked like a man on a mission. Mouth set in a stern frown. Eyes narrowed against the sunlight. He took a deep breath and knocked on the glass, then shoved his hands into his pockets and waited.

Beth held her breath. She was only twenty feet away, but apparently he couldn't see her through the slightly tinted glass. Thank God, because she had absolutely no interest in being seen.

He frowned a little harder and his head dropped, almost as if he could hear her thoughts. His nearly black hair glinted as the wind shifted it, and Beth looked away. She hated that she still found him so attractive.

His next knock startled her, and Beth jumped. The movement drew his eye, and suddenly he was looking right at her. Her heart stammered, and when he raised his hand in greeting, she shook her head.

Eric didn't move.

"Damn it," she whispered. She turned and faced away from him, eyeing her office as if it was sanctuary. But it wasn't a very effective hiding place. She would have to unlock the front door in twenty minutes when the store opened, and Eric didn't look like he was going anywhere.

She glanced down at her clothes, happy she hadn't pulled on leggings and a sweatshirt this morning, as she'd been tempted to do. Instead she was wearing dark jeans and black patent heels. At least she could look good while she glared at him.

She took one deep breath before she turned around and strode toward the door. Eric didn't smile or gloat. He simply watched her solemnly.

The lock slid quietly free, when she'd been hoping it would crack like a whip. "What do you want?" she asked through the small space she'd opened.

"I hoped we could talk."

"No."

"Please," he pressed. "I know there's no excuse, but I'd still like to explain. To apologize. Anything."

He looked tired. And miserable. And still obnoxiously handsome in his cargo pants and black polo shirt. His gray-blue eyes held hers, as if he wanted her to see his sincerity.

And damn it, she *could* see it.

"Fine," Beth snapped. "You can come in. But only for a minute. I'm working." She opened the door wide to let him through and, as he passed, the faint scent of his soap hit her hard. Her knees actually went weak, as if she were leaving his bed again, her body limp with satisfaction.

She touched the door handle to ground herself in the present, then clicked the lock shut again.

She found him standing just a few feet inside, looking over the store as if it were a strange land he'd never visited. True enough, she supposed. The other brother was the one who'd come to the store with a girl.

For a moment, she just waited for him to turn around again, but as she shifted, crossing her arms and then uncrossing them, she realized she felt too vulnerable. She didn't know what to do with her hands. Didn't know if she should look casual or tense or aggressive. So Beth walked past him and moved around the glass countertop to her normal station next to the cash register. It felt better to have two feet of counter between them.

Eric seemed unable to tear his eyes away from the back-to-school display. Admittedly, it was a little different from most. The mannequin was dressed in a white button-down shirt and a short black skirt, and she held a ruler in one hand as she peered above the tops of her black glasses. But the other hand held a whip, and her platform shoes were adorned with five-inch metal heels. Beth especially liked the shiny red apple that was perched on top of the sex-ed books at her feet. It was cute and wicked at the same time, but Eric looked only stunned.

Beth cleared her throat.

"Sorry," he said, swinging around to her. "I mean, I'm sorry about everything. And how you found out."

She kept as little emotion in her eyes as possible, unwilling to be vulnerable for him again.

Eric took a step forward and set his hands opposite hers on the counter. For a moment he seemed distracted by the piercing jewelry beneath the glass, or maybe it was the metal cock rings, but then he shook his head. "I can't really explain why I didn't tell you my real name. It doesn't make any sense. It was wrong, and I knew it at the time."

"But you didn't care."

"It didn't feel real. I don't mean you, of course," he said quickly. "You felt… Yeah."

Her lips started to tilt up, so she pressed them together.

Eric cleared his throat. "But it was all a fantasy, wasn't it? I'm not the kind of guy who meets a beautiful woman and invites her to a hotel room. It felt like I was someone else."

"Your brother?"

He winced. "No. Just not myself."

She wanted to hate him. She *did* hate him. But she also knew what he meant. She wasn't the type of woman who slept with a man just a few hours after meeting him. Not that she'd admit that to Eric.

"You look more like an Eric," she said.

"Do I?"

Beth shrugged. "You can go now," she said icily, determined not to give in to the twinge of understanding she felt for him.

Silence hung heavy for a moment, and then he nodded. "All right. But I wasn't playing a game. I don't want you to feel I made a fool out of you."

She froze. "Excuse me?"

"I didn't," he said quickly.

"Oh, I know you didn't. I didn't do anything wrong."

His eyes widened in alarm. "Of course! I didn't mean to imply—"

"You made a fool out of yourself, Eric Donovan," she said past a tight jaw. "I'm fine. I'm great."

"Yeah," he said softly. "I know you are." His head bowed, but when Beth took a step back, he looked up again. The lines around his eyes looked deeper. "Thanks for letting me in. I just wanted to be sure you were okay."

"I am."

"Good." He left then, unlocking the door and offering a grim wave as he slipped out. Beth just stood there as he left and told herself she was glad she'd never see him again. He was a liar and a cheat, and he didn't deserve her attention.

Unfortunately, she knew from experience that he might still get it.

TALKING TO HER HADN'T helped.

Oh, maybe his conscience was very slightly appeased, but now Beth was in his head, stuck there like a spirit exacting its revenge.

Returning to the brewery didn't help, either. Tessa gave him a thumbs-up and a big smile, which made him feel like a wayward kid. And Jamie ignored him completely, which made Eric want to shove him and start a fight, just so they'd be interacting.

Eric had always been the mature one. Hell, when their parents were killed, he was only twenty-four, but he'd taken on the responsibility of his teenage siblings and the brewery, and he'd done it well. There'd been no partying, no vacations and very little dating in the thirteen years since then.

He'd worked. And he'd parented. And he'd set a good example. He'd done what he needed to do, despite the fact that he'd felt inadequate and scared to death the whole damn time.

But something had gone wrong in the past couple of years. Very wrong. His skin felt as if it had started shrinking, squeezing everything too tight inside his body. And his skull felt too small as well; he wore that tension like a helmet, making it hard to think. He felt… panicked. Which made no sense.

Despite the deal with the Kendall Group falling through, not to mention the trouble that had come after, things were going great. Profits had risen six percent for each of the past four years. A nice, steady growth. Jamie had finally grown up and was taking on new responsibilities. Tessa was happier than ever. And they were all finally getting along.

Everything was *good.* And Eric felt…lost.

He'd lost his hold, somehow. He'd lost control. The plans to expand the brewery into a restaurant were not part of Eric's plans, but he couldn't say no. They were partners, after all, he and Jamie and Tessa. Equal. And yet Eric wasn't equal. Not in his mind. And maybe not in theirs, either. Because he wasn't a Donovan. Not really. It felt like the worst sort of injustice that their dad had left him an equal part of the Donovan business, a cruel joke that Eric was the one to lead the brewery for so long.

Because, despite all the wonderful things he'd done for Eric, despite the role he'd filled, Michael Donovan hadn't been Eric's real father.

Eric could still remember his real dad, though only in broken bits and pieces. He'd come around on the weekends for the first few years after Eric was born. Then only on holidays. Then not at all.

Eric had his father's hair and his eyes. He had his genes. And not a drop of Donovan blood to justify his ownership of this place or the unconditional love that Michael Donovan had shown him.

Thinking about it made Eric's skull feel even tighter, so he rolled his neck and closed his eyes. Even his office felt too small. But he didn't want to spend time near Jamie, so Eric decided to catch up on the bottling schedule. It'd be a bitch working the line by himself, but it would be worth it if it wore him out. At least he'd get some sleep.

Eight hours later, when Eric headed home, he was definitely exhausted, but his mind was still working as frantically as ever.

"Dinner tomorrow!" Tessa yelled just as he escaped, and Eric winced. Sunday dinner with the family was not in his comfort zone this week. But if he didn't show, he'd look ashamed or cowed. Shit.

When he got to his condo—a simple two-bedroom that was nearly ascetic, even to his own eye—Eric made a sandwich, grabbed a beer and turned on a boxing match. Boxing was the perfect sport, in his opinion. There were rules and structure, but it was the most

basic of all competitions. The most primal. Beat the
other guy, literally. All other sports seemed to want to
dance around that issue. "Yeah, you can physically de-
stroy your opponent, but you have to be holding a ball
while you do it." That smacked of dishonesty to Eric,
but maybe he was only feeling sensitive to the issue.

Once it became clear that both boxers in this match
were hitting for points instead of a knockout, Eric
turned off the TV, grabbed another beer and headed
for the shower.

Ten minutes later, he was in bed and clicking on the
TV in the bedroom, his body still as tense as ever.

This was his life. Work. His family. And this white-
walled condo. Yet his family had grown up. Both Tessa
and Jamie had significant others now. They both had
homes they'd taken the time to make their own. And
they'd grown into the brewery, too. Eric's role in their
lives was shrinking, and how the hell was he supposed
to make up the loss?

He'd need to find a hobby. An interest. Or maybe he
could take over one hundred percent of the trade show
duties and spend more time on the road.

The thought wasn't satisfying, but it felt logical. He'd
run it by Jamie at dinner tomorrow. Jamie would probably be happy to avoid time away from his new girlfriend, at any rate. Up until now, the man had never
made a commitment to anyone, but he seemed damned
enthusiastic about his relationship with Olivia.

Maybe that was what Eric needed. A woman.

Unfortunately, Beth was the only woman who
popped into his head, and she was unavailable in so
many ways, starting with the fact that she hated his
guts. But, God, she'd been beautiful today. More beau-

tiful than she had been when Eric had first met her, or maybe it was just that he knew the exact shape of her breasts and shade of her nipples. Maybe it was that his fingers could still remember the way her curves had yielded to his touch.

She was gorgeous in that way '40s pinup girls were. Soft and curved and luscious. The embodiment of sex, even though her smile always kept its distance.

Not that there'd been any smiling today. But the anger in her eyes had mimicked the fierceness of her need in that hotel room. She'd wanted it as much as he had. They'd both been desperate. She'd knelt before him and curved her hands over the top of the headboard, her knuckles white as he'd started to ease into her tight body.

Eric closed his eyes against the flickering light of the television and shoved down the sheets. He closed a hand over his thickening cock and imagined it was Beth's hand wrapping around him. Instead of being pissed when he showed up at her store today, she was happy to see him, eager to pick up where they'd left off.

He stroked, feeling his shaft swell against his own hand, and imagined reaching for her jeans and tugging them down. Then he'd bend her over that countertop and strip down her panties. Would she let him have her like that? In the daylight, in her own store, with only a locked door between them and the rest of the world?

Her belly would be pressed to the cold glass of the counter, her ass naked and plump under his hands. And her sex would be just as wet and tight as he remembered. He'd slide in slow and careful, and she'd sigh with pleasure. Her arms would stretch out, flexing against the invasion. And then she'd beg him to fuck her harder. She'd call him by his real name and it would be perfect.

Eric stroked himself faster, his fingers growing slick with pre-come. In his fantasy, Beth cried out, her back arching. "Fuck me, Eric," she moaned, and he felt that surge of power that came with knowing he could make a woman like her come. She'd shaken in his arms and sobbed, and it had felt like a damned miracle to make a woman like her shatter.

Even in his imagination it was a carnal miracle, and Eric took himself with a brutal grip as he remembered her sex squeezing him.

"Come," Beth ordered inside his mind, and so he came, the heat splashing across his stomach instead of filling her up, but it still felt better than anything he'd done since that long-ago night in that anonymous hotel room.

Eric let his head fall back into the pillow and he finally felt tired. Thank God.

BETH HAD A CLASS TO TEACH on Monday, so she surveyed the store for research items when her shift was over. On Saturday night, the place was busy with couples looking for fun and groups of women who giggled over dildos before surreptitiously placing them in shopping bags. Beth had made the switch from baskets to bags to save people the self-consciousness of browsing while toting around a thirty-two-ounce bottle of lube. Some people got a little funny about that.

When she didn't see anything particularly inspiring in the toy room, Beth went to her office to dig through the boxes there. They seemed to get a new set of factory samples every other day, and she could definitely find some inspiration in those innocuous-looking cardboard boxes.

Sure enough, she found a new model she'd never seen before and shoved the plastic box into her purse with a glance over her shoulder to see who was watching, just as if she was one of those shy customers. This self-consciousness was the bane of her existence. She could help an eighty-year-old couple pick out a set of his-and-her vibrators without blinking an eye, but she couldn't discuss her own sex life without stammering and blushing. Luckily, Cairo wasn't so reticent, and she was always happy to help with the classes.

Speaking of which. "Don't forget Monday night," she said as she waved goodbye to Cairo.

"G-spot!" Cairo called. "Got it!" Her gorgeous smile didn't even twitch. Had she been born with that confidence? More importantly, was there a way Beth could steal it from her and make it her own?

It might be fun for a while. Beth couldn't imagine having the sexual confidence to take on two men at a time. Hell, she was usually a disappointment one-on-one. Not that she was *inadequate*. It was only that men seemed to think of her as an exotic animal. The proprietress of a sex shop. The keeper of strange and shivery erotic secrets. The woman who would touch you in a place you didn't even know you had and make your body weep liquid drops of joy.

Meanwhile, Beth was just hoping she could finally find her G-spot so she wouldn't be a complete fraud on Monday night. But judging by the other classes she'd given, even a complete fraud could delight a store full of willing students. Beth didn't exactly consider herself a master in the art of fellatio, either, but she'd received lots of happy emails after that little seminar.

Speaking of which…Beth ducked back into the store. "Cairo, are you doing the column for next Wednesday?"

"Yep. I'll send it to you tomorrow."

"Thanks. You're the best."

The columns. The classes. It was too much. Annabelle Sanchez, the owner of the store, was coming up with all sorts of new marketing ideas, which would've been fine if she weren't on a worldwide tour to help her find her "inner goddess."

Beth sighed as she drove her car toward home. Sometimes she wanted to kill Annabelle. She really did. Granted, Annabelle was her best friend and the owner of the White Orchid, and Beth loved her like a sister— a New Agey, slightly overbearing sister—but her world tour of self-exploration had gone on long enough. If she wanted classes given at the White Orchid, *she* should be the one giving them, not Beth. If Annabelle wanted a sex column written for the local alternative paper, she should write it. Because Beth certainly didn't know enough to contribute a new topic every week.

Thank God the other girls in the shop had agreed to help. Now they split the column up amongst them, Beth edited it so that the style of each was consistent, and the column was posted under the name Ms. White.

Beth had hoped that slight remove would protect her, but her plan had backfired. Her employees had been so excited that they'd had the first column mounted and framed. And the second. And third. Now all four of the columns were hanging on the wall of the White Orchid, and Beth was widely believed to be the author of all.

Her reputation for sexual knowledge was only growing, and none of it truly belonged to her.

Annabelle was supposed to have returned months
ago, and if she would just come home, everything would
be fine. She could lead the classes. She could write the
columns. But Annabelle kept extending her trip. First
by sixty days. Then ninety. Her latest stop was in Egypt,
to study the sex beliefs of ancient Egyptians.

Beth was pretty sure that half of her impatience with
Annabelle was that Beth wanted to be the one traveling
to other countries to study their cultures. After all, her
major had been anthropology before she'd transferred to
women's studies. Then again, exotic countries weren't
really her cup of tea. No doubt Annabelle was striding
around the teeming streets of Egypt with complete confidence. Beth would be constantly worried about being
mugged or kidnapped or simply standing out too much.

She needed to grow a pair. "Of ovaries," she told
herself. But she was trying. She was. Unfortunately,
her biggest risk-taking success had been Eric, and look
how that had turned out. It had been a disaster. A lovely,
bone-melting, burning hot disaster.

Beth groaned and set him from her mind. It was late,
nearly ten o'clock, and dark as midnight by the time she
pulled up to her apartment, and she still had work to do.

Thirty minutes later, Beth was lying on her bed, staring at the ceiling in frustration, the specialized G-spot
toy clutched in her hand like a broken tool. "There is
no G-spot," she told the ceiling, letting her feet slide
down until her thighs touched the mattress. Guilt immediately washed over her. Whether she had a func-
tioning G-spot or not, plenty of her friends talked about
it. Could she discount the experiences of other women

just because of her own experience? That was the worst kind of condescension.

Beth tossed the toy to the far side of the bed, shoved her book on female sexuality out of the way and reached for the drawer of her bedside table.

There were rows of toys inside. Models that retailed for two hundred dollars. Shapes that might make the layperson frown in confusion, but Beth ignored them all for her innocuous, unimpressive, tiny silver bullet massager. An embarrassment of riches, and all she wanted was this. Yet another boring secret.

Beth closed her eyes and touched herself, trying to relax enough to enjoy it. She needed to enjoy it. The last few days had been really crappy, thanks to Eric Donovan.

Why did he have to be the only man she'd responded to in so long? Why did he have to be the one whose touch had washed over her like electricity? His hand had slipped down her spine like a whisper when he'd unzipped her dress. He'd trailed heat everywhere he touched.

Beth arched her neck and curved her hand over her breast just the way he had, the thumb sliding over her nipple.

The electricity returned, swarming down her body to meet up with the buzz of the vibrator.

She didn't want to think about him. She wouldn't. She was so pissed at what he'd done. But somehow the anger just spiraled deep and made the pleasure burn brighter.

He'd been so serious. So intent. She'd worried that night, like she always did. Worried he wouldn't be as good as she wanted him to be, *needed* him to be. But for once her brain hadn't been able to keep up with her body. Because he *had* been good. He'd kissed her breasts, sucked at her until she'd cried out.

Beth squeezed her nipple hard and gasped at the pleasure.

He'd hardly had to touch her at all, and she'd been so close. She'd begged for it.

Best of all, she'd felt like a goddess as she'd taken him, as she'd arched her back and met his thrusts and gasped at the width of him as he filled her.

She slid her hand down her belly and over her hip, feeling the same skin that he'd felt, touching the same hip he'd gripped in his strong hand as he'd fucked her. And then her body tightened with sudden, surprising speed and she was crying out his name as she came.

Beth's hands were still shaking when her eyes popped open. "Shit," she panted. Had she really just gotten off while thinking about that lying jackass? Had she just gotten off in *record time* while thinking about him?

She groaned in frustration, but her body was limp and heavy against her bed. It didn't seem to give a damn what he'd done; it liked Eric Donovan just fine, no matter what his name was.

She'd tried not to use him as fantasy fodder too often, worried he would become even more powerful in her mind. Afraid that if she relived it too often, she'd never enjoy another man as much as she had Eric. Turned out she'd had good reason to be worried. Even when she hated him, she wanted his body.

"Not fair," she whispered. Not fair at all. He wouldn't leave her alone.

Five minutes later, she hadn't fallen asleep. In fact, she was still lying there thinking about Eric Donovan.

Who was he? Why had he lied? He certainly didn't seem like a skeevy kind of guy. He seemed a hundred percent together. Confident, handsome, successful.

Beth got up, pulled on some sweats and went to her computer. She'd been looking for information on the wrong man last time, so she typed in Eric Donovan's name and waited.

There were still only a few image files. That group shot she'd seen before, and another she hadn't noticed that included him sitting at a judges' table at some beer competition.

Beth looked at the group shot again. Eric and Jamie didn't look like brothers. Not at all. They didn't even look like cousins. Their body language and expressions were totally different.

She clicked around a little while, but there were so many hits about the brewery that Beth couldn't filter out any information about the man. There was plenty about his brother, but nothing out there about Eric. Maybe that was the information she was looking for. He flew under the radar. He didn't rock the boat. He put his head down and did his job and that was it. Maybe he was a little like Beth.

She tried to imagine herself lying to someone about who she was. And she sadly realized right then that she could do it. That it would be a relief.

She sighed and clicked on another tab. News stories about the brewery popped up, and she was already starting to navigate away when a name caught her eye. Graham Kendall. Glancing at the heading again, she saw that it still read Eric Donovan.

"What the heck?" Beth clicked on the story and waited while the newspaper website loaded. When it finally did, Beth pressed her hand to her mouth to stifle a gasp.

"Felony charges have been filed against a prominent member of the Kendall Group. Graham Kendall, son of Kendall Group president Roland Kendall, has been charged with theft and fraud related to break-ins at several local businesses."

Graham Kendall? Local businesses? Beth's jaw dropped.

"Though there's been no comment from any member of the Kendall Group, court records show that Graham Kendall has failed to make several court appearances. Police suspect he fled the country weeks ago. Victims of the alleged crimes include iconic local Front Range businesses, such as Creek Construction and Boulder's Donovan Brothers Brewery."

Beth scanned the rest of the article so quickly that she felt dizzy.

Good God, what had happened? She pressed a hand over her thundering heart.

She knew the Kendalls. She'd gone to school with Graham's sister and she'd been a guest of the family many times. But it wasn't just that. Yes, she'd known the Kendalls for years, and yes, she knew Eric Donovan. But the horror pumping adrenaline into Beth's veins was that she was the one who'd pushed the Kendalls and the Donovans into business together.

She hit Google again, but the results were overwhelming. Both Donovan Brothers and the Kendall family had thousands of hits, and a lot of the sites just kept leading her to lists of Colorado businesses. She found one other news story, but it offered the same information as the first one. What was wrong with modern news media? Didn't they ever do follow-ups?

She tried over and over again, using different search terms and combinations, but she could find nothing.

What the hell had Graham Kendall *done?*

Beth didn't know him well. She'd met him only a few times, because even though she'd been Monica Kendall's freshman roommate, they hadn't been close friends. Monica was a spoiled rich girl and in college she'd hung out with other rich kids. Then she'd pledged her sorority and moved on from dormitory living. But her father, Roland Kendall, had taken a liking to Beth, hoping she'd be a good influence on his daughter. He'd invited Beth over for family dinners several times.

When Graham had been at dinner, Beth had thought he was a typical overprivileged kid, as well. He'd even made a sloppy pass at her one night, but she'd stopped him before it had gone too far. It had never occurred to her that he might be a criminal.

Beth closed the Google window and opened her email. Surely she'd exchanged emails with Monica at some point. She paged through and sorted for long minutes, desperate to find a contact. Her heart beat hard. Beth was the one who'd asked Roland Kendall to consider a partnership with the Donovans. It had seemed like a good deed at the time, though she'd thought she was extolling the virtues of Jamie Donovan, when it had really been Eric.

"Thank God," she muttered as she finally found Monica's email address. She typed out a simple message, asking what had happened between her family and the brewery.

Now she just had to wait. But her mind wouldn't stop turning even long after she hit Send.

CHAPTER SIX

A RAINY EVENING WAS BAD news for the Donovan Sunday dinner. Even though Tessa's house—the house they'd all grown up in—was plenty big, it never seemed big enough on a Sunday. The backyard served as a nice outlet. A place to escape when he and Jamie started arguing. Or when Jamie got too much of watching Tessa and her boyfriend, Luke, make eyes at each other. Or sometimes Tessa sent all the men outside so she and Olivia could talk about them.

But today, they were all stuck inside together, and tensions were running high. "You said you'd bring dessert," Jamie insisted, his tone implying that Eric's word couldn't be trusted.

"That was last week, Jamie. You were supposed to bring something."

"No way."

"It doesn't matter," Tessa interrupted. "I think we'll survive without cake for one night."

"Screw it," Jamie said, tugging his phone from his pocket with a scornful look for Eric. "Olivia's still on her way. I'll have her stop and get something."

"Wow, you're really saving the day," Eric snapped. "Congratulations."

"Guys," Tessa groaned. "Seriously."

Eric paced over to the counter and stole a few grapes from a bowl. "Where's Luke?"

"He'll be here soon. He's been at the station since nine, unfortunately."

"Big murder case?" Eric asked.

Tessa laughed and slapped his arm. "Stop. That's my joke. Anyway, he did get a big murder case this summer, so I had to stop using it. If I can't use it, no one can."

"Simone's back, right?" Luke's partner had been on maternity leave, and he'd refused to have another detective take her place, even temporarily.

"Yes, thank God. She's been back for over a month, which has eased his schedule a little. But he keeps trying to force her to leave work early every night, and I'm afraid she's going to punch him in the face."

Jamie snorted. "Tell her to go for it."

"You'd love that, wouldn't you?" Despite the words, Tessa's smile was wide. Jamie might've had a few problems with Luke early on, but they seemed to be building a cautious friendship now. The main problem was that they were too much alike, and Jamie didn't think a guy like Luke was good enough for Tessa. Actually, neither Eric nor Jamie believed any man was good enough for their little sister, but they were getting used to it. Slowly.

Tessa put Eric to work making the salad, and he was happy for the excuse to turn his back on his siblings and slice tomatoes in the corner of the kitchen. It was painfully uncomfortable to have his family know about Beth. And they hardly knew anything at all. He didn't know how Jamie had lived with being irresponsible for so long. It was a fucking burden, and if Eric hadn't been so stubborn, he would've avoided Sunday dinner like the plague.

Eric felt a flash of sympathy for his little brother. He stole a glance at Jamie before grabbing the lettuce to wash it.

Jamie's plans for adding a menu to the bar had caused a blowup this summer. Okay, a series of blowups. Eric was still sorting through all the things Jamie had said to him. That Eric had made him feel like a second-class owner for years. That Jamie wasn't going to put up with being treated like a little brother anymore.

But if Eric wasn't the big brother, if he wasn't in charge, who the hell was he? He wasn't even a real Donovan, for God's sake. A fact so embarrassing that no one ever brought it up, not even in the heat of the worst argument. But it was there, sitting between them. The reason he didn't look like any of the pictures on the wall. The reason he had an Irish last name and Eastern European features. It was the reason Eric worked twice as hard as everyone else in the family. Because he'd inherited a third of the brewery when he shouldn't have, and it weighed on his shoulders every damn day.

Eric rolled those tight shoulders and grabbed the salad dressing from the fridge.

Olivia finally arrived, a bakery box in her hands, and dessert was taken care of, but Eric and Jamie still weren't talking.

Eric shredded some carrots into the salad and watched as Jamie pulled Olivia into his arms and kissed her until she giggled and melted into him.

Jamie was happy, and Eric was happy for him, but he couldn't shrug off his angry guilt. Maybe he'd screwed up when he was trying to raise two teenagers, but he'd done his best. He'd been trying to motivate Jamie, not make him feel like dirt. But Jamie had cast Eric as the bad guy. And Eric's lie to Beth had made things worse than they'd ever been.

The salad was done, and now Eric was just standing there, staring at the big wooden bowl that had once been their mom's. He could vividly remember her passing the bowl around the table, chiding her husband to stop making faces at the vegetables.

"I'm an Irishman," Michael Donovan would say. "The only vegetables we eat are potatoes and cabbage."

"You're an American," Eric's mom would counter. "You eat salad."

But Eric would always try to push his salad aside with his fork, wanting to be just as Irish as Michael Donovan. Then his dad would wink and take a big bite of salad. "We'd better do what she wants, son. We've got to teach your baby brother to eat healthy, even if it makes us feel like rabbits."

Christ, Michael Donovan had been a good man. The best. And when he'd died, Eric had tried his damnedest to step into those shoes. Apparently, he'd failed miserably.

Eric cleared his throat and wiped his hands on a towel. "Jamie," he said, tossing the towel on the counter and turning toward his brother. "I've been thinking."

Jamie's eyes narrowed as if that were a threat.

"You're busy now with all the restaurant planning. You've got your hands full. So why don't I take over the trade show circuit?"

"What do you mean?" he growled.

"I mean you won't have the time to travel for a while.

With all the hiring and training and the marketing push. It's going to be crazy."

"You hate the shows," Jamie said.

Yeah, he did. But he'd do it for his little brother. Eric shrugged. "It's no big deal. I know you're sort of the face of the company, but—"

"But you'd be happy to take that over?"

Eric frowned at the edge in his brother's voice. "I wouldn't say happy, but we obviously need to shift—"

Jamie laughed. "I can't believe this. I finally get a little more responsibility, and now you want to start chipping away at my public role?"

"That's not it at all. I'm trying to help. I'm trying to be *supportive*." He sneered the word even though he didn't mean to, but Jamie was starting to piss him off.

"Oh, yeah?" Jamie scoffed. "Since when?"

"Guys," Tessa warned.

Eric ignored her and took a step forward. "Since when? Since I got behind this restaurant idea in the first place. Since I told you to go ahead and turn our brewery into something else."

Tessa held up both hands. "We are not supposed to talk about work on Sundays. That's the rule."

Jamie ignored her, just as Eric had. He crossed his arms and offered that tight smile again. "Something else, huh? Something not as good as your ideas for the brewery, is that what you're saying? Is that what you've been thinking this whole time?"

"Something just like every other goddamned brewpub in the state!" Eric shouted.

Now even Olivia seemed alarmed. She got up from her chair and put her hand on Jamie's arm. "Why don't we go watch TV? Is it still baseball season?"

"Don't worry," Jamie said. "This is nothing unusual. I'm used to always being the one in the wrong."

"That's not what I said," Eric interrupted. "I'm trying to help."

"Really? Because you seem to manage just fine with balancing all your work at the brewery and still making the trade show trips."

"You're being ridiculous," Eric snapped. "This is all new for you. It'll take you time to adjust."

"I think it's taking *you* time to adjust, Eric. And I think you don't want me at trade shows, talking up all the changes we're making, because you don't approve."

"Screw you," Eric responded. "This discussion is over."

"Good!" Tessa yelped.

But Jamie shook his head. "No, you don't get to start a fight and pretend you didn't. Not after this week."

"Don't," Eric warned.

"Don't what? Don't bring up what *you* did?"

Tessa said, "Jamie!" but he ignored her and stepped toward Eric.

Eric met him in the middle of the kitchen.

Jamie let all his disgust show in a sneer. "Don't bring up that you completely betrayed me just to get a piece of ass?"

"That is not what happened."

"You used my name. You used the reputation you've spent years sneering at. All because some random chick was putting out and you wanted a sample?"

"Watch it," Eric growled, fury eating up every crumb of guilt that still clung to him. "Don't talk about her."

"*Her?* Because she meant so much to you? That stranger you fucked with *my* name?"

"Jamie!" both women shouted at once, but Jamie just smiled.

"Let me ask you something, brother...."

Eric felt his fists float up slowly, as if they were raised by someone else's arms.

"What name did she call you when—?"

Eric punched his brother. He punched *Jamie.* The moment his fist connected, Eric was already sorry. The regret crashed into him even as furious momentum kept his arm moving forward.

He heard the women scream, heard Jamie grunt, but, thankfully, Eric had been standing too close to get good leverage, and Jamie stumbled back but didn't fall. Nothing broke. Nothing bled. But Eric was sure he heard a momentous split crack through the room.

"Eric!" Tessa screamed. "Eric, stop!"

But it wasn't Eric that needed stopping now. Jamie touched his jaw, eyes blank with surprise, but it took no more than a second for those eyes to flatten into rage. He jumped forward and Eric stepped back.

Jamie's first swing slid so closely past Eric's nose that the breeze danced over his skin. But Jamie's second blow landed square in Eric's stomach. Eric grabbed for him, trying to catch his breath as he wrestled Jamie backward. Jamie punched him in the stomach again, but Eric's stomach was already numb, so he hardly felt it.

He shoved Jamie off and raised his fists again, ready for the next round, but a hand closed over the back of Eric's neck and pulled him back.

"That's enough!" Luke Asher's cop voice was damned effective. Eric froze automatically, as if he had to worry that Luke would draw his gun. Jamie didn't stop quickly enough, and Luke dropped his hold on Eric and lunged forward to grab Jamie by the shoulders. "I said, that's enough! You two can punch each other around as much as you like in private. But you won't do it in front of Tessa."

"You idiots!" she yelled, and Eric could hear the tears in her voice. He winced and dropped his head.

"I'm sorry," he said, pressing a hand to his stomach. It was no longer numb. "I don't know what happened."

"You hit me, you dumb shit," Jamie growled. "That's what happened." Olivia clung to his arm, watching Eric with wary eyes.

"I'm sorry," he repeated. His muscles screamed with adrenaline.

Tessa pointed at Jamie. "You were being cruel. You should apologize, too."

"He *hit* me," Jamie insisted.

"Well, you almost deserved it," Tessa said.

Luke stepped warily back, keeping an eye on both men.

Tessa wiped tears from her cheeks. "You two are getting ridiculous. You're worse than you were ten years ago. What's going on?"

Eric wanted to blame it on Jamie. After all, Jamie was the one who'd caused trouble in the past. But Jamie wasn't doing anything wrong now. He'd settled down. He'd changed. And now Eric was the one swinging in the breeze. He'd actually punched his brother in the face, and despite all the screaming, yelling, pushing fights they'd had in the past, neither of them had ever hit each other before today. "I'm sorry," Eric said again. "I'll go."

He started for the front door, leaving chaos behind him. Tessa was ordering him to stay. Jamie was threatening to leave if Eric didn't. And Olivia made sympathetic noises and urged Jamie to calm down.

For the first time in Eric's life, he walked away from his family. And as the old oak door shut behind him and silenced all the noise, he didn't know whether he felt sad or just…relieved.

CHAPTER SEVEN

BETH TRIED NOT TO LET HER stage fright over tonight's class ruin the whole day. A shipment from their highest-end lingerie line was in, and one of Beth's favorite tasks was unpacking box after box of gorgeous silk. It felt like Christmas to her: exciting and surprising and she always ended up spending a lot of her own money.

The gorgeous silk was even enough to distract her from her thoughts about the Kendalls, but it still weighed heavily at the back of her mind. Monica hadn't responded to the email, and for all Beth knew she didn't even use that email address anymore.

Beth had hit Google again, first thing this morning, but she'd found nothing more than the day before. It was as if no one else cared about this story except her. But the Donovans must care. They'd apparently been robbed and defrauded and violated. Did Eric blame Beth? Surely not. He'd been determined to do business with the Kendall Group. Beth had just facilitated that. And she clearly owed him nothing, regardless.

Beth hung up the last of her favorite baby-doll night-gowns and headed back to her office with a sigh. If she could just find out what had happened with the Kendalls and then get through tonight's class, everything would be fine. For a couple of weeks. Until it was time for the next evening class.

Determined to take control of at least one part of her life, Beth looked up Monica's company, High West Air, and called the main number.

"Ms. Kendall isn't in the office today," the receptionist said with a weary edge to the words, as if she'd spoken them a thousand times over in the past few weeks.

"Can I leave a message? Please tell her that Beth Cantrell called. I truly need to speak with her about a personal issue."

The receptionist promised to deliver the message, but Beth wasn't hopeful. The family had to be in lockdown mode. To her surprise, her cell phone rang a few seconds later. "Hello?"

"Beth? It's Monica Kendall."

It had been years, but the cool voice was immediately familiar. Beth blinked in surprise. "Monica! How are you?"

"Oh, things are crazy. Just awful. I guess that's what you were calling about."

"It was, yes."

She sighed. "I saw your email. I'm sorry I didn't have time to respond."

"It's okay. I know you must be overwhelmed."

"I am!"

She waited a few beats, but when Monica didn't continue, Beth decided to just jump right into it. "I don't really know how to say this, so I'll just be honest. I know someone who works at the brewery—one of the Donovans, actually—but I wanted to call you to find out what had happened."

"One of the Donovans, huh? I bet it's that little slut, Jamie, isn't it?"

Beth actually gasped. She didn't know why. She

didn't even know the man, but Monica's offhand insult sent a jolt of shock through her body. "I…"

"He's the one who got me pulled into this bullshit," Monica snapped.

"Oh. I thought your brother was the one in trouble. The news said he'd left the country." Fled the country was more like it, but Beth tried the diplomatic route.

"This is all Graham's mess. All of it. I had nothing to do with it, despite what Jamie Donovan says."

"Nothing to do with what? I still have no idea what's going on."

Monica sighed in that exact same irritated way she'd used to whenever Beth had been unwilling to sleep in the TV room of the dorm so that Monica could be alone with her boyfriend of the week. "It's unbelievable. Graham got himself into deep shit in Vegas. Gambling. Coke parties. Hookers. What a complete loser. He fell into debt and started dealing with some contacts overseas. You know what I mean."

"No, I don't know," Beth said patiently. Was this some sort of rich people talk?

"Eastern Europeans. The Chinese. There's plenty of money to be made if you're selling the right goods."

"What goods?"

Monica laughed, the sound dripping with condescension. "Social Security numbers, credit card numbers. Very popular items in the emerging markets."

What Beth wanted to say was, "You sound awfully high-and-mighty for a woman whose family is under investigation for criminal activity," but she bit her tongue and waited for the urge to pass. She'd done a lot of tongue biting during her freshman year of college, and it was a little like riding a bike. She still knew how to work Monica Kendall. "But how did you get dragged into this, Monica?"

Monica sighed again, the sound fraught with self-pity and martyrdom. "My first mistake was having sex with Jamie Donovan."

The words stabbed straight into Beth's gut before her brain could kick in. Jealousy rolled through on a horrible, sickening wave, even as Beth told herself it wasn't true. Or actually, it might be true, but it had nothing to do with Beth. Monica's Jamie Donovan was a different man. A different mouth. Different hands. He hadn't touched icy Monica Kendall after he'd touched Beth.

Unless, of course, he made a habit of lying about his name.

"Jamie Donovan?" she finally managed to croak.

"Your *friend?*" Monica drawled.

"No, I… Is he the bartender? Blond hair?"

"Ha. I'd describe it as more a washed-out brown, but, yeah. That's him. I can't believe I let him talk his way into my bed. And then when I wasn't interested in seeing him again, he told the police I had something to do with the robbery."

"Really?"

"Yes. Can you believe it? What a loser."

Jamie Donovan hadn't struck Beth as any kind of loser at all. He'd been handsome and confident, and even in that brief interaction, his natural charisma had been obvious. "So you're under investigation, too? It's not just Graham?"

"It's so unfair. Me! I keep thinking it's got to be some sort of awful joke."

"I can't imagine."

"I knew you'd understand, Beth. You've known me longer than almost anyone."

That was a bit of an exaggeration. Monica had plenty of friends from high school, where she'd been the queen bee. And *known* wasn't exactly the right word, either. Beth and Monica were, at best, acquaintances at this point.

"Beth, do you think you could do me a little favor?"

"Um…" Beth stared warily at her desk. "What kind of favor?"

"If the police were to get in touch with you, maybe you could mention that we had this conversation."

"What conversation?"

"About Jamie Donovan. About how he's trying to fuck me over because I wouldn't let him fuck me sideways." She laughed as if she were delighted with herself.

"Monica—"

"You have no idea what he's like. You know the type—a woman's never said no to him, so he can't accept it when one does. He's spoiled."

Spoiled? Beth took the phone from her ear and stared at it in disbelief. If that wasn't the pot calling the kettle black… "How can this possibly matter?" she finally asked. "Why would the police ever call me?"

"Well, they call me often enough, believe me. So if I happen to mention that you and I had this conversation…"

"Yes, we had this conversation. That won't mean anything to them if they already suspect you, Monica."

"So maybe you could tell them we had this conversation six months ago."

Monica had shocked the hell out of her again. Beth

shook her head and kept shaking it. "I'm not going to lie to the police for you."

"It's not really a lie. I mean, don't you believe what I'm telling you? Jamie and I were supposed to be having a business meeting, and instead he got me drunk on that crappy beer, took me home and took advantage of me. And then when I—"

"He took *advantage* of you? That's not quite how you said it."

"Listen to me," Monica hissed. "I'm not going down for my idiot brother. I don't have a gambling problem. I don't spend too much money on coke and whores. They can throw him in prison for fifty years for all I care, but I didn't do anything wrong. And you…" She took a deep breath as if she were gearing up for a scream. *"You,"* she ground out. "After everything my family did for you, the least you can do is back me up."

"Excuse me? What did your family ever do for me?"

"The dinners, the introductions, the trips to Aspen…"

"There was *one* trip to Aspen, and the dinners and everything else were for your benefit."

"My benefit? What the hell are you talking about?"

Beth didn't want to say this. Monica might be a bitch, but it wasn't easy for Beth to deliberately hurt someone's feelings. Still, there was another condescending laugh lurking just beneath the surface of Monica's voice. Beth could hear it. "Your dad thought I was a good influence on you. He wanted me around because he didn't like those snobby girls you were always hanging around with."

"My sorority sisters? How dare you!"

"Talk to your father," Beth interrupted.

For a moment, Monica sounded as if she couldn't get

any words out of her throat, but she finally managed, with a vengeance. "Look, you little slut. My father let you latch on to us because he felt sorry for you. You were poor and quiet and always carrying around about thirty too many pounds. You owe us, so you'd better back me up if the police get in touch. Understand?"

Beth hung up. There was nothing left to say. Not to Monica, anyway. She waited, shoulders tense and hands clutched together, but the phone didn't ring again. Silly that it could hurt to hear those things from someone she neither liked nor respected, but it stung. She had been poor and shy back then, and she hadn't known how to dress for her figure. Oversize shirts and baggy jeans had been a mistake.

She managed a smile at that understatement. A mistake didn't begin to cover her fashion choices back then. She'd been hiding. But she'd learned. So screw Monica. College was supposed to be the place where you discovered who you truly were deep inside. Beth had made big strides in college and afterward. Monica hadn't changed at all.

Not for the better, anyway.

Beth stared down at the phone, feeling that she should do something. She had to do something, didn't she? A woman who was being investigated by the police had just asked Beth to lie for her. Was Beth an accessory now? She'd never even had a parking ticket.

But she didn't understand. What could Monica have to do with theft? She was hardly going to climb over security fences in her Manolo Blahniks.

Beth did another Google query for Graham Kendall, but she didn't find any new details. Then she pulled up the website of the Boulder Police Department. She couldn't call 911 about something so trivial. But who would she call? The tip line? That seemed melodramatic.

She stared at the phone, biting her thumbnail until she realized what she was doing and forced her hand down.

The thing was…what if part of Monica's story was true? What if Jamie had taken advantage of her? Would the Donovans even want Beth bringing all this up to the police?

She couldn't imagine it. The man Beth had met had been outraged over Eric's lie. Surely, if Jamie Donovan was an immature, arrogant asshole, he would've been high-fiving his brother over a good score. Then again, you couldn't tell what some men were like. Beth knew that from personal experience.

She didn't owe them anything. Even if she had encouraged Roland Kendall to do business with the Donovans, this wasn't her fault. Not really. At most, they were even now, she and Eric. He'd lied to her over and over, and she'd…introduced him to a family who'd stolen and lied and dragged the brewery into an international fraud investigation.

"Crap," she muttered.

She wanted nothing to do with any of this. She certainly didn't want to talk to Eric again. But now she had information that might affect a police investigation.

"Crap." She had no choice.

Beth picked up the phone, but she didn't call the police. She called the brewery instead. Eric wasn't in, so she asked for his voice mail, even as she wondered if a brewery would have a voice mail system. Somehow, she pictured messages being written down on napkins, but then the phone clicked and Eric's voice was in her ear.

Beth closed her eyes at the sound. His voice was gruff and deep and sexy, and she was abruptly taken back to Saturday night and her fantasies about him.

Silence rang in her ear and she realized she'd already heard the beep. "Oh, hi. Eric. This is Beth. Cantrell. I wanted to talk to you about something. Um…could you give me a call?" She left her cell number and hung up, accidentally clattering the phone hard against the receiver.

Cringing, she waited. And waited. Ten minutes later, she made herself get back to work. An hour later she told herself to stop worrying. And by the end of the day, she'd put him from her mind. If he never wanted to talk to her again, so be it. Good riddance to bad rubbish. She'd only been trying to help.

CHAPTER EIGHT

ERIC HADN'T PLANNED ON setting foot in the brewery until Tuesday. He'd worked from home instead, making calls and booking hotels for the winter beer fest in Phoenix in November. He didn't want to talk to his family, and when Tessa finally called, he let it go to voice mail. But by the end of the day, he was pacing the small dimensions of his condo, desperate to get behind his desk and do the last few things on his schedule that he couldn't do from home.

By six-thirty, he'd decided it was safe. Tessa was likely long gone, and if Jamie was still there, he'd be in the front room. Eric could sneak in, shut his door and work for another hour or two before heading back home.

When he saw neither Tessa's nor Jamie's car in the lot, Eric breathed a sigh of relief. Monday was a fairly quiet evening, so they'd left the barroom in the capable hands of Chester, who'd recently been promoted to supervisor to let Jamie spend more time on the restaurant plans.

Eric walked in without worrying he'd run into a family member he owed an apology to, and sat behind his desk with a grim smile. He had fifteen voice mails, but he knew from experience to leave those until he was done with his current worries.

He sank into his work, the only place he could manage to lose himself, and was surprised to look up an hour later and realize how much time had passed. Once he'd sent the last graphics file he owed the ad agency, he picked up his phone and jotted down messages. Distributors, the glass company, a follow-up question from the liquor board. He was in auto mode halfway through, but then a message took him by surprise. A big surprise. Eric wrote down Beth's number and hung up the phone, his heart suddenly speeding.

What did she want? And why had there been so much tension in her voice?

He'd assumed he'd never see her again, and the sudden shift of expectations made his pulse surge. He grabbed the phone and started to dial the number, but stopped before he got past the area code.

It was nearly eight o'clock. He was done here. Why call her when he could use this as an excuse to see her?

"Because you don't want to see her," he told himself even as he hung up the phone. And it was true to an extent. He didn't want to see her, but maybe he needed to. Because every hint of the weariness that had dogged him all day had vanished at the possibility.

She was wrong for him. She hated him. Yet she made him feel alive.

That had to be a tale as old as time, but here he was telling it again. And here he was shutting down his computer and grabbing his phone and setting out for the White Orchid.

"Why not?" he muttered. She might still be at work. And if she wasn't, he could always wander around the shop to find out what secrets it held.

This time when he pulled into the White Orchid,

the parking lot was packed. Monday nights were slow at the brewery, but they seemed to be a hopping time for an erotic boutique. Maybe the stress of getting back to the workweek was too much for some people. They needed a release.

He spied the same red sports car that had been there the other morning and pulled in next to it.

Strangely, even though he'd been so self-conscious about his first trip, this time he didn't even blink. The place was filled with customers who might know him, and he didn't give a damn. He was too focused on getting a glimpse of Beth.

Would she be wearing one of those fantastic tight skirts she'd worn at the expo? The ones that were knee length and showed hardly a hint of skin, but somehow seemed dirtier because of it? Or would she be wearing tight jeans that framed the shape of her thighs? He didn't give a damn which it was, but the anticipation of finding out shot through his body and squeezed his heart tight.

Eric opened the door, expecting to see customers in pairs and groups, spread throughout the store. His eyes were still sliding over the racks, searching out Beth, when he realized that everyone was gathered on one side of the store. In chairs. And Beth was standing in front of them, talking about…

"…the argument about the existence of the G-spot continues to this day, with each side insisting that the facts support their theory. Either that there is no G-spot and it is simply a figment of an overeager doctor's imagination, or that every woman has a G-spot and if she doesn't enjoy that sort of stimulation, she's simply not doing it right. Personally, I can't discount women's experiences on either side of the issue, but we're not here to take a stand either way. We're simply here to help you explore the possibilities, and hopefully have fun while doing it."

A class? Eric listened to laughter roll over the crowd and shook his head. A *class?*

This was what Tessa had mentioned a few weeks ago, when Jamie had chimed in and told Eric he should drop in and see if he could learn a few things from this woman. Eric had nearly choked on the horrifying irony. He'd already had his own one-on-one session with Beth Cantrell, and he'd learned plenty.

But this…

Beth was giving an anatomical description that sounded a bit like a map to treasure. Eric listened closely, because he'd never heard anything like this. The teacher in health class hadn't even mentioned a clitoris, much less a G-spot. Eric and every other boy in his junior high had been left to figure out female pleasure on their own. What a damned injustice, for both the boys and the girls.

But this information was priceless, and Eric considered taking a seat. He considered it, but found he was unable to move, frozen by the sight of Beth gesturing, shaping sexual knowledge with her hands as she coolly discussed the female body. *Her* body. She described female erectile tissue and the correlation to male anatomy, and all he could think about was touching her, making her wet, making her shake and scream for *him.*

Suddenly, she was done talking, and the audience was clapping. Eric blinked from a daze. Was it over? Had he missed it? But no. A dark-haired girl he recognized from the expo took Beth's place and started talking technique. Eric wished he'd brought a notebook.

Beth edged over to stand at the side of the crowd, her back to the wall. She was dressed like the perfect model of an up-and-coming businesswoman, just as she had been at the expo. So how did she manage to make a black skirt and a gray button-down blouse look so... promising? Was it just her generous curves? Was it the schoolteacher vibe that reminded him of that damned mannequin near the register? Or was it the flash of a bright red necklace drawing his eye to her throat and the intriguing glimpse of skin above that first button?

Eric divided his time between keeping an eye on her and listening to what the other woman was saying. Something about pressure and stimulation. Something about female orgasm and—

His eyes slid to Beth again, and she was staring at him, her lips parted in surprise.

Eric straightened as if he'd been caught doing something wrong. He cleared his throat and shifted. She still stared.

Finally, she pushed away from the wall, skirted around the crowd and walked toward him. "What are you doing here?" she whispered, not exactly looking happy to see him.

"Sorry, I only got your message a few minutes ago. I was on my way home, so I thought I'd see if you were here. I didn't realize you were...um, giving a class."

A blush crept up her face. It had to be a blush. But that couldn't be right. Maybe it was pink fury. "What did you want to talk to me about?" he asked before she could start yelling.

"Oh," she said, turning to look around before tipping her head toward the door. "Can we speak outside?"

"Are you done?" He gestured toward the presentation, where the dark-haired girl now had her fingers thrust up inside an anatomical model. Eric tilted his head to the side to get a better view.

"Cairo has it under control," Beth said quickly, wrapping her hand around his elbow. "Let's talk outside."

He tore his eyes from the girl's slender hand disappearing into plastic flesh and followed Beth to the parking lot. She walked all the way to her car, then crossed her arms and paced next to it. Eric noticed her red spike heels immediately. Did she know how distracting they were? Is that why she wore them? Or was it because they made her legs look impossibly long?

"Do you remember that night…?" Her voice trailed off and her pacing faltered. "I mean…" She glanced up, but her eyes slid quickly away from his. "I don't know if you remember this, but at the expo, I told you that I knew the Kendall family."

His mind spun. Out of all his memories of that night, this one had taken very low priority. "Right," he said, crossing his arms in defense. "I'd forgotten."

"I had no idea about…you know."

"Their side project?"

Beth winced. "Yes. I just found out about it last night. I don't know exactly what happened, but I'm sorry."

He tilted his head in acknowledgment, but he had a feeling this was leading somewhere. "All right. Thank you." She was friends with someone who'd violated the security of the brewery and tried to damage Eric's employees. And she hated him. This couldn't mean anything good.

"Would you be willing to tell me what really happened?" she asked.

"Why?" he asked more harshly than he'd meant to.

She swallowed, her gaze sliding away again. As if she felt guilty. As if she'd done something wrong.

"Look," he said. "If you know the family, that's your business. But don't expect me to help them out just because I feel guilty about what I did. If Graham Kendall is someone you know *well*—"

"No! That's not it at all. It's complicated. I've known the family for a long time, and I…"

His heart sank. "And you want to help them?"

"No. I just…I think I might be responsible. That's all."

Eric dropped his arms and stepped back. That hadn't been what he'd expected at all.

"Excuse me?"

Beth hugged her arms harder to herself and paced to the bumper of her car before making herself walk back to Eric.

"Beth, what are you talking about?"

"That night at the hotel. You called me to give me the room number." Her body warmed just saying the words, and she could feel her face turn red. "I was on my way to the elevator when I saw Roland Kendall. I shouldn't have said anything, I know, but I was flustered. I told him I'd heard he was negotiating a deal with the brewery."

"Okay."

"Kendall said he wasn't going to go with Donovan Brothers, but I asked him to give you a chance. I told him you were a good guy. At least I thought I was talking about you."

"Beth, what does this have to do with Graham?"

"Roland Kendall called you just an hour later. I think I'm the one who convinced him to go with Donovan Brothers."

Eric shook his head. "You're hardly responsible for what happened afterward, though."

"Then would you be willing to tell me what happened? Please?"

He didn't look happy about it. In fact, his frown made her want to squirm and apologize and promise she'd never do it again...whatever it was she'd done. "Eric—"

"I'll tell you. The stuff that's a matter of public record, anyway."

She nodded and didn't say a word. She wanted to get his take on it before she told him what had happened. She wanted to know how upset she should be about Monica's bullshit.

"So...Roland Kendall called me and finally agreed to the meeting."

She met his gaze and felt the quiet spark that arced between them. Roland Kendall had called while she was naked in Eric's hotel room. Eric had still been on the phone when she'd quickly scrambled into her clothes and made her escape.

"The meeting went well," Eric said. "Really well. As a matter of fact, we came to an agreement. A month later, we were waiting for Kendall to sign the contract, when the brewery was robbed. All that was taken was one keg and the computers. It was similar to a series of robberies in the area. At first, it seemed like we were a random victim."

She nodded. "But then?"

"Then the detective on the case managed to find a fingerprint, and it belonged to Graham Kendall. It all unraveled from there. Apparently he'd been pulling the same thing in Denver the year before. We just ended up being hit because we were on his radar, I think."

"So that's it?" she asked, folding her arms tighter.

"Basically." Eric's eyes dipped down her body. "You're cold. Here." He pulled his keys from his pocket, and the SUV next to her beeped. The flash of the lights reminded Beth that it was starting to get dark. As she looked around, the lot lights of the restaurant across the street blinked to life.

Eric slipped a coat over her shoulders.

"Thank you," she murmured. The cold leather creaked as she pulled it tighter, but her body heat soon warmed it up. As she grew warmer, his scent drifted up from the coat. She actually had to close her eyes at the smell of his body, his soap. It surrounded her and stole inside on every breath.

"So why did you want to know?" he asked.

Beth opened her eyes and it seemed to have grown darker in those few seconds. She could still see Eric clearly, but he was dimmer now. As if this weren't real. Yearning pushed against her breastbone as if there were no space for it inside her chest. "So Monica had nothing to do with this?"

All the easiness left his body as he stiffened. "Monica Kendall? Why?"

That wasn't the reaction she'd been looking for. Beth sighed and pulled his coat tighter around her. "*Did* she have something to do with it?"

Eric looked away. "If she's a friend of yours, I don't want to say anything."

"She's not. We just happened to be roommates our freshman year at the U. That's it."

"Then why are you asking about her now?"

Beth hesitated. She wanted to hear his side of the story first, but he was obviously suspicious. "Because she called me today. And I want to hear the truth." She knew that what Monica had said wasn't the truth, because Monica wouldn't bother with it if there was a lie that painted her in a better light.

"I'm not sure if I should tell you this." He looked away again, staring at the lights of the restaurant.

"I won't tell anyone. And I think I deserve a little truth."

That brought his face back around, his eyes flashing silver as the distant lights caught them. "You do," he said, and those quiet words made her feel a hundred times better than all his apologies and explanations. "All right. Monica was there the night the brewery was robbed."

"She helped break in?" She was frowning at the ridiculousness of that, but Eric was already shaking his head.

"No. She was in the front room. She had some beer and then told Jamie she needed a ride home. While he was in the back, she unlocked the front door. They left through the back. That's where he set the alarm."

"And she watched?"

"She was right there."

Beth nodded. "And she asked him to take her home?"

"She did."

Beth could tell from the edge in his voice that there

was something he wasn't saying, and she figured it had to do with what had happened when they got to Monica's house. "When Monica called me today, she said that Jamie had given her name to the police because she refused to see him again after that night."

"That's complete bullshit, excuse my language. She came in a few weeks later and started a fight in the barroom. I heard the argument myself. What she said…it didn't have anything to do with him wanting more. Just the opposite."

Beth made her decision then. This story sounded like the truth. It fit what Beth knew about Monica and her creepy brother. "Eric, the reason I called you is… Monica asked me to lie to the police."

"She *what?*"

"I left her a message this weekend, asking what was going on between her family and the brewery. When she called today, she said her brother had broken into the brewery and she was being dragged into it because of Jamie. She said Jamie had given her name to the police because she slept with him once and then refused to see him again."

"That's a pretty amazing lie. But what does that have to do with you lying to the police? You're not even involved in this."

"She asked me to tell the police—if they just *happened* to call—that we'd had this discussion months ago, right after the break-in, before the Kendalls were even suspects."

"Ah. I see. And you didn't want to go along?"

"Of course not! Why would I do that?"

Eric shifted, his foot sending a pebble sliding across

the blacktop. "Because you must hate me. And you probably think we're not very nice people."

"I don't think that. And I don't hate you." She shook her head, trying to sort through the anger she felt at him. "Look, I know it's just a name. It doesn't change what happened. And yet…it does change it, doesn't it?"

He put his fists on his hips and looked down at the ground. "It's the stupidest thing I've ever done. Not the…" His gaze rose to watch her past his lashes. "Not what we did. I wouldn't take that back. But the other. Because I don't want you to regret that night. It kills me that you do."

Did she regret it? Despite her anger, she knew she couldn't. That one night with Eric had been a revelation. Her whole adult life had been dedicated to helping women find sexual fulfillment in their lives, any way they—legally—could. She'd studied sexuality and anthropology along with women's issues in college. She loved learning about the complicated formula of societal mores and personal preferences that helped to form each woman's experience. She understood it all deep inside her heart and mind. And yet she couldn't translate all that useless information into sexual satisfaction for herself.

She couldn't relax. And she couldn't trust. And despite the orgasms she'd fought for tooth and nail, she'd never once been able to lose herself in the experience. Until Eric.

Some chemistry writhed between them. Something like a spark, but so much more vibrant and powerful than that.

"I don't regret it," she finally said, the words drifting away into the midnight blue of the evening sky.

Eric tipped his head as if he hadn't heard her.

"I don't regret it," Beth repeated a little more loudly. And it was the truth.

"No?"

No. She'd do it over and over again, if she wasn't afraid she'd get lost in it. In him.

"You're..." He moved closer, shrinking the space between them from two feet to one. "You didn't have to call me, after what I did to you. You owed me less than nothing. Thank you for being kind."

She started to shrug, but his hand reached toward her, his skin the color of a shadow in the rising dusk. But it felt warm as daytime when his fingers touched her cheek.

"And thank you for not regretting that night."

Beth forced herself not to turn into his hand. Not to rub against him like a cat. But she let herself close her eyes and feel his skin on hers. Her nerves danced. Her breath fluttered in her chest like birds' wings.

She thought he shifted closer. Thought she felt his breath touch her mouth. She held herself still and did not surge toward him, which was the only concession she could manage after her earlier disgust with him. *Don't throw yourself at him. He doesn't deserve it. No matter how good he smells. And how—*

His lips touched hers. His fingers spread along her jaw and tilted her face just enough that their mouths fit perfectly together. Beth sighed, her lips parted and then she tasted him.

Memory flooded her body with all the grace of a crashing wave. She was halfway into a pitiful whimper when light exploded around them and Eric jerked away.

"What the hell?" he muttered.

Beth just blinked like a deer caught in the head-lights. Bright headlights. She touched her fingers to her lips, breaking the spell, and finally realized what had happened. "The parking lot lights," she whispered. "They're late."

Eric shoved his hands in his pockets and glared at the pole that stood right in front of Beth's car. They were directly in the middle of a bright pool of light.

"I'll have to adjust the sensors," she finished weakly.

"You'd better." He managed a smile. "Before you scare the hell out of somebody else."

Beth realized she was still pressing her fingertips to her mouth and dropped her hand. "Do you think I should call the police?"

"Um…huh?"

"About Monica."

"Oh! Jesus, I thought you meant…" He waved a hand toward her and bit back a laugh. "Sorry. It's been an odd week."

"Glad I'm not the only one."

"Yeah." He pushed a hand through his hair and shook his head. "If you're okay with waiting, I'll talk to the detective on the case. He's involved with my sister now, so I can bounce it off him and see if he wants to do any-thing about it. Would that be all right?"

"Yes."

"Okay," he said, running his hand through his hair again. "Then…thank you. I should… Here." He reached into his wallet and took out a card. "The second number is my cell. Call me if you're worried about anything. I don't want to miss you again."

Had he missed her? "Oh," she murmured, realizing

what he'd meant. Of course he hadn't *missed* her. He barely knew her. "I'd better get back in," she said belatedly. "Goodbye."

She walked away, wishing she could go back and kiss him again. Wishing it wouldn't damage her pride to throw herself into his arms and damn the light. Was he watching her? Did he want her to stop?

"Beth," he said, and she spun so quickly that she nearly stumbled. So much for her pride.

Eric walked toward her, smiling as if he knew exactly what she'd been thinking. He reached out and said, "My coat."

She was still waiting for him to touch her, to cup her chin and tilt her head so he could kiss her again. A real kiss this time. Not…

"Oh," she finally managed. "Of course."

"If you're cold, you can—"

"No. Thank you, though." She slid it off, forcing herself back into the damp air and into a place where Eric Donovan didn't kiss her. "Thank you," she repeated.

Shivering, she walked back to the life where she pretended to be a vibrant, sexual woman and away from the life where she actually was.

CHAPTER NINE

"Come on," Cairo pleaded. "It'll be fun."

Beth shook her head. "No. I'm exhausted."

"It's only eight o'clock!"

"I've been here since eight. I hardly got any sleep last night, and it's a Tuesday. Not a big party night for me." She just wanted to go home. After she'd tossed and turned last night, she felt like she could sleep for twelve hours.

"Pleeease?" Cairo pushed, folding both her hands under her chin and watching Beth with wide brown eyes. "Pretty please? I know for a fact that Davis will be there."

"Davis?" For a moment, Beth couldn't place the name. "Oh, *Davis.* How do you know he'll be there?"

"Because he's the guitar player in the band."

Had he told her he was in a band? It sounded only vaguely familiar. Which was exactly why she couldn't see Eric even casually. She'd spent an hour with Davis on Thursday night, and she could hardly remember anything about him. Except for that one unfortunately vivid detail that Cairo had revealed.

"Oh, what the hell," she muttered. Maybe waxed man meat wasn't unfortunate. Maybe it would rock her uptight little world. "All right. I'm in."

"Yea! Come on. They're starting their first set any second."

And that was how Beth found herself at a college bar at nearly nine o'clock on a Tuesday night, playing the part of girlfriend to the band. She was wearing jeans, at least, so she was only moderately overdressed in a silk shirt and heels. Thankfully, Cairo was wearing her normal style of 1950s housewife dress and cute pumps. She even had a little flower in her hair, glowing white against her black bob. They stood out among the college girls in their leggings and layered T-shirts, but at least they stood out together.

Cairo's boyfriend—*one* of her boyfriends—was playing backup on bass tonight. Her other boyfriend had just arrived and was settling into the seat next to Cairo, his fingers already laced through hers. Beth sneaked a look at the bass player, Rex, curious to see whether he'd react. But no. It was totally normal for them. Beth was fascinated every time she saw them together. They didn't seem to struggle at all, while Beth felt as if she was always flailing.

Applause broke out and she realized the song had come to an end. She clapped and smiled at Davis, impressed despite her distraction. He was a great guitar player. Skilled and subtle. He didn't show off. He just played with quiet confidence. Maybe she should give him more of a chance.

The front man was a Jamaican rapper—or he was pretending to be Jamaican. College students had a weak spot for all things Jamaican, after all. Still, the guy was good. Even though Beth wasn't into rap, she had to admit that he sounded amazing with a live band backing him up.

Davis finally stepped off the stage. "Thanks for coming out," he said as he took the chair next to hers.

"You guys sound great. I'm really impressed."

He smiled. "It takes a lot of commitment to keep this up after college. Not as much fun to rehearse after working a full day."

"I can tell you love it," she said. She made herself concentrate on Davis for the next ten minutes, because he deserved it. He was funny. And talented. And she could see the interest growing in his eyes as they talked. She noticed the way his eyes swept down her legs when he turned to talk to the drummer. She even felt a responding warmth of interest. Thank God. It *wasn't* just Eric. He wasn't the only one she wanted.

But…she couldn't lie to herself so easily. Sure, she was interested in Davis. Just as she'd been interested in previous men, some she'd slept with and some she hadn't. But she didn't feel that awful, wonderful need. That temptation to press her face to his neck and breathe in his scent and take him home and let him do anything he wanted.

"You look great, by the way," Davis said, his eyes traveling down to her heels again.

"Thank you."

"I'll admit I have a weakness for heels."

She smiled, feeling pleasant warmth again. "So do I."

"Nothing wrong with that." When he set down his drink, he rested his hand on her knee. Beth's heart jumped. It felt…strange. Was that a good thing? It was better than nothing, which was exactly what she'd been getting lately.

"Hey," Davis said, gesturing toward the stage where

the drummer was taking his seat behind the drums. "We've got another set. We should be done by ten. Will you hang around?"

Would she? Beth looked down at his hand on her knee. It was a nice hand. Elegant. Long. A little callused at the fingertips from playing guitar.

"We could go somewhere," he said.

"Okay. Yes." She nodded, trying to convince herself she was doing the right thing. She needed to put Eric behind her once and for all. She couldn't keep up this one-sided relationship with her memories. And if her heart felt a little panicked instead of excited, well, so be it. She had to get back out there.

"Great." He smiled, and his hand tightened on her knee for a moment as his gaze slid to her heels again. "Then I'll be right back."

Beth tried her best to look anticipatory, but her mind was already working, working, working. Where were they going to go? To his place? They'd only kissed that one time. Was she ready for this? Her heart thumped harder, and when the music started, the screech of the guitar made her jump.

Calm down, she told herself. *You're being ridiculous. You can do—or not do—whatever you want.*

Right. Maybe they would go to his place. And that would be fine. They could just take it from there. They could kiss and see where that led. That was all. See if it felt right. No big deal.

But now his kind comments about her shoes were starting to tumble around in her roiling brain. Beth shook her head. So, he liked heels. Most guys did. No big deal.

But what if he had a *thing* for heels? What if he

wanted her to wear them every time they went to bed? What if he wanted to *lick* them? It wouldn't be the first time that had happened to her. That one guy had—

"Beth!"

She spun toward Cairo, desperately relieved for the distraction.

"Harrison is getting a group together for rock climbing next weekend. Want to come?"

"Oh, I don't climb."

"I don't, either, but it's fun to watch." She took a moment to give Harrison a sly wink and a smile. "You could stick with me. We'll set up a picnic while they're climbing."

Beth laughed, picturing Cairo on the edge of a cliff in a dress and pearls, her tattoos peeking past her sleeves every time she set another dish on the blanket. "That sounds fun."

"I could teach you the basics," Harrison offered. "If you want to try an easy climb."

She cringed. "I don't know. We'll see how brave I'm feeling." But she found the idea surprisingly enticing. A little scary, maybe, but still fun. Which was exactly how she *wasn't* feeling about Davis. Instead…it just felt weird. And that wasn't how it should feel. She was making a mistake. Trying to force the issue because she'd gone home alone last night and gotten herself off, thinking about Eric. Again.

But now she was losing sight of the lesson she'd learned from that night with Eric. She'd finally touched that feeling she'd been reaching for all her life. That place where she couldn't think, because she was too damn busy living in the moment.

That first night, when they'd met at the wine bar…

when he'd touched her, she'd been lost. So lost that she'd spread her legs under the table and closed her eyes and let him get her off right there. Right there, where she could have been worrying about everything, not to mention everyone around them.

"Cairo," Beth said, leaning forward to touch her friend's arm. "I told Davis I'd hang around, but I'm exhausted. I need to go home and get some sleep. Will you tell him I'm sorry? Really sorry?"

"Sure. Are you okay? You've been a little off lately."

"I'm fine. Just running on empty. But this was fun. Thank you so much for inviting me." She tried to catch Davis's eye, but he was watching the singer intently for cues, and he didn't look up as Beth left.

She'd learned something important six months ago, but the lesson was starting to fade. She was capable of utter sexual completion. She could have that feeling she'd been chasing for so many years. The key was listening to her body. It didn't matter how good a man looked on paper or even how interesting she found him. The thing that had always been missing from her life was chemistry.

She'd found it with Eric. She could find it again with someone else. But maybe what she needed was a refresher course. A reminder of just what that spark felt like when it exploded into flames and licked over her whole body.

A shiver stole over her as she stepped outside. Her nipples peaked, but she didn't think it had anything to do with the crisp air. It was the thought of having that again. Of losing herself in pleasure.

Why the hell had they decided on one night, anyway? Why couldn't they have more than that? Why couldn't they do what other single adults did, and use each other when the need arose? It didn't have to mean anything more.

His lie hung over her like a warning, but what the hell did his name have to do with what he'd done to her body? Nothing. Nothing at all.

Beth pictured Eric's card where she'd left it on her coffee table. She thought about calling him. Wondered what he would say. And this time, the adrenaline that pumped into her veins wasn't urging her to run away at all.

ANOTHER EXCRUCIATINGLY tense day at the office had left Eric with what felt like a permanent scowl on his face. His only relief had been the chance to finally get caught up on the bottling, and that noisy, busy room had been his saving grace. Tessa had dared his mood several times, but even she'd finally given up. Jamie hadn't even looked in his direction.

At least Eric's knuckles had stopped aching, which was a nice relief from the constant reminder that he'd hit his little brother in the face.

Eric was just taking his first deep breath of the day as he turned onto his street, but when he pulled up to his condo, he saw Tessa's car parked at the curb. When he saw that Jamie was sitting on his tiny porch, Eric groaned. What the hell was this? Some sort of bad mood intervention? He considered making a run for it.

But then his lights hit Tessa's windshield and, through the rain, he noticed that she was still in her car. That was strange enough to make him pull up and roll down his window. Rain pelted his face as he waited for Tessa to put down her window and talk to him.

"What's going on?" he called out.

"We need to talk this out!" she shouted.

"I'm not up for this right now."

"Too bad!" She rolled up her window to prevent any further discussion, so Eric just sighed and pulled into his small attached garage.

But when he got out, all he saw of Tessa's car was the taillights fading into the night.

"Hey!" Jamie shouted, running out into the rain after her. Once her taillights disappeared completely, Jamie stopped and stared after them.

When he finally trudged back to the porch, Jamie was glaring at Eric as though he might be considering starting another fistfight.

"What the hell is going on?" Eric demanded.

"I have no fucking idea. Tessa drove me over here, going on and on about how we all needed to make up. But when I got out of the car, she locked the doors and wouldn't let me back in."

"She locked you out?"

"And now she just left me here!"

"That little brat," Eric growled. "She's trying to force us to spend time together."

"I'll call Olivia."

Eric rolled his eyes. "Don't be ridiculous. I'll give you a ride. Surely we can stand to sit in the same car for five minutes."

"Or I could just walk," Jamie muttered.

Eric jerked his head toward the car. A few seconds later, Jamie finally gave in and headed into the garage. But when Eric got in, he didn't start the car right away. Jamie shifted uneasily.

"I'm sorry," Eric said quietly. "I'm really sorry that I hit you."

Jamie sighed. "I know you are."

"I don't know what came over me."

"I was being rude."

"You've been rude before, and I always managed to behave like a sane person."

Jamie shrugged and leaned back in the seat, so Eric started the car and pulled out of the garage. Jamie's place was only a few miles away. If it hadn't been raining, he probably would've walked home as soon as Tessa had locked him out.

They were halfway there when Jamie spoke. "I can handle it, you know."

"You can handle what?" Eric asked.

"All of it. All my duties at the brewery. I can handle them. So don't worry."

"I'm not worried that you can't handle it. I was honestly trying to help. You've got Olivia now, plus all the planning with the restaurant side.... That's all I was thinking. That I wanted to help. That's all I'm ever thinking."

Jamie didn't respond, but a few seconds later, he nodded.

And that was that. Everything was fine. Eric pulled up to Jamie's house and Jamie said, "Thanks for the ride," and opened the door. But he paused just before he got out. "Hey," he said. "Everything else aside? She was totally hot."

"Who was?"

"That woman who came to the bar. I would've been damned impressed if I hadn't been so pissed. Way out of your league, man."

"Gee, thanks."

"I didn't even know you had a league, frankly."

"Get out," Eric ordered, but he was trying hard not to smile. Beth *was* hot. She *was* out of his league. And he was damned impressed with himself for even approaching her in the first place.

He felt marginally better when he drove away. Back to his normal amount of tension instead of this new level of anger and regret. He'd made up with Jamie, and Beth was…well, she'd seemed fine when he'd left her on Monday. Though he couldn't quite figure out how he'd ended up kissing her. And why she'd let him.

Who the hell cared? He was smiling as he drove home, so if he could just avoid worrying about anything else until the morning, he'd take that and be happy.

His phone rang, and Eric dug it out of his jacket, knowing exactly who it was. "We made up," he said.

"Yea!" Tessa squealed.

"Good night." He hung up, still smiling as he slowed to a stop at a red light. Tessa was a piece of work, but she always knew exactly the right thing to do. Maybe he should just turn his share of the brewery over to her and let her run with it.

The phone rang again. "Everything's great," Eric said. "So just drop it while you're ahead."

"Oh," a female voice said. Then, "Drop what?"

That wasn't Tessa. Eric tipped the phone down to look at the display. Yep, the voice matched up with the name. "Beth?"

"Hi."

"I'm sorry. I thought you were someone else."

"That's a relief."

The light turned green, but Eric turned the corner

and pulled over to the curb instead of driving on. He couldn't drive and talk to Beth at the same time. She was way too distracting. "So. Beth Cantrell."

"That's me."

He frowned at the nervousness in her voice. "What's up?"

"Oh, I wanted to find out what happened with the detective."

Of course. His shoulders fell a little. "I let him know exactly what you told me. He made note of it. It might come up in the trial, but it won't affect the investigation."

"I see. That makes sense."

"He said he'd get in touch with you if he needed to use your story."

"Great. Okay."

"Okay," he repeated, aware of the awkwardness growing between them. A sign, maybe, that things were better left as they were. They were nothing alike. All they'd had was sex. But goddamn, it had been good sex.

"Thanks—" he started, but Beth cut him off.

"Would you like to come over?" she asked.

Eric blinked, sure that he'd heard her wrong. She'd spoken quickly, after all, the words running together on one long breath. "I'm sorry?"

"Would you...would you like to come over?"

"Tonight?" He glanced at the dashboard clock. 10:30.

"Yes."

He felt that he wasn't quite grasping this. She couldn't mean—

"I know we had an agreement. So I understand if this is over the line."

"No," he said. "No! There's no line. Absolutely not."

"So…"

"Yes." Had he just said that? He wasn't supposed to see her again. That had been the deal. One night. Nothing more.

"Yes?" she asked, as if she were giving him a chance to change his mind.

He should say no. But what the hell was he trying to protect? He wasn't the same man he'd been six months ago. His family and his work…those were slipping away. And if there was one thing that was totally separate from those parts of his life, it was Beth Cantrell.

"What's your address?" he asked.

He thought he heard a sigh of relief from the other end. Had she worried he'd say no? Jesus, he was already putting the car in gear. She gave him the address, and he was on the road. If this was a mistake, he didn't want time to consider it. This was one mistake he was determined to make.

CHAPTER TEN

BETH CAREFULLY SLIPPED ON her favorite new panties, then added the matching bra. Strangely calm, she turned and looked at herself in the mirror, trying to see her body as Eric would see it.

The midnight-blue silk looked amazing against her skin. She trailed her finger along the edge of the bra where her breasts pushed up into enticing mounds. Eric would like it just fine. And it was nice to think of being with him again. He already knew what she looked like. Too curvy for today's standards of the feminine ideal, but just right for him, maybe. And he wouldn't be surprised by her unadorned skin and unpierced erogenous zones. She was the same plain Beth she'd been the last time.

She slipped on a black wrap dress that she loved but had worn only once before. She was always afraid the tie would come loose or the top would gape open, and there she'd be for all the world to see. If that happened tonight, it would only help things toward their natural end.

Last, she put on her favorite black stilettos, trusting that Eric wouldn't feel the need to lick them at any point during the night. "Not that there's anything wrong with that," she said to herself, sighing. Her whole career was based on giving people just what they wanted, after all.

But that didn't mean she had to extend the customer service to the bedroom.

She'd jumped in the shower before calling him, so the last thing she needed was lip gloss and mascara, and she was done. Ready to see him. Ready to figure out the quickest way to get him to her bedroom.

She kicked her workout clothes under the bed just as the doorbell rang.

Wow, he hadn't wasted any time. Which meant he wanted this, too, mistake or not. And who the hell cared if it was right? For once, she was looking forward to sex as if it were a treat instead of a test.

She didn't have to paste a smile on her face as she opened the door. In fact, she had to try hard not to grin like a crazy woman.

Eric's eyes swept down her body. "Hi," he said to her legs.

"Hello." He was wearing a pale blue polo shirt tonight. Was there anything more delightfully preppy than that? She opened the door wide and stepped back. "Come in."

"Thanks." He stopped just a few feet inside and shoved his hands in the pockets of his jeans. "I realized on my way up the stairs that I should've brought something. A bottle of wine. Or maybe dinner?"

"I've already eaten. And I have wine here. Would you like some?"

"Yes," he said quickly.

Beth couldn't hold back the grin as she walked to the kitchen. This was fun. Last time, it had been her, making that long walk to his door. She'd been nervous, wondering what the hell she was doing. Did he feel the same way now? What would he say if she just dropped her dress and walked back into the living room? She pressed her hand to her mouth too late to stop the laugh.

"Did you say something?" he called.

"No, sorry. I just…dropped something."

She was just setting the corkscrew to the wine when she looked up and found him standing in the doorway of the small kitchen. "Did you just get off work?" he asked.

"Yes. No. I mean, I worked until eight and then went out with a friend."

His eyebrows rose. "Oh?"

He thought she'd been on a date, and wasn't that what it had been? One more attempt to set Beth Cantrell up with a man who could push her stubborn buttons? She felt a sudden urge to tell Eric the truth, but she settled for just a tiny bit of it. "Can I be honest with you?"

"Of course."

"There's a man I've been on a couple of dates with. I saw him tonight."

He leaned against the archway with a frown. "Okay."

Just as she was about to let it out, the words dried in her mouth and worry started turning in her head. She couldn't stop it.

The cork popped free of the bottle, so she used that as an excuse to look down. "I'm sorry. I…" Her mind whirled. She grabbed on to the first thought that bounced forward. "Why did you come over?" she asked, wanting him to say it so she wouldn't have to.

"Because you asked me to."

"I know, but… We didn't want to do this, right? We didn't want to see each other again?"

"We agreed it wouldn't be a good idea."

"Right. Exactly. And it's not a good idea." She made

herself look up, but as soon as she saw his dark frown, she chickened out one more time and reached for the cupboard to get glasses. "I'm sorry," she murmured.

"I don't understand. Do you want me to go?"

She loved that he'd asked her that. As if it would be no big deal to drive to a woman's house in the middle of the night just to say hello and make small talk for a few seconds. The lack of pressure helped her mind settle, as if the molecules of her brain could stop bouncing off each other if only things weren't so intense.

She took a deep breath and handed him a glass, then she held on to hers with both hands, hoping it would hold her steady for the next few minutes.

"I was out tonight, talking to this man, and thinking that it was time. You know?"

Eric looked puzzled and sipped from his wine instead of answering.

"It was time for that decision. Were we going to get physical? Did I want to? And all I kept thinking was that I hoped he was like you."

His confusion blanked to surprise. "Like me?"

Beth took a steadying gulp of wine. "Yes. I realized that I was about to go home with this man, and I just wanted it to be what it had been with you."

"I still don't understand. What was it with me?"

Shaking her head, Beth let her eyes drift down to his wide chest. "It was good. Wasn't it?"

When he didn't answer, she got a little nervous. When he still didn't answer, she forced herself to meet his eyes. He looked shocked. "Yes," he finally said. "It was good. Of course it was. For me, certainly."

God, she hoped he wasn't just being polite. "It was

good," she repeated, as if she needed to convince him. "And simple. And easy."

"Easy?" His eyebrows rose at that.

There was no way to explain that, so Beth didn't try. "Tonight, I was wishing I could have that again. And then I realized I could. Or I could try, anyway."

He took another drink, watching her with wary eyes. "We agreed that it was too complicated."

"It doesn't have to be."

His eyes traveled down again, as if he were pondering the simplicity of taking off her dress and fucking her. Her body tingled with awareness. "I thought you were pissed off," he said.

"I was. I am. And I don't trust you. I won't ever trust you."

His mouth flattened.

"But you never told anyone about me, did you?"

"No. Never."

"So you lied. And it hurt. And…maybe you owe me."

When he met her eyes, his gaze was dark and hot, and she knew he wanted this, too. "Owe you what?"

Beth let the power of the moment wash over her. "You owe me the right to know the name of the man who's inside me. Don't you?"

She'd thought she'd seen lust in his eyes before, but now it blazed like a fire. His jaw tightened to steel. Eric wanted inside her. Badly.

"And don't you want to hear your own name?"

"Yes," he growled, his teeth still clenched together.

The word shivered through her body, tightening her nipples. Beth took another sip of wine and started to walk past him. "You look more like an Eric, anyway," she said.

His hand closed around her arm. "You said that before."

He pulled her back until she was standing right in front of him, their bodies separated by only a few inches. She looked into his gray-blue eyes. "You do," she whispered, and it was true. He would never be a Jamie. James, maybe. But Eric sounded clipped and cool. It suited him perfectly.

"Good," he growled. He set his glass on the counter and took hers, as well. When he shaped his hand to her jaw, she thought he meant to kiss her, but he kept his distance. She held her breath as his other hand spread over her shoulder. "So you think I owe you?" he asked softly.

She nodded, but he wasn't looking at her. His fingers were trailing slowly down, following the path of her neckline, and Eric watched his progress with vicious focus.

"Yes," she breathed.

His fingertips dipped lower, pulling the soft fabric out of line. She felt his touch against the sensitive skin along the edge of her bra. His fingertips sneaked just under the silk, still slipping down. Beth shuddered and he looked up.

"I'll give you anything you want," he said.

Yes. That was what she wanted. *Anything.*

"What were you thinking about while you were out with this other man?"

She shook her head. His fingertips left her skin, but he followed the line of the fabric down lower still, all the way to her waist. She felt the slow friction of him pulling the tie that held her dress together.

"You were going to do this with him," he said softly.

"Maybe."

"So tell me what you wanted."

"I wanted…" Beth swallowed hard. "I wanted to feel like this."

He pulled the tie with agonizing slowness.

Beth couldn't quite catch her breath. "I wanted to shiver when he touched me."

The tension of the fabric wrapped around her body suddenly loosened. She closed her eyes as he eased the dress open. His fingers brushed the naked skin of her stomach. She shivered again.

"Like you're shivering now?" Eric asked.

"Yes." She'd forgotten. She'd forgotten this feeling of being seduced. She'd meant to seduce him tonight. To untie her dress and drop it to the floor just to shock him. But in this game between them, he was the one who did the undressing. Just like last time.

And just like last time, she was wet already, her arousal soaking the expensive silk between her legs.

He still didn't kiss her. She felt his whole hand curve around her waist, the edge of his hand resting on the curve of her hip, his thumb fanning slowly across her ribs. She opened her eyes to see him still watching his hand.

"You left too quickly last time."

"I know," she whispered.

"I wanted more." His hand tightened on her hip, and he finally moved forward, but he guided her back.

Beth stepped backward. One step. Two. Her dress fell open. Her back touched the doorway. He loomed above her. "I wanted more," he said again, and then he finally kissed her.

This was nothing like that brief whisper of a kiss in

the parking lot of the White Orchid. This felt…angry.
Rough. Deep. She matched it with her own anger and
frustration, pressing into his mouth, tasting him as he
slid his tongue along hers. Both his hands were around
her waist now, holding her against the wall as he devoured her.

She wanted him so much it felt almost like hate. Why
did it have to be him? Why couldn't it be this good with
someone else? Someone who'd never lied? Who'd never
made a fool out of her?

He pushed the dress off her shoulders, and Beth let
it drop before tangling her fingers in his hair. He had
her trapped against the wall, surrounded by his body,
but she still needed to hold him, to be sure he didn't
change his mind and slip away.

His hands slid down to her hips, and he held her tight
as he rocked his body into her.

Oh, God, yes. He was already hard and big, and she
was already lost. Instead of turning, her mind was spiraling down into a place where she couldn't hear her
own thoughts. All she knew was the way his tongue
slid over hers and his fingers pressed her flesh. All she
could think was that she wanted him inside her.

She turned her face away, and Eric slid his mouth to
her neck and sucked there.

"Eric. I…" Jesus, that felt so good. Especially when
she thought of him moving his mouth lower and lower,
sucking the whole way. "The bedroom," she gasped.

"Yes," he said against her throat.

She led him down the hall, damn glad she was still
wearing her heels as she walked in front of him. She
made sure to add a little extra sway to her hips, and
when she glanced back, he wasn't looking at her face.

But when they got to her bedroom, she didn't know what to do, which kicked her brain to life. It remembered that it was supposed to be worrying, second-guessing, overanalyzing. She stood helplessly for a moment, but Eric took charge, thank God. He seemed to know what to do. Instead of thinking, he took off his shirt, then reached for his belt. Even that was preppy, one of those Cole Haan strips of braided leather, and as she watched him slide the leather free of the buckle, her knees went a little weak.

He looked so...strong. His chest was so wide. His biceps were thick. He probably belonged to a gym. He probably lifted weights while the skinny gym girls swooned. Were those the girls he normally dated? The ones he told his family about and gave his real name to?

Beth shook her head, breaking the thoughts free and sending them scattering. It didn't matter. He wanted her, secretly or not. More importantly, she wanted him. So she stopped thinking and reached for the button of his jeans. She could feel the thick length of him through the rough fabric, and she immediately knew what she wanted.

She slid his zipper carefully down. His hands fell to his sides. Then she slipped her hand inside his briefs and wrapped her fingers around his cock. He was so hot. She eased him free and went to her knees.

My God, he was lovely. A work of art. She hadn't gotten a chance to get up close and personal that night at the hotel. But now she could look her fill. The head was plump and perfect, but from there, his shaft got even thicker.

Beth stroked him, one slow, firm stroke. A tiny bead

of liquid leaked from the tip. She pressed a small, wet kiss to that spot just as she glanced up to see Eric's face.

She couldn't read much. He looked…serious. She licked the underside of his cock, just to see if she could budge his expression. His jaw jumped. Good enough for her. She smiled and licked again, loving the rich, clean taste of his skin.

Eric took a deep breath. "You said I owed *you*."

She closed her eyes and sighed against him. "This isn't for you," she whispered. "It's for me."

Beth wrapped her hand around the base of his shaft, saying a little prayer of thanks for the class she'd given on fellatio this summer. She finally had someone to practice her newfound skills on.

She took it slow, building up, pressing small kisses at first, then lingering ones, letting him feel the moisture of her open lips. Then she slid her mouth over him, pressing her tongue to the underside of his head. His taste settled into her, making her hum with pleasure. He smelled like soap and sex combined, and salt touched her tongue when she sucked.

She eased him deeper, aware of how thick he was, how impossible it would be to take it all. Her clit felt painfully hard as she took as much of him as she could before easing back.

His hands still hung by his sides, but his fingers had curled into fists.

Beth took him deep again, letting him push roughly over her tongue. This time when she pulled back, she stroked with her fist at the same time, and Eric gasped. She used her mouth and hand in slow tandem, knowing the sensations would blend together into one nonstop feeling of—

"Christ," he ground out. Now his hands were open, hovering near her head as if he wanted to take hold of her and thrust deep.

Closing her eyes, she let herself feel everything. His tension. His hardness. The way he seemed to get thicker with each pull of her mouth. This was what she'd always yearned for. Pleasure. Getting it or giving it, that part didn't matter. She just wanted the pure blankness of it. Wanted it to go on forever. She took him over and over again, loving every minute of it. She lost herself in every stroke of him inside her mouth, taking him as deep as she could manage.

"Beth," he breathed after long minutes of silence.

She knew what he was going to say. She could taste it on her tongue.

"Stop," he urged. "I can't…"

But she didn't want to stop. Because his hand was finally in her hair—urging her to stay still or take more, she didn't know. She tightened her fist around him, quickened the slide of her mouth, and felt his hand slip toward the back of her skull. His breath hissed between his teeth, then he groaned and jerked and his come flooded her throat.

It was the most fun she'd had in months.

ERIC COLLAPSED ONTO THE bed, his body warm and completely weak. "That's not what I was planning," he managed to say.

"Oh?" Beth pressed against his side, chuckling softly. Her hand traced light circles on his chest. "I hope you're not disappointed."

His laugh sounded more like a groan.

"So what did you have planned? And when did you start planning?"

"Okay, *plan* may be too strong a word, but I definitely had some major points I wanted to hit." And none of them had started with having an orgasm three minutes into the best blow job of his life.

"Like?" she asked, her hand dipping lower. He didn't think it was possible to get hard again so quickly, but if anyone could make it happen, it was Beth Cantrell.

"Like..." He watched her fingers spread wide just below his rib cage. Her hand looked so feminine against him. "Like I thought I'd spend a little time on you first."

"A little time?" she teased.

"Well, I've got to work tomorrow."

Her nails bit lightly into his skin.

"I thought I'd make you come," he said. "And then I thought I'd slide deep inside you. Maybe make you come again." He pushed up to one elbow, and Beth rolled to her back. "Isn't that what you wanted? Me inside you while you scream my name?"

"I..." Her eyelids fluttered. "That would be good, yes."

"Yes?" He traced the same spot he'd traced before, the rise of her breast against the dark blue fabric of her bra. Her skin...he couldn't describe it, not even in his own mind. *Soft* was an utterly inadequate word.

He reached for the delicate bow at the front of the bra and pulled it free. "You always have these little ties."

"Do I?"

"Yes. I love it." Last time, the ties had been on her panties, and all he'd had to do was pull them free and she'd been naked.

"It's my favorite—" the laces finally gave way, and

he smoothed the dark silk off her breasts "—brand," she finished weakly.

"Mine, too," he murmured, lowering his head to brush his lips over one dark nipple. Everything had been hurried before. Desperate. Now he had time to taste her, touch her. And he was suddenly glad he'd already come, because just this was stirring his cock again, a goddamned miraculous resurrection.

He opened his mouth over her and drew her in, and Beth gasped so sweetly that it made his chest tighten. He knew she was experienced, he knew she'd probably done things in bed that he'd never even heard of. But somehow she sounded like the simplest kiss was a wonder to her. How was it possible for her to be so many amazing things at once?

He found a rhythm with his tongue that made her gasp and writhe, then eased his hand down her stomach and cupped it over the dark fabric that covered her sex. She was wet. Soaked through. He stroked her through the silk, and pressed his teeth to her nipple.

Beth arched up with a little cry, but he wanted to make her scream.

Giving up any teasing, he dragged her panties down and slipped his finger along the seam of her body. Her clit was hard and eager, and when he brushed it, she groaned as if she was in pain.

She was close to coming already, but he wanted to do this right. Thanks to her earlier attentions, he could actually concentrate, and Eric thought of the lesson he'd overheard at the White Orchid. Raising his head, he watched her face as he touched her clit again.

Beth threw her head back. She let her knees fall open and pressed toward his hand. He could make her come right now. Easily. His fingers were soaked. All he had to do was circle her clit a few times and she'd come apart for him. But he didn't want easy. So instead of concentrating on that spot, he pressed two fingers slowly inside her pussy, stretching her.

"Oh, God," she moaned. "That feels good."

When he rubbed the heel of his hand into her clit, her mouth opened on a sigh. Watching her face, he curled his two fingers up and pressed into her body as he fucked her with his hand. He felt it. Subtle, but just what the girl at the shop had described. The faintest little curve of texture in her flesh, hardly even noticeable. He pressed his fingertips against it and rubbed her clit at the same time.

Beth's eyes popped open. "Oh," she breathed. He did it again. Her eyes fluttered closed. She whimpered and grabbed his wrist, holding him tight inside her.

His dick throbbed in sympathetic approval.

"Eric…"

Yeah.

"Don't stop. Just…" Her forehead creased with concentration. Her nails bit into his wrist in sharp points of pain that did nothing but excite him further. He felt her muscles tighten around him as he worked her. Jesus Christ, he wanted inside her. But not until…

"That's… It's…" Words seemed to fail her as she whimpered and turned her face away. Finally, a sharp cry escaped her mouth and she was shaking, her hips bucking against him as she came. "Oh, God," she sobbed. "Oh, Eric."

He waited until her last sobs had passed before he let her go. Then Beth rolled to her side, still panting. He smoothed a hand over the generous curve of her ass, loving the way her hip rose up from his hand. He shaped every curve, then slid the edge of his hand down until he touched wet heat.

"Mmm," she sighed, pushing into his fingers as he stroked her.

"More?" he asked, and his cock strained forward when she eased her legs open at his touch.

Eric pulled a condom from his wallet, rolled it on and pushed slowly inside her from behind. It was…heaven. He held her tight to his chest and fucked her as slowly as he could, drawing it out, burying himself so deeply inside her he felt consumed by her body.

A long time later, when they both came again, Beth didn't scream his name. Instead, she sighed it so softly that he barely heard. And strangely, that was even better.

CHAPTER ELEVEN

HE'D AWOKEN EARLY, GRATEFUL that Beth was still asleep and they could avoid any morning-after awkwardness. They'd have to talk about what this meant, if anything, but not when they were naked. And not when her cheeks were flushed pink with sleep.

Though he'd managed to dress without waking her, he hadn't been cold enough to just sneak out. He was still trying to make up for his lies, after all. Stealing out like a thief probably wouldn't help.

So instead of tiptoeing out the door, he sat down on her side of the bed and smoothed a lock of hair off her shoulder. Beth didn't respond. She was sleeping on her stomach, her head cradled on her arms, and once he'd swept her hair away, nearly her whole back was exposed to him.

In the morning light, her skin glowed, so smooth that his fingers actually ached to touch her. He wanted to run his hand down her spine, put his mouth to her shoulder blade and work his way up to her neck. He wanted to smell her, taste her, *have* her again.

Just the thought of touching her had him hard as a rock already. But if he slipped back into bed and woke her, there'd be talk of breakfast, then talk of *talk,* and he didn't want to walk away this morning with any of that tension. He wanted to fucking float.

He brushed the backs of his fingers over her pink cheekbone. "Beth?"

She sighed.

Eric forced himself not to give in to the warm feeling spreading through his chest. *It was just a blow job, man. Get it together. It was just sex.*

"Beth? I've got to go."

Her eyes finally opened, widening when she saw him sitting there. "Oh!" She twisted around, holding the sheet to her chest.

"Go back to sleep. I just wanted you to know I'm leaving."

"I..." Her gaze slid to the doorway and she nodded. "Okay." She obviously wanted to avoid any awkwardness, too.

"I'll call later," he promised, then got to his feet before he screwed up and kissed her. He glanced back as he left, and he could have sworn he caught her smiling. He smiled, too, but not until he was safely outside.

Hard to believe, but...last night had far surpassed their first night together. That had been hot, yes. Desperate. Mind-blowing. But last night had been all that and more. Including the part where she'd fallen asleep pressed tight to his side.

She surprised him, constantly. Every interaction with her left him less sure of who she was. Funny, considering he'd been the one with the fake name.

She just seemed so...soft. Not just her skin, but everything about her. Soft and so much more vulnerable than he'd ever expected. He was really glad he'd gone to her place, though he still had no idea why he'd gone. Well, he knew *why* he'd gone. There was no question of that. But why had he decided to risk it?

Six months ago, it had seemed the height of danger, meeting her. It had felt foolhardy and wrong, sleeping with a stranger, and a notorious one at that. It had been completely out of character.

But now…now he was a different man. Every part of his life felt uncertain. Hell, he didn't even know what his character was anymore. Compared to that confusion, Beth was solid. After all, there was no question of what he wanted from her, and how much he wanted it.

Three hours later, he was still gliding through his day as if it weren't quite real. He'd showered and eaten. Now it was time to get to work, but he checked his phone as he stepped into the brewery, just in case he'd missed a call from Beth.

"Just the guy I wanted to see," a man said from the dimness of the bar.

His eyes were still adjusting, but Eric recognized Luke's voice. He stuffed the phone in his pocket. "Hey, Luke. What are you doing here so early?"

"I've got news about the investigation."

"Good news?"

"After Monica called your friend, I started pushing a little harder. It seemed suspicious. I mean, more suspicious than the Kendalls usually are. We've found some evidence of how Graham broke into other places. Some were just standard break-ins that he paid local thugs to carry out. Some seemed to be crimes of convenience. Renovations that left buildings vulnerable. Stuff like that."

"Okay."

"But there was one man who struck me as cagey. So after I heard from you about Monica, I pressed him harder. His place was hit late last year. A big catering and event company that had a lot of employees over the past ten years, not to mention all the payment information from clients. He'd always claimed not to know anything about any of it, but he was lying."

"He knew Monica?"

"He slept with her. He's married. That's why he suggested she come to his office. Or maybe she suggested it, he couldn't seem to remember those details."

Eric shook his head. "So it was the exact same situation?"

"Pretty much. Counting the owner of that construction company she slept with, that's three men. Maybe that's all there are. But that's enough to charge her as an accessory."

"You're going to charge her?"

"The D.A.'s leaning hard. They'd much rather she give up her brother." The double doors to the back room opened, and Luke looked up with a smile.

"Hey, Luke," Tessa drawled with the kind of smile for her boyfriend that a big brother shouldn't see. Eric cringed, but Tessa ignored that and walked up to kiss him on the cheek. "Eric, did you and Jamie really make up?"

"We talked. We're fine."

"Good. I still can't believe you did that. God. I'm so mad at you." She glared, but her sternness was ruined by the hug she gave him. "Be nice to Jamie."

"I was trying to be nice!" he protested.

"Maybe you need to learn how to communicate better," she suggested.

"Maybe he needs to learn how to grow up."

Tessa slapped his arm. "Behave."

"Hey!"

But she just shrugged and started straightening tables.

"Anyway," Luke said when he finally dragged his eyes off Tessa. Here was a man who was head over heels. "I'll need to get that information about your friend."

"My friend?" Eric stiffened and glanced toward Tessa.

"The woman. Beth… What's her last name?"

"Right," Eric started. "I'll—"

"Cantrell. Beth Cantrell. I'll need to interview her."

Eric swallowed and watched his sister, who'd stopped shifting things around and was now staring at Luke. "Sure," Eric said. "No problem."

"Beth Cantrell," Tessa said. "I know that name."

Eric ignored her, but Luke didn't, of course. "She's the woman who said Monica Kendall asked her to lie."

"Yes, but—"

Eric spun on his heel. "No problem. I'll see you two later."

"Wait!" Tessa yelped. "I know who she is!"

His neck burned, but strangely, the heat felt like ice crawling down his spine. He stopped, but didn't turn around.

"I met her a few months ago. She runs the White Orchid."

"Oh," Luke said, and then silence fell. Eric could feel their eyes on him. He stared hard at the doors that led to his office, where he could lock himself in and avoid these questions.

"Eric?" Tessa started. "Beth Cantrell called you about this?"

The icy heat worked its way up to the tips of his ears.

"Do you know her?"

Oh, boy, did he know her. "Um," he said, hoping that would suffice. But when he turned around to find Luke and Tessa standing side by side, they didn't seem satisfied with that response. Tessa looked blankly confused. While Luke looked…anticipatory?

"She's a business contact."

"Oh, yeah?" Luke asked. "What kind of business?"

"Business business. Local stuff. You know."

Tessa's eyes just seemed to get wider. "No, I don't know."

Best to throw in a little truth in these situations. "I met her at the Boulder Business Expo last year. Her booth was close by."

"Wait a minute," Tessa gasped, and Eric could hear the pieces clicking into place as if there were a microphone inside her brain.

Oh, no.

"Ohmigod!" She covered her mouth, muffling the next words. "Oh, my God. She's the one!"

Luke raised an annoyingly delighted eyebrow. "The one, what?"

"No," Eric said as sternly as he could, but Tessa dropped her hand from her mouth and pointed it at him.

"You said that woman saw the nameplate at the expo and thought you were Jamie. Holy shit, Eric. You slept with Beth Cantrell!"

Eric shook his head, but he could feel his face showing every inch of the truth.

"Wow," Luke said. "She, ah…she's really the owner of that sex shop?"

"Manager," he murmured past numb lips.

"Wow," Luke repeated. He crossed his arms and looked Eric up and down as if he were reassessing him. "So."

Eric swallowed hard and tried to think of something—anything—to say.

Tessa laughed, a sound of thrilled amusement. "I can't... My mind is boggled. I'm utterly, completely *boggled* right now. Apparently I wasn't the only one hiding my dating life in this family. You're like... That's just... That's *legendary.*"

This was why no one was supposed to know. The scandalized delight on both their faces was all fun and games now, but soon enough they'd be whispering about it. Wondering. And they'd never, ever look at Eric the same way.

"It was just one date. We had a glass of wine." *And I got her off right there at the table.* He shook his head. "That's all."

"You big fat liar!" Tessa crowed. "You said you slept with her!" She covered her eyes, laughing. "Oh, God, you're my brother. I didn't want to know this. She must be... Wow."

"This is not an appropriate conversation—"

"Eric! Are you... You're not one of the men she's written about in her column, are you?"

"Column?" he asked dumbly, momentarily forgetting his intention to spin around and stalk out. "What column?"

"The one she writes for *The Rail.* No. Don't answer. I don't want to know which one you are. You're not pierced anywhere, are you? Never mind! Don't answer that, either." Tessa waved her hands as she shook her head. "No."

"Pierced?" he muttered, his mind veering between horror and awful curiosity. She wrote about sex for a paper? Had she written about *him?*

"Is she—?"

Eric cut his hand through the air to stop his sister's questions. "I'm not going to stand here and discuss her as if she were a news story. Luke, I gave you her number if you need to call. That's the end of it."

"Oh, I think I might have to make a personal visit," Luke drawled.

Tessa elbowed him before nearly collapsing in laughter.

Eric was either going to leave or start shouting, so he chose to leave. He hit the doors too hard and they bounced off the walls with a satisfying crash. For a moment, he considered walking right on through the back room to the door in the far wall. But that would only make the talk worse.

The *talk*. Now he'd betrayed Beth again. She'd forgiven him for the lie, but only after making sure he hadn't told anyone. It wasn't totally his fault, though. She was the one who'd come to the brewery. Granted, she'd rightfully been upset at the time, but clearly she wanted to keep this just as quiet as he did. If people found out, Eric might never get one of those late-night calls again.

"Shit."

Before he even reached his office, he turned and headed back to the front room. "Hey."

Luke's and Tessa's heads popped up.

"Please don't say anything to anyone about this." He looked at Luke. "Not even her. She's a very private person. Uh, despite what you may have read."

Luke nodded. "I won't."

Eric was vividly aware of the silence he left behind. He knew it wouldn't last. As soon as he was safely gone, they'd talk about it. They'd theorize about what a wild woman Beth Cantrell must be. They'd talk about her store and her column. Eric shut his office door and pulled up Google, determined to find out exactly what kind of a wild woman she was.

Were there things she was into? Kinky fetishes that she liked? If so and they kept seeing each other, he was going to have to up his game. Up to this point, both of their nights together had been impromptu. Unexpected. But given time to think about it... Yeah. She'd probably expect more at some point. Thank God that little class had served him well. He'd have to hit the White Orchid website and see what was coming up next. He'd have to read her column.

Assuming there was even a chance he'd see her again. She dated other guys, obviously. Hell, she'd been on a date with someone else last night. But Eric had been the one she'd called for sex.

As for what else she might be up to...Google wasn't helping. Nothing about a column came up when he entered Beth's name. He tried going directly to *The Rail*'s website, and there it was, right on the front page. "Sexuality Personified" by Ms. White. Not a very good cover name, but the name of the column damn sure fit.

While his stomach turned flips, Eric raced through the first column. It was actually fairly tame. "Ms. White" said she'd received several letters asking about a partner's refusal to use condoms. "If he refuses with you, then he's refused with others. This is not okay. N-O-T. We've all had partners who claim not to feel anything with a condom on. Just make clear that he certainly isn't going to feel anything with it off. Not one little thing. Better yet, walk away. And don't let a man tell you that he can't wear a condom because of piercings—yours or his. Genital piercings are very obviously not constructed with sharp edges. Take it from me, piercings are not a problem."

Take it from me?

Eric glanced down at his own unadorned lap. Piercings. Did that make it…better? For her? *How?*

He hit the Archived button and braced himself for what he might find. Only three columns popped up, thank God. One was about transsexuality and dating, a topic which didn't apply to Eric, obviously. One was a rather funny piece comparing men's and women's orgasms. It didn't offer many personal cues, but Eric focused on one sentence intently. "A recent partner confessed that he was sure women's orgasms were much more intense than men's, that he'd never screamed and shaken the way I do. …" So that was someone else who'd made Beth scream and shake. Of course, he knew she'd had other partners, but… Shit. His shoulders suddenly ached with tension.

The last column. Eric swallowed hard. A guide to threesomes. He didn't even read it. He couldn't. Whatever she did when she wasn't with him, that was her business. He clicked away, but his mind kept turning and he opened the threesome column again. Then he closed it.

No. He didn't want to know. She was an amazing force of sex and sensuality. That was what had attracted him. And whatever she did with other men— or women—she'd called Eric last night. She'd wanted him and no one else. *All I wanted was for him to be like you.*

The memory of those words filled Eric with such fierce triumph that he felt like he'd grown taller. He might be vanilla as all hell, but maybe that was her favorite flavor. Or at least the flavor of the month. Let her go out with however many faceless bastards she wanted to, as long as Eric was the one making her come. She could be that hobby he'd been looking for. She'd sure as hell taken his mind off work for a few hours.

Eric glanced at his calendar and bit back a groan. The sales rep for the oven company was coming this morning to give them all a tutorial on working the new pizza oven. As if Eric would ever be anywhere near it.

This was just the first step. Now that the oven was in, Jamie would start bringing in chefs for interviews. Next Sunday the new dining deck would be built, and Eric was still pissed that the brewery would be closed on Monday because the front door wouldn't be accessible.

Then they'd bring in servers, new equipment, flatware, dishes, supplies. But today was the start of it.

The truth was that Jamie had been right. Eric dreaded all of it. He'd been faking his way through it for Jamie's sake, but what Eric really wanted to do was stop everything. He needed time to think. He needed to catch up or make new plans or…

Jesus, he wished he'd stayed in Beth's bed instead of getting up.

Eric was still staring into space when a hard fist rapped at his door. He didn't have to look through the small window to know it was Jamie.

"I'm coming," Eric snapped. By the time he forced

himself out of his office, Jamie and Tessa were waiting with a balding man sporting a thick mustache. Eric introduced himself, but he was distracted by his suspicion toward his siblings. Tessa stood with her arms crossed and her lips pressed tight together. Her eyes touched on Eric and then slid away.

Jamie looked dead serious, and that was hardly a natural state for him. So why was he shooting Eric such a searching look? Had Tessa told Jamie?

Eric scowled at both of them as the salesman began his well-rehearsed spiel. Jamie and Tessa got caught up in it, and within minutes, they were huddled around the oven with the sales guy. Eric listened, but he hung back, watching from a few feet away. Jamie and Tessa tried out the different vents and knobs. They opened doors and adjusted the exhaust.

Jamie grinned as the salesman made a small pile of kindling in the oven and explained that the temperature would need to be kept low for the first day, then gradually heated from there. "What kind of wood are you planning to use?" the guy asked as he checked the exhaust one more time.

"Apple," Jamie said.

"Nice choice." The guy drew a lighter from his pocket and set it to the kindling. And just like that, Eric's old life was over. Flames licked at the tiny pile of wood. Donovan Brothers was no longer just an artisan brewing company. It was a brewpub.

They all stood around staring at the flames, though Eric knew he was the only one who saw the fire eating away at their life. Everyone else saw it as creation.

Finally, the salesman declared the initial lighting a success, and both of Eric's siblings walked the guy out to the front room. Eric stared at the oven for a minute, slightly interested despite himself. He hadn't known what to expect. The only wood-fired ovens he'd ever seen were huge brick behemoths. This oven was stone on the inside, but the outside was galvanized steel just like any commercial oven. It definitely took up too much space, but it wasn't so obnoxious that Eric could reasonably complain about it.

Jamie walked back in, hauling a bundle of wood. "Pretty cool, huh?" he said as he laid the wood out on the floor.

Eric grunted.

"The applewood should be here this evening, but for now, we'll warm the oven with oak."

Eric nodded. "Good. Great." He glanced at Jamie and found that his brother was watching him instead of the oven. That same strange, tense expression was on his face. Eric decided to meet it head-on. "What did she tell you?" he asked.

Jamie scowled. "What are you talking about?"

"What did she say?"

"Who?"

"Tessa."

"I don't know what the hell you're talking about."

Eric threw his hands up. "I can tell by the way you're looking at me that something's up. So tell me what she said."

Tessa pushed through the doors. "What who said?"

"You," Eric snapped. "You told him."

"I did not! I said I wouldn't say anything and I didn't."

"Hey!" Jamie barked. "Care to clue me in here?"

Eric could suddenly see the truth on Tessa's face.

She hadn't said a thing. Shit. "Nothing. You were just giving me a weird look." Boy, that didn't sound guilty at all.

"I was looking at you weird because I thought everything was cool between us, but you're growling at me like a pissed-off bear. What the hell's wrong with you?"

What *was* wrong with him? His conscience had poisoned him and turned him into an idiot. "Nothing," he finally said. "We're good."

"Hard to tell these days," Jamie muttered. "So what are you keeping from me now?"

"Nothing," Eric snapped.

Jamie looked at Tessa, but she shook her head and shot Eric a wary look.

Eric sighed. "I'm sorry I was in a bad mood. It has nothing to do with you. Really. So how long before you can try out the oven?"

Just as Eric had hoped, talk of the oven distracted Jamie. "Tomorrow at the earliest. We'll let it warm through today so we can try it out tomorrow. I'll have to mix up a batch of dough myself. Unless someone else is willing." He gave Tessa a significant glance.

"Oh, fine," she groaned. "I'll make the dough. Have you settled on a recipe yet?"

"I've got it narrowed down to a few. But Olivia recommended I wait until a chef is hired so I can get his or her input. I'd like to have somebody with their own brain, since I'll need guidance."

Great. Another strong personality in the building. Eric shot a look at the tank room. "Just make sure whoever it is gets along with Wallace. We don't need two temperamental creative types in here. Speaking of which… Where is Wallace?"

Jamie and Tessa shrugged, so Eric went to look, happy to have a chance to escape. Wallace wasn't in the tank room or the bottling room. It wasn't like him to not show up. Heck, it wasn't even like him to stay gone on his days off.

Eric headed to his office to check for a message from Wallace. There was nothing on his phone, so he paged through his emails before finally pushing back in his chair and checking his desk. And there it was on the far corner. A letter.

Wallace was off to California. Faron had discovered that her husband had cheated with someone she'd asked him not to date. She was done. So Wallace was off to help her pack. To declare his love. To bring her back.

"Good Lord," Eric muttered. "Seriously?"

This was a firing offense. Wallace couldn't just walk out on the tanks for however many days because he was *lovesick*.

Eric looked over the letter again. He'd be gone for three days. Maybe four. Eric would have to drop all his office work and take charge of the tank room.

His scowl faded a little. He'd have to spend hours in there, scrambling to cover Wallace's duties. He'd be stuck in the tank room for the rest of the week.

A slow smile spread across Eric's face and he felt a strong urge to rub his hands together. Four days would be more than enough time to get a small test batch started. Something fun. He'd have to see what supplies Wallace had on hand. He'd also have to be careful not to use too much of Wallace's special stock of ingredients, or the man would be on the rampage. He'd be unhappy with the intrusion regardless, but he'd just have to deal with it. After leaving them in the lurch, Wallace would deserve to be upset. Still, maybe the sexually liberated weren't so bad, after all. As a matter of fact, maybe Eric had joined the ranks himself.

He wanted to jump up and get to the tank room immediately, but he made himself answer emails and shift his schedule around to deal with distribution problems first. Nearly two hours passed before he could manage it, but he finally slipped into the tank room and closed the door.

Heaven.

He loved this place. Loved the idea of being in charge of product instead of people. It was so much easier. So much more natural for him. The problem was that he wasn't needed here. Wallace had already been the brewmaster for three years when Michael Donovan died and Eric had stepped in to try to fill his shoes. The brewing was the one thing he hadn't needed to worry about. Wallace had it covered. So Eric had taken care of everything else.

And now…Wallace *still* had it covered. His beer won them awards every year. He was highly respected on the national scene. And he was utterly in control of every step of the process.

Eric smiled grimly. "Except when he's not here."

He found a list of things Wallace wanted done while he was gone. "Tanks are only to be touched by Eric or Jamie!" he'd written in huge letters. He would've included Tessa, too, but Tessa had been afraid of the fermentation tanks since their father had told a story of almost getting a hand blown off when a valve malfunctioned. She'd put in her two weeks with Wallace, learned the ropes and then she'd bolted, happy to escape with her life and both hands intact.

Eric read the list and got to work. He'd have to take care of the scheduled duties before he could indulge in experimentation, but he approached the mash tun with a smile. Between Beth calling him up and Wallace going out of town, this was going to be a very good week, as long as he kept his back to the kitchen and ignored everything else.

CHAPTER TWELVE

THE MAN HAD DELIVERED yet another revelation. Beth shook her head as she disassembled the store mannequin, laying all the poor girl's parts out on the floor.

Whatever Beth pretended to be here at the White Orchid, Eric Donovan was her own personal sex class, teaching her things she'd been unable to figure out herself. He was like…a learning aid. Because she already knew everything. She understood it. But she couldn't process it.

Take, for example, the G-spot. She knew all about it. She'd even assumed she might have one. But she'd figured it was like any erogenous zone. What worked for some women might not work for her.

Boy, had she been wrong.

It was so simple that she felt stupid for needing Eric to show her. It was her own damn body, after all. And the answer was easy: all the toys in the world wouldn't do a damn thing for her if she wasn't aroused. Stimulated. Shaking with need.

Sex started in the brain, not the G-spot or anywhere else.

God, even while masturbating she'd been thinking too much. She was going to have to find a way to get past that, because she couldn't keep Eric around as a sexual aid forever. Even if he was such a devastatingly good one.

After all, she'd already learned so much. This time last year, she'd been worried that she was sexually... Beth shook her head, trying to think of the word. Not repressed, but, "Hollow," she murmured.

Yes, sexually hollow. That was exactly how it had felt. Every structure in place, every appearance correct, but nothing substantial to fill those spaces.

Then she'd met Eric and realized that she was full to the brim, and only one ingredient had been missing: chemistry. That had been lesson one. Lesson two had been less profound but just as important—anything was possible when you were truly turned on.

Beth smothered a laugh and glanced around the store, wondering just what else would feel good when one proceeded in just the right way. A new world of possibilities had opened up to her. She glanced down at the whip in her hand, the one she'd just wrestled out of the grasp of the mannequin. One look at that, and she couldn't stop her laughter, imagining Eric standing over her with a whip.

He didn't need a whip. All he needed was that dark scowl and a growled order.

Her laughter died away, and she felt suddenly, completely serious. Eric didn't need props. He was the prop.

But that was all he could be. As much as he turned her on, as much as he brought her to life, she didn't trust him. How could she? And with her history of love, brief as it had been, sex was as far as it could go with Eric. He'd already lied to her, and that was the end of that. Her heart wasn't available to him.

The door opened, admitting a gust of cold, wet air.

Autumn in Boulder was usually crisp and cool, but it had been awfully warm and humid up until this point. Maybe the Indian summer was over. She smiled widely. "Hello," she said to the man walking in. She waved one mannequin arm.

He raised his eyebrows at the limb.

"Can I get you a towel?" Beth asked when a drop of water trickled down his jaw.

"I think I'll live," he said, swiping a hand through his wet hair.

"All right. Let me know if you change your mind. And if you have any questions, feel free to ask me or Kelly. She's in the back room."

"Are you Beth?"

Beth stood, her smile fading as she studied him more closely. He was tall and lean and dark. She was pretty sure she didn't recognize him. "Yes. I'm Beth Cantrell."

The man reached into his coat pocket and pulled out a black leather wallet. But when he turned it around, she saw the flash of a badge. "I'm Detective Luke Asher. Eric Donovan may have mentioned me?"

Beth smoothed her suddenly damp palms down her skirt. "Oh, of course. Hello." She didn't know what caused the rush of sick anxiety in her stomach—the fact that she had to talk to a police detective, or the idea that Eric had already talked to him about *her*.

His eyes traveled over her, and for a moment, she thought he was checking her out, but then she saw that he looked around the shop with the same assessing gaze. He was only *detecting*.

"Is there someplace we can talk?"

She nodded. There was only one customer, and she was in the toy room with Kelly. "My office," she said.

"My partner will be here in just a moment."

"Oh." His partner? Beth's hands started to sweat. This sounded serious. "Should we…?" She gestured vaguely toward the back room, wondering if she was about to be interrogated.

"Sure."

Oh, God, she sincerely hoped that Luke Asher was the bad cop on this team, because even though he was intimidating he seemed like a fairly polite guy. Sure, she could feel his eyes boring into her skull like lasers, but…

Beth used the excuse of stopping at the door to the toy room to glance behind her. She was surprised to find that the man wasn't even watching her. His eyes were still sweeping the room.

She stuck her head through the curtains to the toy room. "Kelly, can you listen for customers? I have to step into my office for a few minutes."

Kelly nodded and gave a thumbs-up. She was chewing gum again. Beth sighed. She'd warned the girl twice. Now she was going to have to write her up.

But she forgot all about Kelly when she heard the front door open and turned to see a beautiful woman step in and give the shop the same sort of assessing look that Detective Asher had.

"This is Detective Simone Parker," he said.

"Oh," Beth said, feeling immediately calm when the female detective smiled. "Nice to meet you."

But her calm disappeared once they were all seated in Beth's tiny office. She pressed her palms flat to her desk, then realized she looked like she was about to bolt and clasped them tight together instead.

"So, is this serious?"

Asher smiled. "It's likely nothing, but I do need to get the story directly from you."

"Is Monica going to get in trouble for this?" As objective as she could be about Monica, Beth had known her for over fifteen years.

He leaned forward. "It's not your story that's causing her problems, Ms. Cantrell. This isn't the first time she's done this. And you know what? She's not even the point of this investigation. I want her brother, and I need to persuade her to stop protecting him."

That surprised her. "Is she protecting him?"

He smiled. "I see you know her fairly well. You're right. Her father is asking her to protect him."

She nodded, even though she really wanted to shake her head. Roland Kendall was arrogant and cruel in business, but he'd always been kind to Beth.

"But his son is already in trouble. He doesn't want his daughter to go down, too."

"I don't want to hurt them," she said quickly. "I just wanted to be fair to Eric. I mean, to the Donovans."

He nodded, his gaze sliding past her shoulder. When his eyes froze, she glanced behind her to the crowded shelves where inventory was stacked. She didn't try to figure out what had distracted him. It could've been any one of the brightly boxed toys. Or maybe the spectacle of all of them together.

The female detective cleared her throat. "We'll do our best to keep you out of this as much as we can," she said.

"Thank you." Beth took a deep breath and told them exactly what had happened. Whatever these people had done, they'd done to themselves, and she couldn't let herself feel guilty about that. Monica was the one who had pulled Beth into this mess in the first place.

By the time they stood to leave, Beth had managed to suppress most of her guilt.

Detective Asher shook her hand. "Thanks for getting in touch with Eric about this."

"Oh, sure," she stammered. "We local businesses have to support each other."

His eyes darted behind her one more time before he smiled and tipped his head. "We'll be in touch."

Beth walked them out, but her relief was premature. Before the door closed behind them, she heard Simone Parker call, "I'll meet you at the station," and turn back around. Beth almost groaned.

"Here," the woman said, holding out a business card. "I forgot to leave you this." But the woman stayed where she was after Beth took the card. Her eyes shifted over the store and her gorgeous brown skin turned suspiciously pink along her cheekbones.

"Detective?"

She cleared her throat. "I saw the sign on the door that you do bra fittings. I just had a baby a few months ago, and…"

"Yes!" Beth said, relieved to be back on solid ground. "Absolutely. Most women wear the wrong size for their whole life, and certainly after having a child, everything changes."

Simone nodded.

"I should warn you that we don't have a selection of sports bras or everyday underwear."

"Right." She bit her lip, her pretty face turning even pinker. "The truth is that someone asked me on a date. It's nothing serious, but it's the first one since…" She waved a hand over her body. "And I'd really like something that isn't cotton or absorbent or just…*sturdy*. But I'm so big now!"

Beth grinned. "I understand. Believe me. And I make a point of buying lines that have pretty bras in larger sizes, because sometimes they seem impossible to find. Do you want to do this now?"

"No!" She looked toward the parking lot in horror. "I think he's gone."

"I'll come back when I'm off duty," Simone said. "Thank you."

After the door closed, Beth found herself standing there smiling. Then she remembered why Simone had been there in the first place.

"Damn," Beth whispered.

If Roland Kendall found out that Beth had told the police about that phone call, he'd never forgive her. The man took good care of his friends and brought ruthless power down on his enemies. But what could he do to her?

"Besides organize a boycott of the store," she murmured. God, what had she gotten herself into? What if her scruples put the White Orchid at risk?

Then again, they'd been boycotted when Annabelle had expanded the building and modernized the storefront. The protests had only increased sales. And Beth couldn't just ignore something illegal because it might cause a blip in sales.

The stress burned in her chest. She tried to close her eyes and let it go, tried to focus on the steady white noise of rain hitting the roof. She was doing the *right* thing. She knew she was. She just needed someone to tell her that.

She retreated to her office and pulled up Eric's number on her phone. By the time it rang for the fifth time, she was regretting the impulse to call him. She'd forgotten that this was the morning-after call. It could be awkward.

A loud hum suddenly burst through the line. "Hi," Eric said.

"Oh, hi! Are you…?" The hum grew to a drone so loud she winced and eased the phone farther from her ear. "You're busy, so I'll just—"

"No, just a second." The drone faded. A loud metallic bang rang through her ear, and then there was silence. "Sorry," Eric said. His voice echoed.

"Where are you?"

"I was in the tank room, but I'm in the bottling room now. It's quiet when the line isn't running."

"I'm sorry. I didn't mean to interrupt."

"It's no problem. Really."

Beth rubbed a nervous hand against her skirt again. "Detective Asher came by. He wanted to talk about Monica. I told him everything she said, so hopefully it will help."

"I'm sorry," Eric said.

"Oh, it's no big deal. It's the right thing to do. Isn't it?"

"Sure, but you sound a little upset and—"

"It's just that I've known them a long time. That's all. And having a police detective walk in here made it into a bigger deal in my head."

"You get used to him," Eric said.

"Is he the one who's dating your sister?"

"Living with her," Eric corrected.

"Oh. Well, I just thought you should know. That he came by. That he's pursuing it."

"I know."

"You know?"

He sighed, the sound echoing around the hard-walled space he was in. "I apologize. He told me earlier. I meant to call you, and then I got busy and… I'm sorry. I should've warned you."

He should have. "I was pretty startled by a cop coming in here to interview me, and then his partner came and it kind of freaked me out."

"I know. I really meant to call, but…"

"I think you owe me again."

"Oh?" he murmured.

She'd said it as a joke, but the silence on Eric's end suddenly felt very serious. Beth sat up straight and breathed out so sharply that it rasped into the phone line.

"Are you asking me to come over again?" His voice didn't echo now. It was too low.

"No, I—"

"Well, if I owe you, I should pay up."

"That's not what I meant," she finally managed to get out.

"Are you sure?"

Was she? Because her body had come to startling life at the idea. "We agreed this couldn't be a regular thing."

"We did. But two nights? That's hardly regular." His voice was still soft, but there was no mistaking the calm sternness of his personality. He made everything sound so reasonable. "Is it?"

Beth's gaze fell on the box of faux-fur panties that sat next to her desk.

She needed to stretch her wings. This wasn't about Eric, this was about her. But working on herself was a long-term goal. In the short term, her choices seemed to be Eric, or fantasies about Eric to help her get herself off. What the hell kind of choice was that? He seemed more than willing to help her out, even if he hadn't actually applied for the job of sex assistant.

And she wanted him. Wasn't that enough? "You're right," she found herself whispering. "Can you come over tonight?"

"Yes."

"But we can't keep doing this."

"I know."

"You have your life," she insisted. "I have mine."

"I couldn't agree with you more. But tonight…"

"Yeah," she breathed. "Tonight."

A loud boom echoed through the phone, and Beth heard a distant voice speaking.

"Okay," Eric said. "I'll be right there." When he spoke to her again, his voice was a quiet rumble. "What time?" he asked softly.

She glanced at the clock—2:45. Beth wanted to say *now*. She could do it. Cairo would be at the store in fifteen minutes. Beth could be home in thirty. And they could be naked within seconds. She could have him inside her, pushing deep, filling her until she screamed.

"Eight," she said, forcing herself to say the reasonable thing, instead of the "God, I need it right this moment" thing.

"I'll be there," Eric said.

When he hung up, Beth set her phone carefully on the

desk, clenched her hands in fists and ducked her head to hide the slow grin spreading across her face. She'd spent her whole career serving the needs of others—it was time to serve the hell out of her own. If this was a mistake, she was going to milk every last drop of pleasure from it before the regret set in. Every. Last. Drop.

CHAPTER THIRTEEN

WHEN THE REGRET CAME, it hit her like a collapsing brick wall. Actually, there was no metaphor needed. It hit her with all the force of opening her front door and finding her father standing there instead of Eric Donovan.

"Daddy!" she squeaked, immediately regressing to her guilt-filled adolescence. "What are you doing here?"

He winked and slipped off the old-fashioned hat he always wore when he put on a suit. He was a big fan of elegance. And modesty. Beth tried not to think of how much cleavage she was currently showing in this dress.

"I was in town for a doctor's appointment."

"Are you okay?" she gasped.

"Healthy as a horse. It was only a checkup. And then I went out for dinner with an old friend, and when I realized how late it was, I thought I'd take you out for dessert before I headed home."

"You should have..." She dropped the thought when she remembered he didn't own a cell phone. "Don't you think you should start back now while it's still light? Mom will be worried."

"Oh, she worries anyway. I'll call and tell her I'll be late. Unless you have other plans." He finally seemed to notice her dress and craned his neck to look behind her.

"I... No, I just..."

"You won't believe who called me up for dinner to-night, *querida*. I don't think I've seen him since..."

Her father heard the footsteps on the stairs at the same moment Beth did. He looked down, and Beth stepped forward.

Eric bounded up two more stairs before his head rose and he stopped with comical suddenness. In fact, he nearly pitched face-forward with the momentum, but he grabbed the railing and saved himself.

Her dad smiled. "I see I'm interrupting."

"No!" Beth said. Eric seemed frozen.

"Come up, come up!" her dad said, waving Eric forward.

He looked warily at Beth, but took one more step, and then another. Beth had no choice but to back into her apartment and let them both in. The landing wasn't big enough for the three of them to stand around, with all that awkwardness taking up so much space.

"Hello! I'm Beth's father," her dad said with an enthusiasm that deepened his faint accent.

"Um, Eric, this is my dad, Thomas. He just happened to be in town tonight! Dad, this is Eric."

"Pleased to meet you," Eric said as they shook hands. His gaze slid to Beth's and she cringed and shook her head.

"The pleasure is mine," her father said. "But I can see you two were on your way out. I'll leave you to your evening."

"Dad. No. I'll just—"

Eric interrupted. "I was just stopping by. You should spend time with your daughter."

"Thank you!" Beth said. "You and I can go out, Dad. I'll see Eric another time."

Eric started backing away.

Her father eyed him, and then his weathered face broke into a wide smile. "I have the perfect solution. We'll all have dessert and drinks together. I'd love to get to know some of Beth's friends."

Beth almost choked on her tongue. Eric wasn't even a friend. He was just a sex partner.

She realized she'd been shaking her head for a full ten seconds. "No, Dad."

"Come. You haven't introduced me to a gentleman friend since high school."

Oh, my God, why was he bringing *that* up?

"Mr. Cantrell," Eric started, but Beth cut him off.

"Dad, no. Eric doesn't want to go out with us. He was only—"

"Of course he does," her dad said, and now there was steel behind that smile.

Eric swallowed. Loudly.

"He wasn't staying long!" she insisted.

Her father frowned.

Eric's face blanched. "I think dessert would be wonderful," he said in such a rush that she barely understood him.

But her father must have understood perfectly, because his smile was suddenly natural again and he slapped Eric on the back. "Yes. Wonderful. Let me just call your mother and tell her it'll be another hour before I leave."

"There's a phone in the spare room!" Beth said as if there wasn't a phone right next to the couch.

Just an hour, Beth prayed. *Please, just an hour.* Not that it mattered. As soon as they were done, Eric would bolt into the night without looking back.

Her father disappeared.

"Ohmigod," Beth whispered, grabbing Eric's arm. "Why did you say yes?"

"I had to! You said I wasn't staying long, and I just… I had to say something!"

"But not that!"

"You basically told him I was here to have sex with you! What was I supposed to say?"

"Are you kidding me? I was going to say you were picking up a CD."

"A CD? Who the hell even has CDs anymore?"

"Eric!" She shook his arm hard. "Do you really think my dad knows that? He's seventy-three!"

"I panicked, all right? I wasn't planning on meeting your family tonight."

Beth let go of him and covered her face with her hands. "Oh, God, I am so, so sorry. This is a disaster. Just…" She froze, then glanced toward the hallway. "Just go! Now! Before he—"

Her father stepped into the hall, shooting his cuffs and straightening his tie. "Your mother's been appeased. I promised to bring her a piece of pie. Is there a place with good pie around here? How about that place we had brunch, *querida?*"

She gave one last, best effort. "I don't think they're open in the evenings, Daddy."

"Nonsense. I looked at the dinner menu when we were there. I thought I might take your mother back sometime. What was it called?"

"Karen's," she murmured. The place was a fifteen-minute drive away, and her dad would want to linger.

"That's it! Let's go. My treat."

Beth gave Eric one last, long, helpless look. He just

cleared his throat, apparently unwilling to be rude and
bow out. Admirable, she supposed, but she desperately
wished he was a low-life bastard at that moment. "I'll
get a sweater," she said, sighing. His gaze slid down
to her breasts, then shifted away so suddenly that she
thought she saw his eyes spin.

She felt like a guilty kid as she walked to the closet
to grab her most modest button-down sweater. But she
always felt that way around her father. It was the one
reason she let her mom talk her into keeping the White
Orchid a secret. Because Beth would rather die than see
heartbroken disappointment in her dad's eyes again.
That one time eighteen years ago had been the worst
moment of her life. So she pulled on her sweater and
pretended she'd been doing nothing wrong and she was
still the nice girl she'd been before her father had found
out she wasn't.

ERIC WAS DROWNING IN mortification. At some point during the evening, he just expected to keel over, stone-cold
dead from guilt. The things he'd been thinking about
doing to Beth. The things he'd meant to do as soon as
he got her alone.

But her father didn't know that. He couldn't even
suspect it. Could he?

At least Eric had gotten a free pass on the ride over.
He'd stuttered something about taking his own car, just
in case. Just in case of what, he had no idea, but he'd
escaped. Admittedly, he'd had a brief impulse to simply
drive home, but that would definitely be the last straw
with Beth. And he really, really wanted to see her again.
He just didn't want to see her sitting next to her father.

The man was just finishing up a story about living

on a ranch in Argentina as a boy. "So your father was a rancher?" Eric asked Thomas politely. Eric immediately took another sip of his wine, hoping the bottle would be gone soon.

"No, my father was an Englishman. A banker. He came to Argentina on business and fell in love with my mother. He never left."

"She must have been a beautiful woman."

"Oh, she was, Eric. In fact, my Beth looks just like her."

"Oh, Dad, that's not true," she said.

"It is true," he insisted, covering her hand with his. "You're a beautiful woman. But you know, your grandmother had six kids at your age."

She sighed as if they'd had this conversation many times. "I'm not going to have six kids."

"No, but one or two…" His eyes slid to Eric. "With a very lucky man."

"Eric is just a friend," Beth jumped in.

"Come, *querida*. You don't dress that way for a friend."

Beth pulled her sweater tighter and cleared her throat. "I'm very busy with work," she said, but her normally confident posture had lost a little of its strength.

Her dad shook his head. "Selling ladies' foundation garments. With a college degree."

Eric was slightly confused by that description, but he was more confused by Beth's reaction. She met his gaze, her eyes widening as she gave the faintest shake of her head. "I'm not a salesperson," she said as she turned back to her dad. "I'm the manager."

He waved a dismissive hand. "Working in a store

like that, it's no wonder you haven't met a gentleman yet. It's nothing but women all day!"

She shook her head, but her dad turned to Eric.

"Why do you think my Beth hasn't settled down?"

Eric pictured Beth standing in her store, surrounded by lingerie and vibrators and little trays of jewelry that looked suspiciously like nipple rings. He pictured her giving classes on sex and dating men with piercings that marked their bodies like damned picture books. He swallowed hard and looked at her in desperation. *Why hadn't she settled down?* Didn't her father know anything about her?

Judging by the way she shook her head again, he didn't.

Eric must have looked completely frozen, because Beth spoke for him. "People marry later these days. I'm not in a rush."

"All your old friends in Hillstone have gotten married and had children."

Eric watched her face stiffen. She looked…angry. "All right. People who aren't in Hillstone marry later. None of my friends are married," she said. "And I won't be getting married anytime soon. Jeez, I swear, you're getting worse than Mom."

"I want to be a grandfather before I die." Without missing a beat, he turned his smile on Eric. "So, tell me about your family."

Here was a subject Eric could handle. He gave her dad the abbreviated version of his family story, but Eric was focused on Beth the whole time. She looked younger and softer. And maybe a little lost. Her dad kept a loose hold on her hand as the waiter came to take their plates away. Her father had ordered a cheese course with wine. Beth had eaten only half a cracker.

"Sounds like you're an enterprising young man," her dad said.

Eric didn't know about the *young* part. Though he felt a bit like a teenager tonight, caught between the girl he wanted to feel up and her eagle-eyed father.

"You must be a very special man to have taken all that on at such a young age," her dad continued, raising his eyebrows.

"I just did what had to be done," Eric said. "And there are plenty of men who have jobs and families at twenty-four. It's nothing special."

Her dad slid his eyes toward Beth. "He's a good one."

"Dad," she said flatly, a pink flush spreading over her cheekbones.

"Do you like my daughter, Eric?"

Oh, Jesus. Eric snatched up his glass of wine to buy a moment. Did he *like* her? More like he wanted to drive her straight home and carry her into his house and straight to his bed. So far his relationship with Beth Cantrell had been about fifty percent lust and fifty percent guilt, but tonight was tipping it out of balance.

"Of course, Mr. Cantrell," he finally said. "She's a wonderful woman." He added, "Everybody likes her," trying for a compliment, but it ended up sounding suspiciously like a cop-out.

The server came to offer the dessert menu again, and Eric and Beth stared at each other while her father discussed pie with the waitress. "And what about you two? Would you like something?"

"No!" they both said.

Beth squeezed her dad's hand. "You need to get

home, Dad. It's late. If you get into an accident, Mom will never forgive you."

"That's true," he conceded. "Especially if I spill the pie."

Beth nodded solemnly while Eric said a quick prayer that this was almost over. It was still sinking in. His stomach still felt high in his throat from the moment he'd looked up and seen her standing there with a dapper older gentleman. Not what he'd expected from the evening. Not at all.

And yet, it was fascinating to watch Beth be someone else. Not the sexy, confident, unflappable woman from the White Orchid, but the daughter of this man who was obviously a big believer in old-fashioned values. She crossed her legs and slumped a little in her chair, her eyes on her father's hand as she tapped her thumb against his.

When she looked up and caught Eric's gaze, she mouthed, *I'm sorry,* and suddenly all this was hilarious. Absurd. How the hell had a no-strings-attached night of sex ended with him meeting Beth's father and answering pointed questions about family and values?

Eric suddenly couldn't stop a smile. Beth looked away, but he saw her mouth tighten at the edges.

"Well, it's been a pleasure," her dad said as he stood, setting his hat on his head with a flourish.

Beth stood. "Where are you going?"

He gestured toward the waitress, who approached with a box that clearly held a whole pie. "I've got to get this home to your mother. But you two stay and enjoy. I ordered you apple pie à la mode. To share."

"Dad—"

"Nonsense. Eric will see you safely home, won't you, Eric?"

"Of course," Eric said, standing, as well.

Her dad signed the check and shrugged his coat on.

"Thank you for the wine, sir," Eric said, putting a lot of thought into the right pressure of his handshake, which was strange. What could it matter what kind of impression he made on Beth's dad?

He was still mulling that over as Beth finished hugging her father. Their pie arrived, vanilla ice cream pooling in the plate as it melted.

"Oh. My. God," Beth groaned as she collapsed into her chair. "I can't…I don't even know what to say. I'm… *horrified,* to say the least."

"It's all right," he said, as if it were.

"Eric. *God.*"

"He's very nice."

Beth stared at him as if he'd lost his mind. Maybe he had. Eric took a bite of pie.

"How can you eat?"

He set down the fork when he saw the slight green tinge to her face. "So, your parents don't know?"

"Know what?"

"About the White Orchid?"

She covered her pale face with her hands and took a deep breath. "My mom knows. But not my dad."

Eric thought of the man's perfect posture and elegant suit. The jaunty hat and manicured fingernails. "I think that's probably a good thing."

She dropped her hands, her eyes wide with surprise. "Do you?"

"I'm not saying you *should* hide it, but I can understand why it seems like a good idea."

"You don't think I'm a horrible person?"

"Do you think he'd want to know?"

"No," she said quickly. "I don't. But I can't honestly say I've lied for his sake. My mom doesn't think I should tell him, but I feel so guilty."

"And relieved?" he prompted, understanding perfectly.

"Yes." Her shoulders slumped. "And relieved that I can say it's my mom's idea."

"Come on. Eat your pie. The ice cream is melting."

Beth didn't reach for the pie, she just set her hands on the table and looked at him. "You're really nice, you know that?"

Eric cleared his throat and picked up his fork. He wasn't nice at all. Sure, he almost always did the right thing, but it was rarely because he wanted to. It was because he felt he should. And he was still haunted by what his sister had told him a few months ago.

When she was fourteen, only weeks into mourning her parents' deaths, she'd come downstairs to find Eric sharing a beer with a friend. And Eric had said something horrible. And she'd overheard it and never said a word. *Of course, I'd walk away if I could. But I don't have a choice.*

He wanted to put his fist through a wall every time he thought of it. Such a small thing to say. And so cruel. And the worst part of it was that he'd meant every word. Tessa had recognized the truth in his voice and lived each day with the fear that he might leave. If things got too tough. If she got bad grades. If Jamie pissed him off. She'd honestly thought that Eric might pick up and run. And sometimes he'd damn well wanted to.

So, no, he wasn't a nice guy. He was just a guy trying desperately to be as good as the man who'd adopted him and given him the Donovan name. Eric had hoped he'd grown into Michael Donovan's shoes, but he'd long ago realized he never would.

Beth finally picked up her fork and took a small bite of pie. Then another. Eric was distracted from his brooding by the memory of the last time they'd shared a dessert. She'd seemed unattainable then. A dark beauty whose sexual promise surrounded her like an aura. He'd watched her eat just as she was doing now. Delicate bites. The flash of a tongue. The fantasy of that mouth.

She wasn't unattainable now. Now he knew how to make her come. With his hands. And his mouth. And his cock.

But it wasn't just that. He'd cracked a little of her mystery tonight. She wasn't a sexual goddess sprung whole from Zeus's head. Tonight, Eric had gotten a glimpse of the girl she'd once been, and a hint at the woman she was now.

"So you haven't taken any men home to meet your parents?" he asked.

Beth's fork froze halfway to the pie. "No."

"Nothing serious?"

"Not really. And I don't usually—" She looked startled by her own words and bit them off.

"Don't usually what?"

She cleared her throat. "We talked about this at the hotel. I don't usually date men like you."

"What kind of men do you usually date?"

Beth took another bite and shrugged.

Eric pushed harder, not quite knowing why. "What about the guy you went out with last night? What's he like?"

She chewed her pie very thoroughly, clearly buying time. Took a sip of water. "He's an artist. And a musician." Her lips curved in a small smile. "His name is Davis, after Miles Davis."

"Ah, I see." And he did see. Artists. Musicians. Guys with interesting lives and jobs that weren't nine-to-five. Men who were pierced, if her column was any indication. She'd joked once that being seen with Eric would hurt her reputation.

Still, she'd chosen him. Eric tried to appease the jealousy that rose up over these men who were cooler and younger and got to hang around Beth twenty-four hours a day.

"What about you?" she asked. "What kind of girls do you normally date?"

"I don't date much. When my brother and sister were younger, it was complicated."

"You really raised them by yourself?"

"Well, they weren't little kids. Tessa was fourteen when our parents died. Jamie was sixteen. But I couldn't close down bars and have women over. So mostly it was just…" He didn't know how to say it. "Occasional hookups."

"Like this?"

"No." He watched her lick ice cream from her fork. "Not like this."

Their eyes met, and there was that thing between them again, that flash of lust that pierced through all his guilt and responsibilities. He wanted her. Now.

"Are you ready?" he asked.

Beth looked nearly as affected as he was. She nodded and pushed her chair back, rising to her feet even before he stood. Eric took her hand and led her out to his car. He pulled out of the lot and drove toward Boulder, his eyes focused on the road ahead.

"Your place?" he asked quietly.

"Yes."

And not another word passed between them. They didn't touch. Not even as he parked and opened her door. Not as they rushed up the stairs to her apartment. They slipped inside and she locked the door and then they were kissing.

Hard to believe it could be better this time, but there was something pushing his need to a new intensity. Frustration or jealousy. Something harsh. He fisted his hand in her skirt and pulled it up, sliding his leg between her knees as she backed into the wall.

Her hips tilted and the heat of her sex was pressed to his thigh.

Eric was already hard, his dick straining and heavy. He pulled back to unbutton her sweater. Beth reached for his belt.

As soon as her sweater was open, he shoved it down her arms then pushed the soft fabric of the dress down, too. She was trapped, held against the wall, and Eric slid her bra strap down and freed one of her gorgeous breasts.

When he ducked down to close his mouth over her nipple, Beth gasped, and the desperation in that sound made him even rougher. He bit her, scraping his teeth over her nipple as he sucked, and she cried out with a sound between pleasure and pain. He licked gently to soothe her, then bit again, loving the way his name broke in her throat. Going to his knees, he exposed her other breast as well, and gave it the same attention until she sobbed his name. When he finally tugged her dress all the way down, Beth freed her hands and twisted them in his hair, sliding down for a wet, deep kiss that left them both on their knees.

Impatient, she pushed him until he sat back, then she took off her bra and shoved her dress totally off. "Take off your shirt," she said.

Eric's eyes devoured the sight of her kneeling in nothing but underwear and heels. "My pants," he suggested as he whipped his shirt over his head.

But when he reached toward his waistband, her gaze dipped down, assessing. "Just unbutton them."

He obeyed without question.

Beth moved forward and put a hand to his chest. She trailed her fingers around his nipple, making him shiver in surprise. When she put both her hands to his chest and urged him back, he laid down just to see what would happen next. Beth knelt above him like a goddess, her eyes dark and devouring his body, lips parted as breath stole hard from her throat.

"I love your body," she whispered. "I love looking at you. Take it out."

Eric stopped breathing entirely. There was no mistaking what she meant. Her gaze was locked on his hands as they reached to slide his zipper down. He pushed his boxer briefs slightly down, wrapped his hand around his cock and drew it out.

Beth inhaled sharply, her breasts jumping with the movement. Her nipples were so hard that they'd drawn to tight peaks.

"Stroke yourself," she whispered.

The shock twisted around his cock like another hand. He tightened his fist and stroked.

Beth's eyes widened. She caught her lip between her

teeth and watched with fascinated intent as he worked himself slowly. Voyeurism. Exhibitionism. He didn't give a damn what it was that made her want this; all he knew was that jacking off had never felt this good, ever. His shaft got thicker in his hand, growing for her, craving her attention.

Beth set her lip free and ran her tongue over the pink mark she'd left. He wanted that mouth on him. Licking his head while he pumped his fist. He wanted her mouth open for him as he came.

But no, he wasn't going to come like this, because Beth was moving toward him, crawling over his legs. But then she did exactly what he'd pictured. She slowly lowered her head until it hovered just over him. Eric tightened his grip and held still for her.

She licked at the liquid leaking from the tip, sighing as if the taste made her happy.

Eric closed his eyes and tried to breathe past the pressure already starting to build. She licked him once more, then twice, before easing farther up his body.

He opened his eyes when she settled on his thighs.

Beth sat straight. Though *straight* was the wrong word for a woman like her. She was all generous curves and softness. Even as he took in the glory of her breasts, she cupped them in her hands, and her thumbs skipped over her nipples.

"More," she said, nearly breathless.

Obedient to a fault—the fault that he might screw this up and come too soon—Eric stroked himself again.

"You turn me on *so much*," she whispered, squeezing her nipples as she watched his hand. "How do you do that?"

It was a mystery and a miracle to him. He just shook

his head. Her breathing grew more rapid. He matched his pace to the rhythm she set.

He'd never done this in front of a woman before, and the depravity of it filled him with such dark joy that he could hardly breathe. That he would do this for her. That she would want him to. He could see that same darkness in her eyes as she watched.

Was this one more thing she was into? Piercings and threesomes and this? He'd do whatever the hell she wanted, anytime.

He stroked faster, watching her fingers tighten around the dark buds of her nipples. But Beth shook her head. "Don't come."

Fuck. He froze, squeezing his shaft in a merciless grip. Air shuddered from his lungs.

"Don't come," she murmured again. She put her hands to the floor and eased higher.

He let go of himself just as she pressed her satin-covered sex against him. The pale gray fabric immediately darkened where he leaked moisture against it. Eric laid his head to the floor and groaned.

"I want to watch you finish sometime, but not tonight."

Sometime. She wanted him to do that again, another time, another night when they'd be together like this. He pulled her down and kissed her as her sex pressed against him with torturous force. She kissed him back, but she only gave him her tongue for the briefest moment before she rose up again. Her weight settled against him. She smiled, then rocked her hips, the slippery fabric dragging along his tight skin.

She slid over him, her eyes fluttering shut with pleasure. But if she was content with this, Eric sure as hell wasn't. It was too much. He needed in her. In her mouth or her pussy, just inside.

Eric wrapped his hands around her waist and lifted her, following her over, kneeling between her spread legs as she stared up at him in surprise. He yanked her panties down, shifting one of her legs over to pull them off. When she spread her legs again, Eric growled. That was what he wanted. He pulled a condom from his pocket and tore it open with fingers that weren't quite steady.

Then he rolled it on and pulled her hips higher. "Watch me," he ordered. It was his turn now, and she did as he asked, coming up on her elbows so they could both watch as he pressed the head of his cock into her.

"Oh," she breathed, her stomach sucking in as she took a deep breath. He moved slowly, watching as her pussy stretched to accommodate his width. Her dark hair glistened with moisture.

She made a small sound as he pushed farther, and Eric looked up to find her mouth open and gasping for air. Her cheekbones stood out against her flushed skin. "More," he said, pulling back a fraction of an inch before surging deep.

"Oh, God," she cried, her back bowing, thrusting her breasts high. She fell to her back then, and Eric fucked her. The harder he fucked her the more she seemed to like it, so Eric gave up any idea of subtlety. He tucked one arm behind her knee and spread her wide so he could get even deeper. She was a tight vise around him, as if he were tunneling through her body.

"Eric," she panted. "Ah, God. Yes."

Yes. Yes, she wanted it hard and rough, and he was still filled with that dark joy and that jealousy and that need to have more of her. Their bodies slapped together as he pulled her leg higher and thrust hard and fast.

When Beth reached a hand down to rub her clit, Eric slowed so he could watch, but he kept a steady rhythm, watching as his shaft worked in and out of her and her fingers desperately circled her clit.

Her muscles squeezed him tighter. "Just…" she whispered. "Just a little more. Please. Just…"

One second, he told himself as his blood surged hard into his dick. Just one second and he could—

"Oh, *God*," she screamed. Her hips surged up to meet his, shaking against him as he thrust. Her nails clawed into his arm, deep enough that he grunted, perfect enough that he felt himself seizing up, and then it all crashed into him and he came in a nearly painful release. The most intense orgasm of his life. It surged over and over until he could hardly breathe.

As his senses began to return, he realized that a bead of sweat was rolling down his jaw, his knees were killing him and his arm burned where Beth had scratched him. And she couldn't be too comfortable against the cold tile of the entryway. But she looked like something beautiful and wild, stretched out, her eyes closed, sweat shimmering against her brow as she panted.

Eric leaned down and pressed a kiss to her damp neck. "Hey. You okay?"

"Mmm," she moaned, not moving a muscle.

He slid out of her body, wincing at the sensation against his overloaded nerves. He winced again when he forced himself up, his knees screaming at the movement. But every twitch of discomfort was a sweet reminder of what they'd done.

After disposing of the rubber, Eric zipped up and crouched down next to Beth. "Come on. I'll help you up."

She shook her head, and what the hell could he do but smile with self-satisfaction? She still wore her shiny red heels, and not one other thing except for the finger marks he'd left on her thigh. He touched the marks carefully, but she didn't grimace.

"You really know how to make a guy gloat, you know that?"

She finally opened her eyes. "You deserve to gloat," she said as she reached up to his outstretched hand.

"Come on. I'll tuck you in."

"Oh." She blinked, but then nodded and stood up as he tugged her.

"Unless you want me to stay?"

"No, you should go. You've had quite the evening, what with that impromptu family dinner."

"I'll stay," he insisted, but she shook her head.

"Go."

Jesus, he'd really screwed this up. But what could he do? He was still wearing his shoes and jeans. All he had to do was slip on his shirt. And Beth had toed off her heels and was switching off lights. She moved slowly, at least. Deliberately. As if her knees weren't quite steady.

"I'm off tomorrow," he said, his heart tripping against his ribs with the risk of putting himself out there. "Let me stay?"

Beth's hand touched the wall and she held it there as if she needed the support when she met his eyes. "You're sure?"

Thank God. "Yeah. I'm sure."

"All right then. Come to bed."

He picked up his shirt and grabbed her clothes as well, then followed her down the hallway that already felt familiar, and his body relaxed as if he were coming home.

CHAPTER FOURTEEN

SHE WOKE TO THE SOUND of a phone ringing. Not her phone. Beth opened her eyes just as she felt the bed dip. The soft slide of fabric against skin was unmistakable in the quiet room.

"Hello?" Eric said in a low voice. "Yes, I'm fine."

Beth thought she heard the notes of a woman talking on the other end of the line.

"No, I'm still in bed," he murmured. "Yes, I'm alone. I'm not talking strangely.... Because I have a headache, that's why."

He cleared his throat and glanced over his shoulder toward Beth. He looked guilty, and Beth was suddenly worried he wasn't as single as he'd claimed. Maybe that was why he'd lied. Maybe that was why he didn't want anyone to know.

Eric turned away again. "Look, I don't want to talk about this right now. I'll be there in a few minutes, all right?" He hung up and cleared his throat.

"Trouble?" Beth asked warily.

"Not really."

Her pulse stuttered before speeding up. Did he have a girlfriend? Was he cheating? Her mind began to replay the conversation in the brewery. There'd been no indication either way, had there?

"My sister," Eric finally said, sighing. "She thought I was talking like I didn't want to wake someone up."

"Oh." Beth dropped back to the pillow. "So you were."

"So I was."

"Eric, you're not involved with anyone, are you?"

He jerked around to frown at her. "Involved?"

"Do you have a girlfriend?"

"No. Of course not. I wouldn't be here if I did."

Beth shrugged. "You never know. And considering how all this started, I just suddenly worried that was the reason you'd lied."

"No. That wasn't it."

"Okay." She looked at the clock and bit back a groan. "It's almost nine."

"I'll go," he said, his voice still a little distant. But when he glanced back at her, his mouth quirked in a half smile. "Thanks for letting me stay. It was nice."

It had been nice, lying in her bed together, watching TV in the dark. It had also been way over the line.

He must have seen the hesitation in her eyes, because Eric gave a careful nod and reached for his jeans. "I've got to go into work anyway. Problems on the line."

She nodded as if she knew what he meant. "Thanks for…everything," she said, stumbling over the last word.

His back tensed. "Sure."

"I'm sorry again, about my dad."

He shook his head and leaned over to put his shoes on.

For some reason, Beth couldn't stand the silence. "Will you call me if something more happens with the investigation?"

Yeah, his back was definitely tense. "Is that the only reason you want me to call?"

Clutching the sheet to her chest, Beth sat up. "What do you mean?"

"I mean… I guess I don't know what I mean. Just that this is starting to get…"

"Awkward?" she suggested.

"No." He yanked hard at his laces, then stood up. Beth forgot that she was having a serious conversation and let herself be distracted by the muscles of his arms. "It's getting a little intense, and it feels weird that— Hello?"

"Sorry." Beth forced her gaze up to his eyes. They were smoky blue and pissed. She was a little startled at how intimidating he looked. Hard and nearly cruel. It reminded her of the way he'd taken her on the floor of her living room.

His jaw looked like stone. "All I'm saying is that we're spending time together. More time. And you don't even trust me."

"No, I don't trust you. I told you that from the start."

"I know I lied to you." He paced away. "But I haven't lied to you since, have I?"

"It doesn't matter," she said. "This isn't about trust. This isn't a relationship. It's just…" She tried to think of a word that wasn't insulting. "Casual."

"Right. It's so casual you don't want people to know about it."

"What?" she yelped. "You don't want people to know, either!"

Eric ran a hand through his dark hair, messing it up even further. "I know. But it's not that I don't want people to know, I just…"

She raised a haughty eyebrow.

"I just want this to be private."

"That's the same thing, Eric."

"Regardless, we made that agreement when it was only one night. But now…"

"Then we should stop," she said quickly.

He crossed his arms and stared down at her as if she were an insolent child.

She shrugged. "What? You're right. I don't trust you and I never will. We only meant it to be one night. Then we agreed on two. But it's getting out of control."

His eyes slid toward the hallway.

"I like it out of control," he muttered.

Beth closed her eyes. So did she. She was getting wet just thinking about how bold she'd been last night, and how wild it had made him. And how he'd fucked her on the floor like a beast. They'd barely made it through the front door. "I like it, too," she admitted. "But I don't know what you're asking for."

He sat down facing the hallway. "I don't know. Maybe I want to feel like I can call you."

"Of course you can call me."

He glanced over his shoulder. "I want to call without feeling like I'm intruding on your real life."

"Yet you don't want to talk to your sister in front of me."

"I was trying not to wake you."

She lay down and stared at the ceiling. "That's hardly the whole truth, Eric. Don't pretend it is."

He cursed softly and she felt the bed shift as he moved closer to her. "All right. Here's the truth. My sister figured out who you were. Luke and I were talking about you and he said your name. She recognized it and connected the dots. She knows you're the woman who came into the brewery. The one I…"

Beth nodded.

"And as soon as it came out, they were looking at me with different eyes. Wondering what we'd done. Imagining what you might see in me. You're almost like a celebrity."

Yeah. She could understand that. Because it had always felt like that on her side, too. Except she lived with it on every single date. At least Eric could walk away if he wanted.

She was suddenly painfully glad he didn't want to walk away. "It's the same for me, you know," she murmured. "It's the flip side."

"I get it."

"You're nothing to hide, Eric. But I want it to be private. Like you do."

"Are you still dating other men?"

She opened her eyes and met his gaze. "What?"

"Are you seeing other men?"

"I've spent the last two nights with you. I haven't had time to see anyone else."

"That's not an answer."

"To be honest, I haven't thought about it."

His jaw jumped as if he were grinding his teeth together, a pulse of frustration beneath his skin. "I'm not asking to bring this out of hiding. With that column you write…"

She felt a sudden shock of horror. He knew about the column? How? She imagined him reading it and—

"If you could respect my privacy. Not mention me by name."

"Of course!" she said quickly.

"Everything in my life, everything I do and I am… it's for my family. My siblings. My father. My name."

"I understand. I'd never put your name out there."

"It's not that I'm embarrassed by you, Beth. You're amazing. I just… I don't know what this is. What we're doing. But I need it. For me. Just for myself. And maybe that's why I like that no one knows. Does that make any sense?"

She didn't know why, but it did make sense. It felt… *safe* this way. She nodded.

Eric cleared his throat. "And I guess what I want is to know that when you're with me, it's just me. That it's private. That you're not seeing anyone else. For however long. A few days. Whatever it is."

That was what he wanted? Privacy and exclusivity? As if she needed anyone else's attention after spending the night with him. As if she had the least bit of interest in another man's hands on her.

"If that's not your style, that's fine, but I can't read that column and wonder if—"

"Of course," she interrupted. "Of course I won't see anyone else right now."

His shoulders relaxed a little. "Yeah? I don't want to try to change anything for you."

"I never see more than one person at a time," she said with complete honesty.

He arched a startled look over his shoulder. "Never?"

She shook her head, frowning at the disbelief in his voice.

"Okay," he said.

"And you can call me," Beth whispered. "You can call and it can still be secret."

He was quiet for a long time, and since he was facing

away from her, she couldn't read his expression. Was he angry? Offended? Finally he took a deep breath and said, "I'd like that."

God, so would she. She nodded as he turned toward her. He touched her cheek, then brushed a quick kiss across her mouth before he stood. Her heart made a slow turn in her chest as he left.

She just sat there holding her breath until she heard her front door close.

What the hell was she doing? She didn't trust him. He didn't want anyone to know they were lovers. It was all wrong, and yet she felt infatuated.

Was it just the sex? Or was his secrecy the thing she liked?

She had to be at work before eleven, but Beth let herself curl back beneath the covers anyway. They were crisp and cool and she stretched her limbs out, reveling in the feel of her naked body against the cotton.

The sex was reason enough to feel giddy, but maybe it was his reticence that she liked. After all, her heart had been broken by a man who hadn't been able to keep his mouth shut. No, actually, her heart had been mashed into unusable pieces by a man who'd never even intended to keep his mouth shut.

She hadn't been like the other girls in her high school. She'd been tall and curvy and dark, and it had seemed like ninety percent of the other girls had been slender and sweet. Beth had grown breasts and hips in fifth grade, and from then on, she'd done her best to cover them with baggy jeans and sweaters. Those efforts had kept boys at bay, though that hadn't been her goal. Not exactly. She just hadn't wanted them making comments about her boobs.

But her senior year, she'd finally landed a boyfriend. Christopher West. He'd taken her to homecom-
ing. They'd dated for months. She'd fallen in love. And
she'd lost her virginity. The sex had been fine. Nothing
spectacular, but nothing awful, either. And if she wasn't
that into the sex, she'd certainly been into the idea of a
boy liking her. That part had been exhilarating, that a
boy she loved would be so desperate to have her. That
he'd beg and moan anytime she said no. He'd needed
her. He'd loved her. He'd thought of her every moment
they were apart.

Beth had suddenly found herself transformed from
a girl no one noticed into a girl who could drive a boy
to fits of lust. So she'd liked the sex just fine.

During spring break that year, Christopher's parents had been working, so there'd been lots of sex at
his house. And then she'd made the worst mistake of
her life. When Christopher had brought out a Polaroid
camera and asked if he could take pictures of her, Beth
had been flattered he'd want them. She'd thrilled to the
idea that he'd thought her beautiful. So she'd said yes.

She burrowed deeper under the covers at the thought.
How many hours of her life had she wasted, wishing she
could go back to that one stupid moment and change
her words? *No,* she'd say. *Not in a million years.*

But no matter how hard she'd prayed, the past always
stayed the same. She'd posed naked for him. She'd shyly
spread her legs. She'd even let him take a picture of her
on her knees in front of him.

Whatever his intentions had been at that point, the
responsibility had been too much. He had dirty pictures
of his girlfriend. His friends had been teasing him about
dating the chubby girl for months. He wanted to prove

that the chubby girl was just as hot as their girlfriends. Hotter, even.

Or that had been his explanation later.

Whether he'd meant to hurt her or not, he'd shown the pictures to some friends at a party. Then he'd brought them to school. Someone had grabbed the worst of them and passed them all over.

Beth had been ruined. *Ruined.* There was no room in high school for a girl who would let a boy take X-rated photos. She'd worn an invisible scarlet letter that begged for insults and abuse. She'd been lower than garbage. And then her parents had been called to the principal's office....

When she felt the tickle of tears inching down her face, Beth pressed her hands to her eyes and shook her head. Why was she thinking about this? This wasn't high school. She didn't have to answer to anyone.

But it had been there all this time, hadn't it? Part of her inability to relax with a man was caused by her constant fear that he would talk about it. That he'd describe her and what they'd done. That he'd laugh with his friends. That he would use what they'd done as a trophy, especially now that she was running the White Orchid.

Eric had been right. Being the manager of the store was a little like being a local celebrity. Not that she'd done anything to earn fame, but just working at the store brought infamy. And instead of bragging about it, Eric didn't want anyone to know. That felt safe, despite his lies. Safe to have sex with him, but not safe to love. She could rely on that, at least.

She let a few more tears fall for that seventeen-year-old girl. Those last months of school had felt like the end of her life. In a way, they had been, because she'd never been that girl again. That Beth had been destroyed.

But she was someone better now, so Beth made herself get up and shower and dress for work. She dressed down because she felt like it. No need to try hard to look sexy when she felt sexy all the way to her bones. So she wore jeans with her heels, and a flowy little black top, and she pulled her hair back in a ponytail. She felt like a new woman and she looked like one, too.

When her phone rang there was only a small bit of hoarseness in her voice to betray her earlier emotions. "Hello?" she answered as she locked her door and started down the steps.

"Ms. Cantrell?" The voice wasn't familiar, so Beth was cautious.

"May I ask who's calling?"

"Ms. Cantrell, this is Yvette Page with Mr. Roland Kendall's office. Mr. Kendall would like you to stop in for a few moments today. The address is—"

"No," Beth interrupted, stopping on her front stairs to try to catch her breath and calm her suddenly thundering heart. There was only one thing he could be calling about. "I can't today. I'm working."

"Oh," the woman said, genuine surprise obvious in that one syllable. Apparently not too many people said no to Roland Kendall. "Perhaps you could rearrange your schedule. He was quite insistent."

"I really can't," Beth said. "It's impossible. Please convey my regrets." She hung up before her voice could start shaking. Did he really think she'd show up to his office like one of his children, ready to be browbeaten into obedience?

What could he want, anyway? She'd already told the

police. There was no taking that back. So he obviously just wanted to punish Beth for what she'd done. When her phone rang again, she immediately hit the button to decline the call. It was either Kendall or his secretary, and Beth didn't want to talk to either.

Just as she'd expected, when Beth finally made it to her car, the message indicator on her phone chimed. It was from the same number that had called the first time, but when Beth listened, it wasn't the secretary's voice.

"Beth," Kendall barked. "I don't know what you think you're up to. After everything I've done for you. I brought you into my home and exposed you to a life-style you'd never even dreamed of. And this is how you repay me? With lies about my daughter? I don't know if this is envy or jealousy. I don't give a shit what it is. But you're going to stop this immediately or there will be repercussions in your personal and professional life. In fact…" His words trailed off, and Beth wondered if he'd just remembered that his diatribe was being re-corded. "Get your ass down here or you'll regret it," he finally muttered before the line clicked dead.

"Oh, sure," Beth breathed. "I'll be right there."

He hadn't been specific, but Beth was sure he meant to harm the store in some way. After all, how else could he hurt Beth? The White Orchid was the most impor-tant thing in her life. It was personal *and* professional. She felt sick that what she'd done could harm the store and Annabelle.

Too flustered to try to calculate the time in Egypt, Beth decided against calling and sent a text instead. *Please call when you can talk. XO Beth.*

Annabelle needed to know what was happening, just in case, and the sooner the better.

As she drove toward the store, Beth tried her best to put it from her mind. It was no big deal. It would be fine. She'd told the police her story, and if Kendall really got nasty, she'd tell the police that, too.

Reassured by her temporary bravado, Beth managed to walk into the White Orchid with a smile.

"Hey, Beth!" Kelly called. "You look cute!"

"Thank you. Why does it smell like tea and ginger in here? Not that I'm complaining."

"That tea lady stopped by this morning. She said something about gearing up for winter?"

"Linda Fallon? The one with the tea shop?"

"That's her."

Beth had met her at the expo that spring, and Linda had claimed that several of her teas contained ingredients to increase female libido. "I told her we'd do a display this winter, so she's right on time. Did she leave more samples?"

Kelly pushed a box forward on the counter. "Yep. She also brewed up a cup for me. She carries an electric kettle in her car. How cute is that?"

Beth grabbed the box and headed for her office. Maybe she'd actually try some out this time. Before, she'd thought it would be wasted on her barren sex life. But now… Then again, maybe Beth didn't need an increase in libido at the moment. She was cruising along nicely. Smiling, she took another deep breath of spiced air and hurried to her office.

She felt good again, as if the walls of the store insulated her from the outside world. It was a fantasy world, after all. And if an erotic boutique wasn't about relaxation, what was?

Determined not to spend the day holed up in her office again, Beth decided to finish the fall cleaning. The racks were getting crowded, and people in Colorado didn't need swimsuits in October. She marked down the swimwear and moved it to the clearance rack to make more room for Halloween items. Annabelle had always been sure not to let the shop degenerate into a costume store, but they wanted to be festive. And what could be more festive than a naughty nurse uniform?

Beth eyed the mannequin who was dressed in a female soldier outfit that featured hot pants and a sleeveless camo shirt. Not exactly practical for jungle wear, but the customers seemed to get a kick out of it. They'd nearly sold out. She moved some of the plus-size bustiers up to the front, too, because their buxom clients often complained about the challenges of finding sexy outfits in their size. Beth could sympathize. When she shopped for bikinis, the size of the little triangles that were supposed to cover her breasts was laughable.

She was just wiping the tops of the racks with cleaner when the door opened to admit a deep male laugh. "I know I've been way too busy," the man was saying, "but I swear I'll be home early tonight to make it up to you. In fact, maybe I'll even have a present."

Beth turned to greet the customer, and her smile froze on her face. The man froze, too, phone still pressed to his ear and green eyes getting wider by the second.

"Uh, Olivia," he said. "Can I call you back?" Jamie Donovan slowly lowered the phone and stole a quick glance around the store. When he looked back to her, his eyes fell to the spray bottle and rag she clutched in her hands.

"Oh," he said softly and blinked several times.

Beth was still frozen, but when her hand squeezed hard enough, the bottle released a mist that made her jump.

"Hello," Jamie said.

"Hello," she repeated. She shouldn't be surprised to see him here. He was a past customer, after all. But somehow she hadn't thought of this, and knowing what she'd done with Eric the night before… "Can I help you find something?" she asked automatically, because she couldn't think past the automatic at this point.

"Oh, I…" Jamie glanced around again, and his cheeks turned faintly pink. "I was looking for a gift. I'll just…browse."

"Okay."

But he didn't move, he just rocked back on his heels a little and stuck his hands in his pockets, a gesture that reminded her of Eric. "So, you work here?"

"Yes."

"Ah. We were never actually introduced." He stepped closer and reached out a hand. "I'm… Well, I guess you know my name."

"Right. I'm Beth." She shifted the rag to the other hand and gave his hand only one good shake before moving back. "Anyway, I'd better get back to work or—"

"Beth!" Kelly stuck her head out from the back room. "There's a woman on the phone who does henna tattoos and she asked to speak to the manager."

Beth met Jamie's gaze and watched his eyes widen even more. "Excuse me," she murmured. She'd never been so happy to get a call from a vendor. Not only did it get her away from Jamie, but after a few minutes on the phone with the woman, Beth realized she was actually proposing a good idea.

"I know you have occasional gatherings at the store," the henna artist said, a little breathless with nervousness. "I'd love it if you'd consider hiring me to give tattoos."

Beth knew what henna tattoos were, but she let the woman explain her process and her experience with the art. "If you'd be willing to come in and maybe give a demonstration, I'd certainly consider the idea."

They arranged a time later in the week and settled things within moments, but when Beth hung up, she stayed in her chair. She needed to give Jamie time to do his shopping and get the heck out.

Then again, what did it matter? She had no reason to be embarrassed. Eric might not be happy that another person in his life knew about her, but Jamie didn't *really* know. He didn't know that she and Eric had seen each other last night. And the night before.

She'd just decided to brave another awkward meeting and was pushing up from her desk when her cell phone rang. Beth dug her phone from her pocket and gratefully sank back down.

"Beth!" Annabelle cried, her voice clearer than it had been in months. "Are you okay? Is everything all right?"

"I'm fine!" Beth cut in.

"Oh, thank God. I miss you so much. When I got your text, I swear my heart melted."

Beth smiled. Annabelle approached friendship like she approached everything else—with passion and enthusiasm. "I miss you, too. Really." *Really.* "Are you still having fun?"

"Fun doesn't even describe it. I can't believe how content I feel. How whole. I feel like I've been reborn."

Beth nodded, happy for her friend, but the truth was that Annabelle had said that exact thing after a Bikram Yoga class the year before. "That's amazing. I'm so happy for you. But have you given any more thought to when you'll come home?"

"Oh, Beth, it all feels so far away."

Beth nodded, frowning. "Okay, but I need to tell you something, Annabelle. I'm worried that I've caused some trouble for the store." She explained exactly what had happened, leaving out her affair with Eric. "I don't think I could have handled it differently," she ended.

Annabelle gasped. "Of course not. You did the right thing!"

"I don't know what he's thinking, but he's a powerful guy with political connections. I'm worried about that state representative who was making noise last year."

"The one who proposed the bill that would've made it illegal to sell sexual paraphernalia within a mile of a public school."

"Yeah."

"It didn't get out of committee. Don't worry about it."

"But if Kendall decides to put money behind this guy... I just can't figure out what else he might be thinking. God, I'm so sorry, Annabelle. If he—"

"Whatever that bastard tries to do, he won't have any more effect than every other campaign against the store. We are a Boulder institution. Everyone knows the White Orchid isn't some seedy sex shop. It'll be fine."

"I hope you're right."

"Beth, you couldn't do something to hurt the store if you wanted to. It's as much your baby as it is mine. Actually, I've been wanting to talk to you about that."

"Babies?" Beth asked in confusion, wondering if Annabelle had met a nice Egyptian man and decided to settle down.

"No, not babies! The store! I'm thinking it might be time for a change."

"What kind of change?" Beth asked warily. If Annabelle added anything else to Beth's plate, she was going to have a breakdown.

"I've become involved with a women's organization here. Naeemah—I mentioned Naeemah, right? She runs a women's group that works with poor women to help manage microloans and start their own businesses."

"Right."

"Well, I'm kind of...I'm kind of in love with it, Beth. I don't want to leave."

"You don't?" Beth asked, though the words barely got past the sudden tightness in her throat.

"No, I don't. It's not that I want to keep traveling. It's not that I feel like I'm on vacation. I feel like I'm home."

Beth nodded because she couldn't speak.

"What I'm trying to say is that...I'd like to offer you the opportunity to buy the White Orchid."

"What?" she managed to rasp.

"We talked about it a few years ago, remember? The idea that you might like to buy the store someday, that I could pass it on to you. And you certainly work as hard as any business owner right now. You're doing my job, plus your own. You're amazing, and you're the only person I would trust the White Orchid to."

"But…but what are you going to do?"

"I thought I would buy a little house here near the women's center. And I could just…work. Help people."

Beth realized that she was nodding over and over. "I don't know what to say."

"Don't say anything yet. It's a huge decision, Beth. One of the biggest you'll ever make. But I know you're made for bigger things than just being my manager. The store already belongs to you. You can do this. It's everything you've wanted."

She was still nodding.

"Think about it. I'll call next week, and we'll talk details."

"Okay."

"And please be careful about Roland Kendall. I'm not worried about the store, Beth. I'm worried about you."

Beth smiled automatically, but her stomach felt like a boulder as she hung up the phone.

To own the White Orchid. It was her dream. Or it had been her dream, years ago. But she'd spent the last few months just wishing Annabelle would come home and take her place as the rightful head of the store. The face of the White Orchid. The one who knew exactly what she was doing. Without her, Beth just felt…scared.

But if the White Orchid was hers, she'd be a business owner. Her dad would be so proud.

"Oh, sure." She sighed. He'd be proud until he found out what the business really was. Ladies' foundation garments, indeed.

She had money saved, though she'd bit into her savings account with the new car this year. Still, her credit was great, the store had a steady, predictable income; there was no reason to think she couldn't manage a small business loan. She could likely buy the business itself from Annabelle, while only leasing the building.

Looking around the crowded office, Beth made herself take a deep breath. She loved this place and the people who worked here. She loved helping the customers and putting them at ease. And she'd been planning for this moment for a long time. But she'd never expected it to come so soon.

And she'd never expected it to feel so terrifying, if terror was the emotion making her feel sick to her stomach.

"Beth?" Kelly called. "Are you off the phone?"

"Yes," she whispered, then cleared her throat and spoke more forcefully. "Yes!"

"Do you know when we're expecting more glasswork? This twelve-inch guy is scaring people off!"

Beth made herself set aside her thoughts and get back to work.

Jamie was gone, and Kelly was waving around the black glass dildo as she talked to a middle-aged woman in a business suit. Just another day in the office.

CHAPTER FIFTEEN

"IT'S GOING TO HAVE TO BE replaced," the mechanic said as he poked at the rotor. "It's throwing the whole system out of whack."

That didn't sound like a strictly scientific diagnosis to Eric, but he grunted and nodded. "Fine. How long?"

"Five days."

"*Five days?* Are you kidding me?"

"It's coming from New Jersey."

"On what? Horseback? Can't you rush it?"

"That is a rush."

"Jesus," Eric spat. "Do you know how much this is going to screw up my distribution schedule?"

The mechanic shrugged.

"Why didn't you see it the first time you were poking around in here? Or the second?"

The guy shrugged again, and Eric immediately decided to call someone else next time. Someone with a goddamned work ethic. "Order the part," he growled before slamming out of the bottling room.

"What's up?" Tessa asked when Eric stalked into the kitchen.

"The line's down for five days. We'll have to ramp up keg production." His mind was already rearranging schedules. "Once the bottling is back up, we won't have time for kegs, so we'll stockpile them now. As it is, two grocery store orders will be late. Goddamn it, when is Wallace coming back?"

"Leave him alone. He's rescuing his true love."

"True love and Wallace Hood. God save us all."

The mechanic emerged and sneaked out the back door without another word.

"I hate that guy," Eric muttered. He glanced down at Tessa's hands, which were wrist-deep in flour. "What are you doing?"

"Making pizza dough." She tilted her head toward the oven. "The oven's hot enough."

"Where's Jamie?"

"He's running an errand. So…" She pushed down on the dough and flipped it over onto the floured surface. "Where were you this morning?"

"In bed," he snapped.

"Ah. But whose bed?"

"Mine."

"That's weird, because I called your home phone first."

"I was sleeping," he said.

"Uh-huh."

He wanted to walk away, but he was afraid Tessa would take that as a sign of guilt, so instead he reached for the tray of glasses that had just emerged from the washer.

"You know," Tessa drawled as she wiped her hands on a towel. "Now that I know you have a personal life—"

"I don't," he cut in.

"—I'm seeing you in a whole new light. I kind of wonder if I've been missing things all these years."

"There's nothing to miss." He sighed.

"Oh, really?"

Eric shoved a dirty tray in and started to brush past his sister, but she reached out and grabbed his arm.

"So what's this?" she asked. "A whole lot of nothing?"

Eric glanced at his arm, already shaking his head in denial, but then he saw the marks. Four perfect red crescents where Beth's nails had bitten in. Not deep enough to draw blood, but deep enough to leave vivid evidence.

"Unruly customer," he said quickly.

"My God, you're really bad at lying."

He jerked his arm away. "Some of us haven't spent years sneaking around."

"Just months?" she asked with a smile of triumph.

"No. You're way off base with this one."

"Nice try. Those are nail marks on your arm, Eric Donovan, and you were *not* at home this morning. You're still sleeping with her!"

"That's ridiculous. Why would she want anything to do with—?"

The doors to the front room swung open with a dramatic whoosh of air.

"Well, well, well," Jamie drawled, strolling in like the Cheshire cat.

Eric rolled his eyes. Just what he needed. Another smart-ass sibling causing trouble. "Whatever you're about to say, drop it," Eric warned. "I'm not in the mood."

"Drop it?" Jamie crowed. "How could I drop the most amazing thing I've ever seen?"

Eric glanced at Tessa, who shrugged. "Is it something to do with the new oven?"

"It's at five hundred fifty and going strong!" Tessa chirped.

Jamie's smile widened. "Oh, no. It's not that. Not at all."

"All right." Eric sighed. "The bottling line is down for five days. My brewmaster is missing in action. And you've got to find a chef. We've got shit to do, so if you could just give us the big news already, that would be great."

Jamie just grinned for a few more heartbeats. Then he said, "So I went into the White Orchid today."

Eric groaned, though his ears were filled with the strange, muffled squeal that came from Tessa's direction.

"Dude," Jamie said, laughing. "Dude, *seriously?*"

"I know, right?" Tessa gasped.

"Wait." Jamie looked at Tessa. "You knew about this?"

"I just found out!"

"And you didn't tell me our brother was a goddamned rock star?"

Tessa shook her head, but she clapped her hands at the same time. "He swore me to secrecy! I wanted to tell you!"

"That's enough," Eric snarled.

"Oh, no," Jamie answered. "No, it's not nearly enough. You went out with the manager of the White Orchid and *you didn't tell me?*"

Tessa bounced up and down. "He's still seeing her!" she blurted out.

"Goddamn it, Tessa!" Eric roared.

She slapped a hand over her mouth. "Sorry," she squeaked from behind her fingers.

Jamie shook his head. "No shit? Man, it's always the quiet ones who surprise you."

Eric's face felt so hot he expected it to melt off at any moment. He opened his mouth to deny it, but the lie sat like clay in his throat. He wasn't ashamed of her. It wasn't that at all. He just…wanted her for himself.

"I went to apologize," he said quietly. "Just like you told me to, Tessa. Then she called me about Monica Kendall. That's it. It's no big deal."

"Oh, it's a big deal," Jamie countered.

"Come on." Eric put up his hands in surrender. He saw Tessa's gaze shift immediately to his scratched wrist, so Eric dropped his hands. "Even if…even if I… She's just a regular girl."

Jamie shook his head. "I seriously doubt that."

Tessa giggled and Eric was pretty sure his face turned from red to purple. "I'm obviously not still see-ing her," he snapped. "Do you think she'd see me again after I lied to her?"

Tessa's face fell. "I guess not."

Jamie slapped his shoulder. "One time or twenty, I take back everything I ever said about you. Everything. Even the part about you being an asshole for using my name. If I'd known you were using it for—"

Eric pushed past him and headed for his office. He closed the door so he couldn't hear them talking, but the low murmurs still filtered through the wood. He should've run to the tank room instead, but it was too late now. He sure as hell wasn't heading back into the kitchen.

He didn't know why it panicked him that they knew about Beth. It didn't feel like modesty or embarrass-ment. It felt like *greed.* This was his and his alone.

Something that had nothing to do with Jamie or Tessa or anyone else, for once. Something that belonged to him, no matter what his name was or who people wanted him to be.

Feeling only slightly calmer, Eric popped open his cell phone and tapped Beth's name. "You could've warned me," he said when she answered.

"About what?"

"My brother."

"Oh," she said. Then, "Oh, no! I completely forgot."

"You *forgot?*"

"I'm sorry. I've got a dozen things going on at the store. And… Oh, Eric. I know you didn't want anyone else to know."

He couldn't be mad at her. After all, she was being pretty damned accepting of the secrecy. And the Donovan family wasn't her problem. Eric sighed and leaned against the door. "It's okay. It was your turn to forget this time."

"I'm so sorry. What did he say?"

"What you'd expect him to say, I guess."

"What's that? I've always kind of wondered."

"Wondered what?" Eric asked.

"What people say about me."

Eric shook his head. "I wouldn't let him say anything about you. That's not the way we were raised. But he did call me a rock star."

"Yeah?" He could hear the smile in her voice. "That sounds about right."

"Very funny."

"I'm serious," she said, her words softer now. "You certainly fucked like a rock star last night."

Eric's face flushed hot again, but this time there was

nothing unpleasant about it. In fact, the heat felt damn good as it sank down through his body. "That was all you," he murmured.

"Oh, no. Not even close."

He tried to think of something witty to say. Or something sexy. Or just a few words that might make sense when strung together. But his brain had gone into Neanderthal mode at the husky appreciation in her voice.

"You make me forget things," she said. "Everything I worry about, I can't worry about it with you."

"What do you worry about? Is there trouble in erotic paradise?"

"Yeah," she said on a laugh. "Yeah, there definitely is."

Eric felt his smile fade. "What's wrong?" He wished he was still in her bed, talking to her about this. Wished they could just be quiet and serious together. But she didn't trust him, and as the silence grew, he knew she wasn't going to answer.

"I wish we could start over," he said softly. "You can trust me. Everyone counts on me, you know."

"It doesn't matter. I don't trust anybody," she said.

It could have sounded like bravado or defensiveness. But Eric heard the quiet truth in the words. "Why?"

He heard movement on her end, the ebb and flow of sound as if she was walking, then he heard a door open and quiet birdsong floated through the phone. Beth sighed. "Because you can't ever really trust anyone, can you?"

Eric closed his eyes and paged through his memories, trying to find a way to convince her. But maybe she was right. He loved his sister, but she'd told him plenty of lies, trying to protect him. And Jamie—they'd been brothers for twenty-nine years, yet sometimes Eric felt that he hardly knew Jamie at all. But there were some people who never faltered. "Your dad," he said. "He's someone you can trust."

She was quiet for a dozen heartbeats. Birds trilled their daylight songs. Eric was just starting to smile, thinking he may have convinced her, when she let her breath out on a quiet sigh. "No," she whispered. "Not even him."

His heart stuttered at the sadness in her voice. Eric didn't understand. He thought of the polite man he'd met. The man who'd held Beth's hand and gone to so much trouble to bring his wife just the dessert she'd wanted. "What do you mean?" But he knew she wouldn't answer. She was telling him that she couldn't.

"Who do you trust?" she asked instead.

"I trusted my mom," he answered with complete honesty. "And I trusted Michael Donovan."

"Michael Donovan? Your dad?"

"Yes. My dad." Not his father, but his dad. The only real dad he'd ever had.

"Was he a good guy?"

"The best."

"You said it was a car accident?"

Eric opened his eyes and stared at the far wall of his office. "Yes. They were both killed instantly."

"And afterward, you stepped in?"

"I tried."

"I'm sorry," she whispered. "I can't imagine what that would be like."

"It was..." Eric tried to find the right words. He always knew what to say about it, knew how to deflect attention away, because for years everyone in Boulder had known the story. Everyone had known who Eric was trying to fill in for and how impossible it was, for so many reasons. "It was…" It was what had needed to be done. What his brother and sister had needed. What had been expected, even as people pretended it was heroic. It was… "Terrifying," he finally said.

"I'm sure," Beth responded as if he'd said something perfectly normal.

But she didn't understand what he meant. Sure, he'd been scared he would screw things up. But more than that… "I wished there was somebody else. Anybody else." Jesus. He'd said it. He'd finally said it. The truth. The words hovered out there, just past his mouth. He could feel them waiting to crash around him. "I didn't want to take any of it on. My sister heard me say that once, when she was young. So maybe you're right."

"About what?" she whispered.

"I was supposed to save her, but I became just another person she couldn't trust."

"That's not true," she said. "You did your best."

"We're all doing our best."

"Oh, Eric," she said with a small, sad laugh. "That's absolutely not true. And I might not trust you, but I can tell you're a nice guy when you say things like that."

Nothing had crashed. She hadn't run away screaming. She still thought he was a nice guy.

Beth Cantrell was a fool, but he liked her. A lot.

Eric could hear the sounds of the brewery past his door. His sister was laughing. Jamie gave a shout of triumph. They were probably loading a pizza into the oven right now, both of them excited about the future of the restaurant. And all he could feel was resentment, because he didn't belong here. He was a placeholder, and placeholder was only a temporary position.

"I'm not really Eric Donovan," he said.

The sound of an engine roared over Beth's side of the line. "What?" she asked.

"Nothing. Are you working all day?" He was supposed to be off, and Jamie and Tessa were going to spend all day baking pizzas and trying to pull him into the fun. "Can I see you?" he asked.

"Yes," she said.

"When?" Eric held his breath, and for a long time, she said nothing. How many times were they going to do this? A dozen? A hundred?

Finally, Beth cleared her throat. "Meet me at my place in an hour."

Eric hung up, still holding his breath. As he slipped the phone back into his pocket, he emptied his lungs on a long, careful sigh. Beth Cantrell was his hobby. She was like yoga and meditation and a workout all rolled into one.

The truth was, day off or not, he should be working until midnight. He had to clean up this distribution mess, plus he was covering Wallace's duties as well as his own. Eric had more than enough to fill up the whole damn week, Sunday included. But instead of calling to apologize to the two grocery store accounts that weren't going to get their shipments, Eric sat down at his desk and pulled up Beth's column.

She'd said she wasn't seeing anyone else, and she'd promised not to out him, so what would she have to write about?

Plenty, apparently.

Even if she wasn't dating anyone else, there were

still extracurricular activities to be found. "We all have that special drawer next to the bed," the column started. "Or maybe it's a box in your bathroom or closet. Maybe you've hidden it in your dresser. But there's no reason to keep your box of toys hidden! Didn't your teacher always tell you it's nice to share?"

Eric didn't blink once as he read the column. It was short and sweet, but the message was clear: a little showing off never hurt anyone. After he read it the first time, he read it again.

Last night Beth had asked him to touch himself in front of her. Had she been looking for reciprocation?

He showed up at her place fifteen minutes early and spent the whole quarter hour pondering the question.

CHAPTER SIXTEEN

EVEN FOR BETH, THERE WASN'T time to think. She jammed two hours of work into an hour of time, just in case her lunch break ran long. "Please, yes," she muttered as she very carefully kept her car at the speed limit through her quiet neighborhood. She had to be back by three to meet with the lighting contractor, but that left her two hours. With Eric.

When she pulled up, Eric got out of his truck, and the sight of him left her feeling strange and shivery inside. She'd never been hit with lust like that before. She'd read that women were just as susceptible to visual stimuli as men, but she hadn't believed it. After all, she'd never asked a guy to dress up in tight red underwear and leather and pose for her. But now she could see it. She could feel it. That the sight of him was enough to turn her on.

He stood aside when she approached, then followed her up the stairs. They didn't even look at each other, as if that would somehow hide their intentions from anyone watching.

Her apartment was beginning to feel like a cheap motel room, but she didn't care. She'd waited her whole life to feel this sort of easy lust, and she wasn't going to bother with shame about it now. She unlocked her

door and led him in, and this time she walked straight
to the bedroom. Eric followed without a word.

It was all fantastically dirty.

They were here in the middle of the day for only one
reason. This wasn't a date. It was sex. So Beth undid
her top button and moved on to the next one. When
Eric saw what she was doing, he raised an eyebrow and
pulled his polo shirt off.

She couldn't resist him. She was worse than a teenage boy ogling a naked woman. His chest was *perfect*.
Mouthwatering. She had to reach out and spread her
fingers over the muscles. She had to drag her mouth
along his collarbone and taste his skin.

How could it be that he affected her more every time
she saw him? How could she want him more after each
night they spent together? Now it was as if all their
chemistry got mixed up with the things they'd already
done, and the things she'd fantasized about doing. It all
twisted up together until she felt as if she'd explode.

Eric cupped the back of her head and brought her
mouth to his, and the taste of his mouth was even better than his skin. When he turned her toward the bed,
she went willingly, letting herself fall across the mattress as he covered her with his body. His back was gorgeous hot skin beneath her hands. His spine the perfect
concave path to follow all the way to his ass. The rough
fabric of his cargo pants stopped her, but she loved the
reminder of his preppy clothes, too. The way he looked
so upstanding in public and got wild and rough in bed.

When his hand shoved up her skirt, he lifted up a little, and Beth smiled. She knew he'd love what she was
wearing. The black garter belt. The stockings. The—

"Christ, you are so hot, Beth. A fantasy." His hand

spread over her bare thigh, and he watched himself touch her. His thumb eased up, just brushing the thin fabric of her panties. He did it again and she gasped.

"I like you like this," he whispered. "Completely dressed. Totally turned on. Like you have a secret."

Beth watched his face as he reached for the bows at the sides of her panties and eased them off. He looked angry again, the way he always did in the midst of sex, and that turned her on, too.

This time, when his fingers slid over her, there was no fabric in the way, and Beth arched into him with a small cry.

"You're so wet for me," he whispered. His eyes stayed on his hand as he touched her with only the faintest pressure. Then his gaze finally rose to hers. "I read your column."

Beth shook her head, thoroughly distracted by the torturous brush of his fingertips. "What?"

"Your column. I want you to do that. For me."

Beth blinked, trying hard to think past what he was doing to her body. The column. "Oh," she said. "The column!" It had been about… Her gaze shifted to the table next to her bed as he finally stopped teasing her to distraction.

Cairo had written that particular column. Beth had never played with her toys in front of anyone, and the thought was…

"Will you?" he asked.

Would she? She could just tell him the truth. That she wrote only a few of the columns and hers usually leaned toward the scholarly end of the spectrum. That she'd never done this or half the things her coworkers described in their writings. She could tell the truth and let him see the real her.

Or she could just go with it, and do what he'd asked her to do. He looked so stern and demanding as he waited for her answer. And Beth knew exactly what she'd say. "Yes."

Eric rose up, his gaze traveling down her body from her half-buttoned blouse to her pushed-up skirt. His eyes narrowed at the sight of her exposed sex and pale thighs framed by the stockings. Beth eased her knees a little farther apart.

"Stay right there," he growled.

Still looking at her, he tugged open the drawer of her bedside table, but when he glanced inside, a little jerk of shock went through his body. He actually stepped back, his eyes widening.

Beth fought the urge to cover her eyes.

"Wow," Eric said.

"We, um, get a lot of free samples."

"I guess so. I don't…" He leaned closer. "Are these all for…?" He frowned down at the drawer. "Maybe you should pick one."

She didn't know whether to laugh or hide her face, but what the hell. She was a sexual fantasy, wasn't she? So instead of grabbing the closest toy and slamming the drawer shut, Beth edged her knees just the tiniest bit wider. "But you told me not to move."

Eric looked from the drawer to her, and his dark frown transformed almost instantly into a wicked smile that made her stomach twist. He didn't smile like that very often, which was a good thing. That smile was more than charming; it *promised* things. Filthy things.

And sure enough, he reached into the drawer with no trepidation at all.

"You're right. You should definitely stay just like that."

Beth breathed a sigh of relief when she saw what he'd chosen. Nothing monstrously big or festooned with pulsing appendages. Just a simple white vibrator with textured ridges along the underside. She could handle that. Even with an audience.

Beth pretended complete confidence when she took it from him, but a few moments without Eric's touch and her brain had kicked back to working life. What if she got performance anxiety? What if she couldn't make it happen? It wasn't like she had a hundred percent success rate.

But she had him to look at this time. And the hard light was back in his eyes as she turned the dial and nervously licked her lips. And as soon as she touched herself with the toy, she knew she needn't have worried. She was already turned on. For him. Her body already tight with arousal.

Beth put one hand behind her on the mattress to brace herself as she arched her back. She dragged the cool shaft over her hot sex and whimpered as the vibration pushed brutally through her nerves.

"That's the prettiest thing I've ever seen," Eric growled.

Instead of closing her eyes and trying to pretend he wasn't there, Beth watched him through her lashes as she worked the toy against her slick flesh.

His jaw tightened, his eyes on fire, and her body responded, wanting to please him, wanting to do anything for his approval. And when he reached for the buckle of his belt, every nerve in her body tightened. Her nipples drew to hard buds, her clit swelled against the pleasure pulsing through it.

The belt buckle clinked, then there was the delicious sound of sliding leather shivering through her, nearly as effective as the vibrator itself.

Beth wanted to whimper like a needy animal when he pulled down his zipper. Though she managed to clench her teeth against the sound, there was no stopping her moan when he drew his cock free. He was huge. The skin tight over his swollen flesh. The head already slick with need.

The sight pushed her too close to the edge. She had to shift the vibrator lower or she'd come within seconds. And she didn't want to come yet, because Eric had fisted that gorgeous cock in one hand, but he used the other to guide her off the bed and onto her knees.

"Don't stop," he ordered when her hand faltered and she braced herself against his leg.

So she didn't stop. Instead, she slid the vibrator over her clit one last time, then down. Down, until she could push it deep inside and fuck herself while Eric wrapped her hair around his fist. She opened her mouth for him, and there was hot approval in his eyes as he rubbed himself against her open lips.

Groaning again, she slid her tongue under him, trying to draw him in. He pushed in a little, but slowly pulled back, leaving her whimpering for more. Instead of giving her more, Eric held her still and stroked himself, only the head of his cock pressed to her tongue.

She loved it. The tightness of his fist in her hair, the fullness of her sex as she pushed the vibrator deeper, the knowledge that he was using her just the way he wanted. This shouldn't be her fantasy: on her knees in front of him, mouth eager and open. But at that moment, it felt like everything she'd ever wanted.

All those years of need and desire were building to a heavy weight between her thighs. A shaking, pulsing weight that pressed harder and harder against her clit. Every breath she exhaled was a small moan that kept the same rhythm as Eric's stroking hand. Her thighs shook. Her hips jerked against her own hand.

When she felt Eric's fist tighten to a brutal hold, Beth sighed and pressed her tongue tighter to him. Grunting, he held her still as he came, and when she pictured what she must look like for him, it was too much. She cried out as the climax took over her body and turned her inside out. It went on and on until she was so sensitive she could only shake and sob.

When Beth came to her senses, she was crouched on her knees, her forehead pressed to the rough fabric that covered Eric's thigh. Eyes open, she panted and stared at his shoes. Had she really just done that? Had that been her?

The sound of him zipping up his pants rang in her ears, and she had the disconcerting thought that he was about to throw money on the table and leave. Disconcerting, because the idea sent a thrill through her spent body.

But he didn't, of course. He lifted her up and slid her onto the bed, then waited for her to edge over before he collapsed, one arm slung over his eyes.

"Jesus Christ, Beth."

She sighed. "I know."

He lifted his head for a moment before letting it collapse to the pillow again. "And you're still dressed."

"Am I? I'm too numb to tell."

"That was…"

"Crazy," she whispered.

"Yeah."

This was getting a little scary. Not because the sex was rough and wild, but because it got more intense every time. That night in the hotel room, that night that had changed her life—it seemed so mild now. Just another round of good sex. But the more time she spent with Eric, the more she needed from him.

"What did you say on the phone?" she asked softly. "Just before we hung up?"

He shook his head. "I don't know."

"Because I thought you said something about not being Eric Donovan."

His chest rose on a sharp breath. Beth turned onto her side to watch him, but his face was still mostly covered by his arm. His muscles were tight beneath his skin.

"Michael Donovan wasn't my father," he finally said. "He adopted me when I was eight. My real dad was never around. He didn't give a shit."

She didn't feel any shock at the words. He didn't look anything like Jamie. She might have suspected, if she hadn't been so distracted by their lies. "But if he adopted you, your name is Donovan, right?"

A tight smile flashed over his face. "Yeah. I didn't lie about that part. But it feels like a lie, sometimes. It always has."

She laid her head on her arm and wrapped her fingers over his biceps. "He treated you differently?"

"No. Never. But I knew. And I made damn sure to be the son he wanted. Not because he demanded perfection, but because I wanted to give him that. He deserved it."

Beth didn't say anything. She understood. She'd wanted to be perfect for her dad, too.

"But then he died, and I had to be more than a perfect son. I had to be a dad and a brother and a business owner. I had to be the disciplinarian, and the breadwinner, and Christ, I had to be Tessa's mom, too. When she needed to see the doctor or buy a prom dress. I just…"

Beth realized she was pressing her nails into his skin and made her hand relax.

"That night, when I said I didn't know why I lied, that's only partly true. I know why I didn't bother correcting you. Honestly, it hardly felt like it mattered. My real name or not my real name, I don't know who I am lately. My siblings are grown up. They don't need me anymore. I'm a Donovan brother who's not even a Donovan. And that night felt like the first real thing I'd done in years."

She took a deep breath and blinked back tears at his words, because she knew exactly what he meant. Hadn't she been faking her way through life for a while now?

When she'd first started working at the White Orchid, she'd loved every single day. The idea of sexual freedom had been a revelation. That there were people in the world who thought sex was good and right and something everyone should enjoy.

She'd left high school so ashamed, so beaten down by what she'd done. And Christopher… He'd recovered within a week, his guilt seemingly wiped clean by awkward apologies to her family and with no price to pay among their peers. He'd been a stud, while Beth had been a slut of the highest order.

Leaving for college had been a relief, but it had been terrifying all the same. Boys, in particular, had terrified her. It had seemed they were predators lying in wait, constantly on the alert for any sign of weakness. Any hint that a girl might be interested in sex or that she might drink too much or just…just *like* him. As if she had to control their needs as well as her own, because God knew she'd be punished for giving in to either one.

Sex had felt like a trick and men like con artists, and her body…her own body was a Judas of the worst sort.

She shuddered to think what her life would've been like if she hadn't stumbled onto a human sexuality class. It had been disguised as part of her major: anthropology. But it had really been an exploration of different societies' attitudes toward sex, and how it affected their gender stereotypes.

Beth had been hooked. The next class had been all about women's sexuality through history. Then another on gender roles and power. Finally, she'd learned enough that she'd asked to see a counselor in the student services center, and just talking about what had happened to her had freed her.

When she'd finally taken a two-week-long internship at the White Orchid, Beth had felt like she'd found a place where she almost belonged. Almost. If she just tried hard enough. She'd been working toward completely belonging for years. She'd dated the men her friends had expected her to date, not the men she really wanted. But now…

Beth eased Eric's arm down until he finally let it fall. His eyes were wary and tired when they met hers. "I felt the same way that night," she admitted. "I feel that way now. Like it's just us here. Like I'm not who everyone expects Beth Cantrell to be." Ironic, maybe, considering she was sexual with him, but true all the same.

He wasn't part of her circle of friends. He wasn't real life. And that was why she liked the secret of this, she realized. Not only would he not tell anybody, but even if he did, they wouldn't be people she knew. They couldn't smile to her face and then discuss her when she left the room.

All these years and those last months of high school were still eating at her like acid. How pitiful was that?

"But you're just who you are," he said. "Aren't you?"

Beth rolled to her back and stared at the ceiling. "No. Not really. I…" She cleared her throat and tried again. "I…"

Seconds ticked by, and Beth could hear her own heart thumping a sad beat in her ears. Eric touched her then, his hand spreading over hers, their fingers sliding together. She held on tight.

She couldn't trust this man, could she?

She tried one more time. "I…wasn't always this person. I used to be someone different."

"Who?" he asked.

God, she wished it was dark, but the blinds were open and the afternoon sun was too bright to offer more than faint stripes of shade across the bed. "I was quiet. Shy. Plain. I was lonely, and then I fell in love, and a boy broke my heart."

"Bastard," he murmured, and Beth smiled.

"I thought I'd never trust anyone again."

"And you haven't."

"No," she said, realizing the truth even as she spoke the words. "No, but I'm starting to trust myself."

She felt him turn toward her, but Beth didn't look at him. She felt raw and naked in a way she hadn't felt even when she was on her knees for him.

"Only now?" he asked.

"Only now. But maybe my timing is good."

He squeezed her hand. "Does that mean you'll tell me what was stressing you out earlier?"

She shrugged. "The owner of the White Orchid is thinking of selling the store."

"I'm sorry. That's some shitty uncertainty. What will you do?"

"I don't know." She deliberately misunderstood him, but her answer was still the same. "We're like a family there. I can't imagine leaving."

"Do you think you'd have to?"

"I think I might." She was beginning to realize that that was the choice she faced. Because if she decided not to buy the White Orchid, then she knew she was telling herself she couldn't stay there forever. Either the store was her future, or her future lay somewhere else. But where? She couldn't imagine.

"What would you do?" he asked, his thumb feathering along the edge of her hand.

Beth closed her eyes and lost herself in that feeling. She'd never been offered physical comfort by a man, because she'd never been able to get past the initial stages of awkward intimacy. This was…nice. If only it was midnight instead of 2:00 p.m. She could just lie like this all night, her hand cradled in his, his shoulder pressed to hers.

"I don't know what I'd do," she finally admitted. "I like helping people. I like that some people come in lost and embarrassed and I make them feel better. And

I like that women want to be happy and fulfilled and we can help them find that."

"I never thought of it that way."

"It's not just about the naughtiness or the sex. At least once a week a woman will confess to me that she's never had an orgasm. Can you even imagine life without orgasms?"

"No," he said flatly. "That's not something men have to worry about."

"Exactly! And those are just the women who are brave enough to come into the store. There are so many who aren't."

"Is that why you write the column?"

Her eyes popped open. No, that wasn't why she wrote the column. She did that because Annabelle had asked her to, and because it was good publicity for the store. Maybe that was why her heart wasn't in it. "Whatever happens, I'll figure it out," she said. "But I was a little lost today. So thanks for meeting me."

"Of course. It was no problem."

She laughed at the wry humor in his voice. Here was the perfect chance to end the conversation. To get up and make noise about going back to the store. But Beth just lay there and held tight to Eric's hand. She couldn't trust that he wouldn't hurt her, but she knew without a doubt that she felt safe right now, and it had been a very long time since anyone had given her that.

"I know you must be busy," she whispered. "But if you're not, can I see you tonight?"

He watched her, waiting for her to meet his eyes, but she couldn't look. She couldn't. "I told you I'd give you anything you want," he said.

Beth turned her head away so he wouldn't see the tear that slipped down her cheek. It wasn't sadness. It was just relief.

CHAPTER SEVENTEEN

SHE DROVE STRAIGHT BACK to the store, her relaxation sneaking away with each second. It was almost three and she couldn't be late for her meeting, but she just wanted to be alone for a few more minutes.

And, if she was being truthful with herself, she wanted to put off going back to work. When Eric had asked, she'd been honest about her reasons for loving the White Orchid. But some of those reasons were starting to fade, taken over by the feeling that she was faking her way through every day.

She also didn't want to let go of her afternoon with Eric. Her pulse sped at the thought of him. She'd see him again tonight, which was both thrilling and frightening. They were getting too close, too fast. Still, she wanted more. More time and sex and secret moments. More of this life she'd never had before.

She rolled down her window, knowing her hair would be a wild mess, but she didn't care. Maybe they'd all think she'd been rolling around in bed. Maybe she'd let them.

She pulled up to the store at 2:58, acutely aware that in four more hours she'd be leaving again, going back to him. To his place this time, to his bed. Was he thinking about her right now? The idea that he'd read her columns, that he thought of her when she wasn't with him... Did he fantasize about her the way she had him?

Beth was so distracted by her thoughts as she grabbed her purse and got out of her car, she didn't notice the man who emerged from the backseat of an SUV a few spaces down. Not until he said her name.

"Beth," the man barked. She stumbled to a halt as Roland Kendall strode toward her.

She took a step backward, casting a quick glance around to be sure they weren't alone. But it was a busy afternoon. The door of the shop opened and customers walked out. A runner passed by on the sidewalk. She wasn't alone.

"What do you want?" she asked.

"I want you to drop this."

She took another step back, hoping to put some distance between them. His balding head was flushed red, his narrow eyes glinting with anger.

"This isn't about me, Mr. Kendall. The police have all the information."

"You did this," he snapped. "And you'll fix it."

"That doesn't make any sense. They already know what Monica said. I can't take that back, even if I wanted to."

"You can't take it back, but you can fix it. And you will."

She shook her head. "No, I—"

"Call the detective and tell him you lied. Tell him you made it up because you've always hated Monica and you wanted to hurt her."

"He won't believe me."

"It doesn't matter. If you take it back, they can't use

it in court. You'll be a labeled an unreliable witness, just as you should be."

Beth was tired of backing away, so she stood her ground and put her hands on her hips. "I'm not going to lie to the police for Monica. She's the one who dragged me into this, and I'm not exactly happy about that."

"You misunderstood her," he countered. "Whatever you think she said—"

"I know what she said. I was there. And it's not fair for you to treat me like the criminal when Graham and Monica are—"

Roland's hand shot out and wrapped around her wrist before she could pull away from him. "I like you, Beth. I always have, but I will not let you ruin Monica's life. I will ruin this store and I'll ruin you."

"Let go of me." She pulled back hard, and her wrist slipped through his hold. "Get out of here."

"Listen to me. Graham is gone. There's nothing I can do for him. But I won't have Monica dragged into this. Please."

Beth froze at that word. A word she'd never heard pass Roland Kendall's lips. This man who'd always seemed impervious and cocky—for a moment, fear flashed in his eyes.

Beth couldn't help her surge of sympathy. She'd known him for too long. "They want him. *Graham.* That's all."

"I can't betray him. He's my son."

"I'm sorry." She clutched her purse tight beneath her arm and edged around him. "I can't help you."

"This is my family," he snarled. She kept walking, but his next words made her stop. "I'd think you'd understand about family, considering how much you love your father. Children might not always do the right thing, but we still love them."

She spun back to face him. "What are you talking about?"

"I had a lovely dinner with your father the other night. I wanted to find out what was going on in your life that would make you lash out at old friends like this."

Beth shook her head. No. This couldn't be right. Her dad had gone to dinner with an old friend. He'd said, *You wouldn't believe who called me....*

"Your father looks great, by the way. And he couldn't stop talking about you. But I was confused."

"No," she murmured.

"He has some strange ideas about what you do for a living."

"Did you tell him?" she asked, skipping any protests or denial. Roland Kendall hadn't made millions of dollars in the past decade because he was an idiot.

"I didn't tell him. But I will."

She'd misunderstood his plans. Or simply underestimated him. Yes, he could hurt the store, but that was long-term revenge. But here was a threat that could be acted upon with nothing more than a phone call.

"Call the detective and tell him you lied," Kendall said. "I don't want to do this to you, but I will."

Beth walked away without responding. What was there to say? She wasn't going to beg this man, but she realized she also hadn't said no. Before she even made it through the doors of the store, Kendall had stalked back to his SUV. A driver hopped out and opened his door.

The man had a driver and plane and God knew how

many houses. And she'd made an enemy of him. It didn't matter that she'd done the right thing. He'd probably ruined people for far smaller things than hurting his family.

Thankfully, the meeting with the lighting guy took only a few minutes, because Beth's mind was spinning. As soon as he left, she called her dad, trying to keep the panic from her voice.

"Beth!" he said with such happiness in his voice that she had to swallow tears. "How are you?"

"I'm good, Dad."

"I've been meaning to call you. I can't tell you how much I liked your gentleman friend. He's exactly the kind of man you should be seeing. Serious, smart."

"Dad, we're only friends. I need to ask—"

"Then you should do your best to make it more. You're thirty-five now. It's time to settle down."

She clenched her eyes shut. "Who did you go to dinner with the other night?"

"I thought I told you! It was Roland Kendall. Can you believe that? The last time I saw him was at your graduation. He took us all to dinner afterward. In fact, I tried to pay for dinner this time, but he insisted, and I confess, I let him. He can afford it, after all."

"Dad… What did you talk about?"

"Oh, what old men always talk about. Our families, our lives. We both want grandchildren, of course. We laughed that both our daughters had forgotten the important things in life. Speaking of which, that Eric really likes you. I think there's more to this than you're revealing to your father."

She pressed her palm to her forehead. So much more.

"I'm proud of you. I worried for a while. After all

that nonsense. You work too hard, and you never come home. But you're a good girl. I know you'll end up with a good man and a good life."

She pressed her hand harder to her head, trying to counter the pressure inside. "Daddy," she whispered. "I'm not…I…"

"Oh, I know you don't want to talk about it now, but it'll happen. You two were trying so hard to hide it. I had trouble keeping a straight face!"

He sounded so happy. And proud. That she wasn't an unwanted single woman. That her horrid indiscretion was far behind her. That she might actually make him proud by marrying a nice man and settling down. He sounded the way he used to sound, before she'd broken his heart and his pride and almost destroyed his love for her.

And for a brief moment—just one heartbeat—Beth hated him.

"Dad, I've got to go."

"Hold on. Your mother wants to speak with you."

"No—" But it was too late. She could already hear her mother's giggle as she picked up the phone.

"Your father tells me you're dating a nice young man who owns his own business! Oh, Beth. Your dad was so impressed with him."

Her mom started on about the pie, and Beth held herself very still, hating the way her heart sped as if she were an eager puppy being praised. Eighteen years ago, her father's approval would've changed everything. Now she was just sorry that she still wanted it so much.

And she could have it. She could leave the White Orchid, date a nice preppy guy like Eric, settle down, find a job she wouldn't have to keep secret. And that incident in high school would never be thought of again. It would cease to exist, overshadowed by the fact that she'd turned out to be a good girl, after all.

This was her chance. She could start over. Walk away from a life that no longer felt as though it fit.

But the trouble was that nothing fit her anymore. Good girl, bad girl, prude or slut. She wasn't any of those things. Or she was all of them.

"Mom," she finally cut in. "I've got to get back to work."

She hung up and squeezed her eyes shut.

Hell, she didn't even know what she wanted anymore. Ten years ago, she would've been relieved if she were forced to tell her father the truth. But the last few years had been nice. Comfortable. She finally felt close to him again, and now Kendall was going to ruin it. Her father would be mortified and ashamed. Her mom would flutter around like an upset bird as he called her terrible names. Beth wasn't sure she could do that again. But she couldn't imagine lying for his approval anymore, either.

Cairo popped into her office. "Hey, can I take my break?"

"Yes, I'm sorry. Of course." Beth forced herself to smile as she smoothed down her hair and stood up.

"You need some blush," Cairo said before disappearing.

God, she needed a lot more than that. But Beth got out her compact and dusted blush on her pale face before adding a little color to her lips. She looked perfectly normal. Confident and poised and successful. She looked like a fraud. But she strode out to the floor with a smile, winking at Cairo to let her know she was free.

"Can I help you?" she asked a nervous woman who was clutching her purse in two hands, eyes wide as she looked over the piercing display.

"Oh!" She jumped a little, but her face relaxed when she saw Beth's smile. "Hi. I don't know. I'm just looking, I think."

"For anything in particular?"

The woman blinked several times, her hands tightening on the purse. She looked about twenty-five. An engagement ring glinted on her finger, but other than that, she wore no jewelry or makeup. A woman who wasn't looking to be noticed.

Beth leaned a tiny bit closer. "It's okay," she whispered. "Look around. It's only women here this afternoon. If you have any questions, you can ask me."

Her hazel-gold eyes swept the room before focusing back on Beth. "Okay. Um. I wanted to look at…um… massagers? But I don't see any. Do you…?"

"They're right in back behind that curtain."

"Oh!" Her eyes went even wider.

Beth gave her the gentlest smile she could manage. "There's no one in there right now, so if you'd like, you can go look by yourself for a little while. I'll come in and see if you have any questions in a few minutes. How does that sound?"

"I… Okay. I guess that would be good." She hurried toward the curtain as if she were afraid she'd lose her courage.

Beth wondered if the woman's fiancé knew she was here. Probably not. Most of them didn't. In fact, according to her customers, a lot of men were intimidated by the idea of a woman finding pleasure with something that didn't involve them.

Eric definitely didn't have that problem. That man had sexual confidence in spades. Or at least bravado. Same outcome, as far as she was concerned.

That part with him was easy, at least. But what would she say to him about Kendall? The truth? A lie? Nothing at all?

She wouldn't know until she decided what the truth was for herself.

Did she want this store? Was she still a part of it? She thought about it the rest of the day. The shy woman bought herself a surprisingly large and detailed vibrator, her cheeks flaming scarlet-red the whole time. A group of friends came in to buy supplies for a bachelorette party. And Simone Parker came back in without her badge to buy a gorgeous white lace bra.

It was a good day. A happy day. But at the end of it, Beth still had no idea what she would do.

CHAPTER EIGHTEEN

ERIC WENT BACK TO WORK, because he didn't know what the hell else to do with himself. He had hours to kill before he saw Beth again, and his shower took only five minutes, and cleaning up his condo took only ten, so he shrugged on a Donovan Brothers T-shirt and jeans and headed to the brewery.

A good thing, considering that he walked into a disaster zone. As soon as he opened the back door, smoke billowed into his face. "What the hell's going on here?" he barked, waving his hand in front of him as he rushed inside.

"It's fine!" Jamie's voice shouted from the vicinity of the new oven.

"Fine? I'm calling 911!"

"There's no fire, damn it! Just open the back door before the sprinklers go off!"

Eric spun around and dove for the door, propping it open with a cement block they kept nearby. By the time he ran back in, the smoke was already starting to clear.

"Jamie, what the *hell?*"

"The exhaust malfunctioned."

"Well, shut the damn thing down!"

Jamie threw him a disgusted glare. "It's a wood-burning oven, Eric. I can't throw a switch."

"I told you we should've gone with gas."

"And I told you that the wood adds more authentic flavor. But we both know you don't give a shit about the food, right?"

"Yeah." Eric laughed. "I actually care a lot more about not burning the brewery down than I do about your fucking pizzas, Jamie. Big surprise."

"It's just the exhaust. Nothing was burning down."

"And now what? Just hope it doesn't happen again?"

"Obviously," Jamie said through clenched teeth. "I'm going to call the rep right now. But I've got the vent locked open, so it's fine. All right?"

"No!" Eric shouted. "It's not all right. None of this is all right. Wallace is gone. The line is screwed. You almost burned the place down. And in a few weeks…" Eric forced himself not to say it.

Jamie threw the wrench he was holding into one of the cabinets. The crash prompted Chester to poke his head through the double doors. "Guys? Everything okay?"

"I got the exhaust fixed," Jamie growled.

"Okay." Chester looked doubtfully between Jamie and Eric before nodding. "Sure. I'll just leave you alone then."

As soon as the doors closed, Jamie stalked forward. "In a few weeks, what?"

"Nothing," Eric muttered.

"Bull. I know exactly what you were going to say, and I am so sick of your shit, Eric. You agreed to this. I'm not asking you to jump in and pretend it's your life-long dream, but if you don't get that fucking chip off your shoulder, I will knock it off."

"We going to fight again?" Eric snapped.

"If we need to, I'm fully prepared to kick your ass.

But I'd rather you just live up to the agreement you made this summer."

"We didn't make an agreement."

"You said you'd support me."

"And I haven't?" Eric threw his hands up. "How much money have we invested in this? I've agreed to everything you wanted. The menu and the concept. The new tables, the new front deck. The oven and fridge and freezer. We're doing everything you want!"

"And you resent every damn minute of it."

"I don't. I don't resent it. It just has nothing to do with me."

Jamie's jaw dropped. "You're kidding, right? We're equal partners here. You can't just pretend this part of it doesn't belong to you, just because you're not in charge anymore."

"I never wanted to be in charge!" he yelled.

"That's a lie," Jamie said with a bitter laugh. "You ran the brewery on your own for years, and you still ran it on your own even after Tessa and I took our places. I'm sorry that couldn't go on forever—"

"I didn't want it to go on forever."

"Of course you did."

"I didn't even want to be in charge in the first place. Do you get that, Jamie? I didn't want it!"

Jamie shook his head with another bitter laugh. "Whether you wanted it or not, you sure as hell took to it like a fish to water. But you're not in charge, Eric. You're not the owner. And you're not our dad."

Eric put his fists on his hips and let his head drop. "Yeah. You don't have to tell me. I'm pretty clear on that count."

"Then stop sulking around here like I'm a rebellious

kid who won't do what you want. This is what *I* want. And I'm making it happen. I'd like you to get behind me, but if you won't do that, at least get out of my way."

"Fine. But do you really think this is what Dad would've wanted?"

Jamie's jaw dropped. "*What?* What he would've wanted? I have no fucking idea. He's been dead for thirteen years, Eric. Who knows what he would've done with the place? And for godssake, you're not the keeper of everything Dad believed in. You don't get to lay claim to that."

"Yeah, I'm clear on that, too. Believe me." Eric let his head fall back and stared up at the ceiling. A few faint wisps of smoke still lingered near the lights. "I'm happy for you, Jamie. I swear I am. And I want this for you. But for me…Jesus, for me I want something else, and I don't even know what it is."

"What are you talking about?" Jamie growled.

"I don't know, man. I don't know. Just…" He waved a hand at the oven. "Just don't burn the place down, all right?"

"Eric," Jamie started, but Eric stole out the open door and into the shade of the afternoon.

He didn't know where he was going. Just away. Anywhere but there.

He drove for miles, and it felt good. It felt free. But would he keep driving even if he had the chance? Where would he go? Even in his imagination, his mind always turned back to Donovan Brothers. He loved that place. It was all he knew, and despite all his doubts and resentments and anger, he could never think of anything he'd rather do with his life.

Maybe, instead of worrying that he wasn't needed

anymore, he should be making damn sure he was invaluable. Jamie was right about one thing. Eric had been sulking like a kid who hadn't gotten his way. So he didn't want to turn the brewery into a brewpub. Big deal. He hadn't wanted to take over the whole operation at twenty-four, but he'd done it and he'd done it well.

"Screw this," he muttered, pulling a U-turn on the deserted county highway. If his plans for the future of the brewery weren't good enough, then he'd come up with new plans. And Eric suddenly realized just where he'd gone wrong.

He'd been concentrating too hard for too many years. He'd put his head down and forgotten to look around. More importantly, he'd forgotten to look back. He had boxes of Michael Donovan's old files in the spare bedroom of his condo. And even though his goal for the past thirteen years had been to run the brewery just as their dad would've, he hadn't looked through those boxes since the day he'd packed them up a decade before. Maybe it was time to look again.

CHAPTER NINETEEN

BETH HAD BEEN NICE ENOUGH to bring dinner, and Eric had carefully laid out plates and silverware and wineglasses on his small table. But the bags of takeout sat unopened on the kitchen counter and one of the plates lay cracked in half on the dining room floor. The other plate was wedged under Beth's naked shoulder. Eric, still buried deep inside her body, tried to catch his breath while he prayed to God she hadn't landed on a fork.

"You okay?" he asked, lifting her enough to slide the plate free.

"I'm all right," she said with a sly grin. "How about you?"

He stood straight, and Beth gasped when he slid farther inside her. Despite the fact that he'd come already, he was still half-hard. "You sure you're done?" he asked, when she stretched and took him a little deeper.

"For now." She sighed.

"Are you hungry?"

"Famished. I somehow forgot to eat lunch today."

He was more than half-hard when he finally pulled out, overwhelmed with images of what she'd done with her mouth over her lunch hour. But when her stomach growled, he decided the reminiscing could wait till later. Though not much later if their recent past was any indicator.

When they finally sat down to eat lukewarm Chinese food, Eric found himself smiling as he chewed.

"You're in an awfully good mood," Beth said.

He raised an incredulous eyebrow. "I'm going to feel a little insulted if you're not."

She laughed. "I admit I'm still a tiny bit stressed. But I don't think I've ever seen you smile like that before."

"Well, I've never had sex on a dining room table before."

"No?"

"I won't ask if it's your first time, but I don't mind telling you it's mine."

"And how was it? A little scary? Were you nervous?"

He chuckled as he reached for his wine. "Like a teenage boy, my eagerness overcame my nerves. In fact, just like a teenage boy, I forgot to think about your needs."

"That's odd. I seem to recall a pretty intense focus on what I needed."

"Yeah, but utensil danger didn't occur to me until after we were done."

Beth laughed until she had to wipe tears from her eyes, and Eric realized she had been tense, even after the sex. "Are you worried about the store?" he asked.

She nodded and took a long drink of wine.

"Has anything changed?" he pressed.

"It's just…complicated."

"Yeah. Believe me, I get that."

"Are things still complicated at the brewery?" she asked. She clearly wasn't in the mood to discuss her problems, but Eric was fine with that. It had been a big deal for her to open up earlier today. As briefly as he'd known her, Eric knew without a doubt that it wasn't easy for her. What he didn't understand was why it meant so much to him that she was starting to trust him. It was just a fling. Nothing else. And if he wanted to share things with her, that was nothing more than another basic need.

"Well," he said, leaning back in his seat, "my brother and I almost came to blows again today."

"Again?"

"Unfortunately, yeah."

"Is that something brothers do?"

"Not us. Not normally. But things have been tense this year. All this crap with the Kendalls."

She flushed and looked down. "I'm sorry."

"Come on. It's got nothing to do with you. I'm just sorry you've been dragged into it. And there's plenty of other crap going on to stress me out. Jamie's adding food to the menu. My brewmaster fell in love with a married woman and disappeared. And I'm just... spiraling."

"Because you don't know what to do?"

"Yeah. But I'm going to try to figure it out."

"Me, too." Her eyes were soft and worried as she pushed her food around on her plate.

"I'm glad we've decided to see each other, though."

She glanced up, surprise flashing over her features. "Me, too."

"Are you going to stay? We could watch a movie. Hang out." Eric was surprised by the hope that squeezed his chest so tight. They'd already had sex twice today. So what was this painful need knotting him up inside?

Beth looked down, and he knew she was going to say no. *No, this isn't a love affair. It's not a relationship. It's just desperate, frantic sex that neither of us want*

*anyone to know about. We're using each other and you
already want too much.*

She ran a hand down her skirt. "I'm not exactly
dressed for hanging out. Do you have something I could
wear?"

He let his breath out slowly, hoping she wouldn't
notice that he'd been holding it. "Yeah, as long as you
don't mind a T-shirt that's way too big for you."

"A T-shirt would be great."

Yeah, that would be great. Her lounging around in
panties and a shirt, her gorgeous legs curled up beneath
her. Her thighs bare. "Bedroom's at the end of the hall.
My shirts are in the dresser. I'll put the food away."

Strange that he'd just had her on this very table, but
she looked shy now as she said thank-you and stood
up. But he felt it, too. That painful anticipation when
they were together. That newness of finding out what
made her laugh, what turned her eyes sad. They were
so intimate, and yet he knew almost nothing about her.
Was her real name Beth or Elizabeth? Had she played
any sports in school? What did she like on her pizza?
What kind of music did she like?

Beth was a closed book with him. Was she like that
with everyone?

He was shoving food cartons in the fridge when he
heard Beth clear her throat behind him. That brief sound
was all mischief and for a moment, beautiful images
flashed behind his eyes of what sorts of kinky little outfits she might have actually smuggled inside her purse.
But when he stood and spun around, Beth was standing
there in a T-shirt and bare legs just as he'd expected.

"Perfect," he said, and then he noticed the pale gold
scrap of fabric in her hand.

She held it up with a quirked eyebrow. "What exactly is this, Mr. Donovan?"

For one blessed heartbeat, he had no idea what it was. "Underwear?" he guessed.

"Oh, it's underwear," she drawled, and then he remembered.

"Oh, shit," he breathed, his face going slightly numb with the shock of it. "I can explain."

"Yeah? You can explain why you stole my underwear six months ago and now you keep them hidden in your dresser drawer?"

How the hell had he forgotten that? Every time he opened the second drawer on the left, there they were, accusing him of being a pervert. Reminding him of how she'd looked that night in the hotel room when he'd unzipped her dress and slid it down.

"I didn't steal them," he said carefully. "You left them behind."

Her cheeks pinkened, and she covered her mouth, but it looked like she was hiding a smile. Please, God, let it be a smile.

"I thought it would be rude to just leave them there. You might have called, looking for them later."

"I might?" she asked.

"I don't know! I just…took them."

"And what have you been doing with them since then?"

"What?" he gasped. Now the pictures flashing through his mind weren't so pleasant. "Nothing! They've just been in my dresser, taunting me like a damned telltale heart!"

"Oh, God," she gasped, and she was definitely smiling now. In fact, she was laughing like crazy. "The telltale heart?"

"Seriously, I felt like a pervert."

"I'm sorry," she gasped, tears leaking from her eyes.

He finally relaxed, though he couldn't quite bring himself to join in her laughter. "You should be. What kind of girl forgets to put her underwear back on, anyway?"

"The dirty, slutty kind?" she gasped, laughing even harder.

"Exactly. And I had to live with that shame."

Her laughter finally subsided to giggles. "Are you sure they stayed in your dresser the whole time?" She held the pale silk panties in front of her hips. "You never tried them on?"

"No!" he yelped.

"You sure? A lot of guys are into that."

"I'm sure as all hell." He narrowed his eyes at her naughty smile. "Why? Is that one of the things you're into?"

"No, but I try to stay open-minded. If you wanted to try them on..."

"I do not," he said emphatically. "Though I wouldn't mind seeing them on you again. Or off."

She disappeared back down the hallway, and Eric followed her. "What are you snooping in now?"

"Nothing," she answered, stuffing the underwear in her purse. Thank God, he was finally free of the responsibility. "There's not much to snoop in here." She glanced quickly around at the bare walls. "You are definitely a stereotypical single guy."

Beth took a brush from her purse and began brushing out her long dark hair.

His heart skipped at the sight of his old T-shirt rising up her thighs every time she stroked. He leaned against the doorway to watch. She was beautiful in heels and tight skirts, but she was even prettier like this, relaxed and natural, her makeup worn off.

"So…" he ventured. "Can I ask what you *are* into?"

Her brush stopped, midstroke. "What?"

God, her thighs were gorgeously full. Tonight he'd have to make time to explore every inch. When he glanced up, she was staring at him, but when their eyes met, she started brushing again.

"What do you mean?" she asked.

"I don't think it's any secret that you're more experienced than I am. Or at least more adventurous. So is there anything I'm missing out on?"

"With me?"

"In general, I suppose. But yeah. With you."

Her eyes slid away. She put the brush down and swept her hair back from her shoulders. What was it? What didn't she want to say? His pulse sped with a mix of excitement and trepidation. He wasn't a prude, but there were some things he probably wouldn't try, even with Beth. Then again…there were a lot of things he would.

"I'm not into anything," she finally said.

His excitement smashed into bits at his feet. "Come on. I can handle it."

Her mouth turned up in a brief smile. "Is there something you want me to be into?"

"No."

She sat down on the plain black comforter that covered his bed. This room was too spare for a woman like her. She deserved to be surrounded by pillows and silks and bright colors.

"Eric...I'm not that exciting."

"Ha!" That was the most ridiculous thing he'd ever heard.

"I'm serious," she said quietly. "I know what people think. I get that. But I'm just a regular girl."

There was no amusement in her tone now. As a matter of fact, she sounded so somber that Eric's neck prickled. He crossed the room and sat down next to her. "I didn't mean anything by it."

"I know that. It's just that I...I'm nothing more exciting than this." She spread her hands over her bare thighs. "Honestly. That's not to say I haven't tried things. I've explored the options, just because of my job and my friends, and...in the end, I'm only...regular."

Did she think he wanted something more than what they had? Did she think he expected her to perform tricks? Eric took her hand and cradled her curled fingers in his. "There's nothing regular about you, Beth."

"That's nice of you to say, but—"

"Nice? Are you kidding me? You think I'm being nice? When I say there's nothing regular about you, I mean every single time I touch you it blows my mind."

She rolled her eyes. "Eric—"

"I can't believe we're having this conversation. Whenever you call me, I think you've got me mixed up with someone else. That you've made a mistake, because what the hell could you need from me?"

Her hand turned until she could weave her fingers between his. "I'm not like this with other men, Eric."

"Like what?"

"Normal."

"Christ, what does that mean? You don't have to tone things down for me or keep the training wheels on or whatever it is you—"

"That's not it." She tried to tug her hand away, but he wouldn't let her, and eventually she relaxed again. "That's not what I mean at all. What I mean is that it's comfortable with you. It shouldn't be, but it is."

"Comfortable? Are you sure that's a good thing?"

Beth took a deep breath, her lips parted as if she was about to say something. But then she just sighed and laid her head on his shoulder.

Comfortable? Like a harmless friend? He didn't get it. He felt alive with her. So aware of her that it hurt sometimes. And she wanted to…what? Braid his hair? "Beth—"

"You have no idea how nice it is to feel comfortable."

He frowned. "I don't think of sex on a table as being comfortable," he grumbled. "Or on the floor."

Beth lifted her head and smiled at him as if he was being silly. "No?"

"No!"

"Well…" She kissed his neck, her lips pressing softly just below his ear. "What about right here?"

He tried to maintain his irritation as her words whispered over his neck. "Right where?"

"Right here in bed?" She turned and put her knees on the bed so that she straddled him. "Wouldn't that be comfortable?"

"I'm beginning to hate that word."

"Are you?" She pushed him down until his back hit the mattress. "That's too bad." She whipped off the T-shirt so quickly that Eric blinked in shock at the sight of her bare breasts. "Because I love being comfortable with you."

"Well…" He blinked again, or else his eyes fluttered shut a little when she rolled her hips into him. "I guess *hate* is a strong word."

HE DIDN'T UNDERSTAND. Beth could see that. But she couldn't explain without revealing everything, and she couldn't do that now. Not tonight, when it might be their last night together. Still, maybe she could make him understand with her body.

She pushed up his shirt and pressed her breasts to his skin. "It's so nice to feel I can do anything with you. But maybe that's just me."

She kissed him finally, a slow, deep kiss as he spread his hands over her naked back, but when he slid his hands beneath her underwear and pulled her tighter, Beth broke the kiss and pushed up with a smile. "But maybe comfortable isn't kinky enough for you. Is that it?"

He answered her smile, then flipped her over so quickly she shrieked. "You've made your point," he growled.

"Have I?"

"Yeah." Eric slipped his fingers beneath her underwear, then he cupped his hand over her sex. "But I still say you're using the wrong word."

She was sensitive from too much sex already, and when his fingers slid along her, Beth gasped at the shock of pleasure. Suddenly, her mind was working again. Moving too fast. The sex wasn't mindless anymore. It was…*full*. Of emotions. And worries. And fears that it meant too much. Because she didn't want it to stop tomorrow. She didn't ever want it to stop.

As he stroked her, she slid her leg along his, opening herself to him, letting herself feel the pleasure and the anxiety all at once.

Tomorrow, if she called Luke and lied to him, Eric wouldn't understand. He wouldn't forgive. And she'd never feel his fingers slide inside her again. She'd never arch into his touch with a whimper.

His thumb strummed her clit and she cried out. "Is that comfortable?" he murmured.

Beth shook her head. It wasn't. It was wonderful and awful and too much.

"I don't want to be easy to you, Beth." He slipped free of her and his strong hand curled over her hip to turn her over. She went willingly, laying her cheek to the bed, closing her eyes against the bittersweet anticipation.

He didn't understand. She couldn't tell him.

His hand shaped her ass, his fingers pressing rough into her flesh when he squeezed. His other hand wound into her hair, and this time when he slid his fingers along her sex, she sighed his name.

She loved him like this. Intense and in control. She loved it that he held her still and stroked her until she begged. "Please," she whispered.

But she had no idea what she was begging for, because even after she came, even after she cried out and arched up and her body clenched around his fingers... she was still whispering, "Please."

CHAPTER TWENTY

"ROLAND KENDALL CALLED. He's ready to deal."

Eric dropped the hose he was using to clean a tank, slipped off his gloves and switched the phone to the other ear. "Are you serious?" he asked Luke.

"They seem pretty intent on talking. He and his lawyer are heading over to the D.A.'s office right now, and I'm on my way to meet them. I think the pressure finally worked, and just in time. We were working up the arrest warrant on Monica Kendall and we made damn sure he was aware."

"Great news. Call me as soon as you know."

Eric hung up and got back to his cleaning with a smile. This year was finally starting to shape up. He'd been at work for two hours, and things were falling into place. The two grocery accounts had been fine with waiting a week for their shipments, the mechanic had called and said the piece would be in a day earlier, and the microbatch Eric had started was almost ready for second fermentation. He was thinking he'd probably age it just for kicks, but he could make that decision later. Hell, he was free to do whatever he wanted for a few more days. Wallace had finally called to say he'd be back on Tuesday.

In the bigger scheme of things, Graham Kendall might be coming back to the United States to face trial.

It wasn't as if he'd murdered anyone, but damn, it would feel good to see him get time for the hundreds of people he'd stolen identities from.

And then, of course, there was sex with Beth. Secret, smutty, comfortable sex with Beth.

Eric grabbed a broom and swept soapy water over to the drain in the center of the tank room, grinning like a madman the whole time. There must be something in the ventilation system at the brewery. He was just as lovesick as everyone else.

Startled by the thought, he froze, the broom still poised above the floor. That wasn't what she'd meant by *comfortable,* was it? It wasn't about falling in love. Sure, he liked her. A lot. What was there *not* to like about the woman? She was gorgeous and smart. Soft and sexy. And maybe even comfortable, despite the fact that he still wished she'd chosen a different word.

"No," he said aloud, resuming his sweeping. He wasn't lovesick. He was just obsessed with the best sex he'd ever had in his life. Totally normal. It'd be weird if he *wasn't* walking around with a smile.

Nodding to himself, Eric hung the broom up and headed to his office. Jamie would be in soon, and Eric wanted to talk to him before he got too caught up in his plans to bring in a chef to interview tomorrow. "Tessa?" He stuck his head in his sister's door.

She covered the phone with her hand. "Yeah?"

"When Jamie comes in, would you two come to my office?"

She frowned at him, but nodded as she got back to her call.

The strange calm he'd felt for the past twelve hours

was still with him. When Jamie knocked on his door a few minutes later, Eric looked up with a smile. "Hey."

Tessa pushed past and dropped into her chair with a glare. "What's going on, Eric? I don't like this."

"Don't like what?"

She pointed at him. "This."

"Everything's great."

Tessa's green eyes narrowed and she shook her head. "Whatever you think you're doing, don't do it."

"Calm down. I just wanted to apologize to Jamie." He looked at Jamie, who'd taken a seat in the other chair and seemed much less concerned with the meeting. "What you said the other day... You were right. I haven't been truly supportive of the changes you're making. I've spent the past thirteen years trying to do exactly what I thought Dad would've wanted for the brewery. Every decision I've made has been about his vision, what he planned, what he valued."

Jamie stiffened. "I care about his memory, too."

"I know. What I'm saying is the only motivation I've had is doing things the way Michael Donovan would've done them."

"Why? I don't get it."

Eric sighed. "Yeah, I know. You don't get it because you don't have to. You don't need to constantly wonder what he'd do, because you're his blood, Jamie. You come by it naturally."

"What the hell are you talking about?" Jamie grumbled.

"I'm talking about this." He pushed the sketches forward. "He never talked about this. Not with me, anyway. But it turns out Dad had the same ideas you did, Jamie."

Tessa picked up the sketches with a frown. "What are these?"

"I went through some of Dad's old things last night. I haven't looked at them in more than ten years, and the last time I did, I was just searching for help on keeping the brewery afloat. I wasn't thinking about expanding. But he was."

Jamie took the papers that Tessa offered and frowned down at them as he paged through. "Okay," he said, obviously not as blown away as Eric had been.

"Look at the plans, Jamie. They're rough and simplistic, but some of his sketches of a dining area look almost exactly like your plans."

"I guess."

"Don't you get it? He was considering adding food. Not pizza, but an actual restaurant. I've been thinking that it's wrong to change the brewery this way—to change *his* brewery—but I've just been stubborn. I'll stop resisting. I'll completely support your ideas for changes from here on out. As a matter of fact, I'm thinking maybe we haven't gone far enough."

Jamie looked up from the sketches, his eyes hardening. "What do you mean?"

"I mean I think you've come up with a great rollout plan. Artisan pizzas cooked in a real stone oven. It's a great idea. Better than anything I could've come up with. But if it goes well, maybe we should think about expanding next year. We could add more items, extend the hours. Heck, we could even consider adding a sunroom that we could use in the winter and the summer. I could oversee a second expansion while you run the restaurant."

Jamie set the sketches down, taking the time to carefully align the papers with the edge of Eric's desk. "Are you serious?"

"Yes."

"You've finally decided that my idea doesn't suck and won't ruin the brewery."

"Yes," Eric said with a smile. "Although I wouldn't quite put it—"

"And at the very same moment you decided that *maybe* I have a decent plan, you also decided it isn't good enough."

Eric's smile faded. "What?"

"You'll let me have my little pizza joint while you work on something bigger and better."

Tessa touched his arm. "Jamie."

"What? That's what he's saying."

Eric huffed out a humorless laugh. "That's not what I'm saying at all. I'm saying you were right. That even without knowing it, you still understand what Dad wanted."

"Jesus, this isn't about Dad. Why do you always turn it back to him?"

"Stop," Tessa cut in. "The important thing here is that Eric is supporting you, Jamie."

Jamie laughed. "By telling me he can do it better?"

Eric leaned forward, his shoulders tightening to rock. "I'm trying to compliment you, damn it. Why is it so hard for you to see that? I'm saying our dad would've been proud of you."

Jamie's jaw turned hard. "That's not up to you to decide. It's not up to anyone. He's dead, Eric. I can't get his approval, even if I deserved it."

"Fine, but lucky for you, you don't need it. You don't have to work for it at all. Even when you're just doing things your way, you're a lot closer to staying true to him than I could ever be."

Tessa shook her head. "What are you talking about?"

"It doesn't matter!" Jamie shouted. "I can't live my whole life wondering what Dad would think about it. He's been dead for thirteen years! What is your god-damned obsession with this?"

"Obsession?" Eric snapped. "It's been my fucking job since he died. To step in and do what he would've wanted. To try to take his place in this world, as if any-one could. Not that you ever fucking appreciated a *moment* of what I've done for you."

"Oh, for godsake. Is that what this is about? You being a martyr?"

Tessa hit Jamie's shoulder. "Stop it. He gave up ev-erything for us."

"That's not what I meant," Eric said quickly. "I love you. It's just that—"

Jamie laughed again. "That you expect us to do ev-erything your way for the rest of our lives because you put in a few years when we were teenagers?"

"I put in *a few years?*" Eric snarled. "I gave up my whole fucking life so I could keep the brewery going for you two. It was five years before you could even wash a goddamned glass in here, Jamie. And seven for Tessa. Do you think my dream was to push papers around on a desk forever? To be a father before I'd even grown up? I gave up my life so I could move back home and try to fill Dad's shoes the best I could for an ungrate-ful little shit who resented everything I did for him!"

Jamie's smile was tight and angry. "You aren't Dad, Eric. And it drove me crazy that you pretended you were."

Eric surged up, shoving his chair so hard that it crashed into the wall and tipped over. "Jesus, I know I'm not Dad! I'm not even his fucking son, am I?"

Tessa stood up, too, but Jamie just leaned back in his seat, looking bored.

"Eric, don't say that," Tessa pleaded.

"Why not? It's true, isn't it?"

"No, it's not true," she said, anger in her eyes. "It's not true at all."

But Eric looked down at Jamie's flat expression. He wanted to hit him again, as if he could beat into Jamie how much he loved him, how much he'd do for him, how desperate he was for him to have a good life. "I wasn't even working here when he died. Did you know that? I got a place in Denver and I was working at a bottling plant for experience. And you know what? He didn't care. You two were the ones who were supposed to take over."

Tessa shook her head. "He left the brewery to all of us, Eric. He wanted you here."

"No, he needed me here for you. When I told him I was thinking of going out to one of the old breweries in the East, he didn't raise one objection."

"Did you need him to?" Jamie sneered. "He was a great dad to you, but you needed him to ask you to stay? Maybe he felt like you didn't give a shit about him because you wanted to work anywhere but here."

Eric swallowed hard against the frustrated rage wanting to escape from his throat. "That wasn't how it was," he growled.

"If you don't want to be here, if you don't think you belong, then you sure as hell don't need to stay here and give up your life for us, brother."

"Jamie, *stop it*," Tessa yelled.

"Are you not hearing him?" Jamie said. "He gave up everything for us. He never wanted this job or this family."

"Fuck you," Eric snarled, stalking toward the door. "Do whatever the hell you want with this place. It's all yours."

"Eric!" Tessa screeched.

"Leave it alone," he muttered as he walked out.

"No. No, I won't leave it alone!" She chased after him. For a moment he thought she was going to leap right onto his back, but she just stomped her foot. "You stop right now, Eric Donovan."

Eric sighed and stopped halfway through the kitchen, but he didn't turn around.

"You promised me you wouldn't leave. You told me just a few months ago that we were a burden—"

"I didn't say that."

"Okay, *I* said we were a burden, and you said you didn't want to be free of us. So you're stuck."

Jesus, she could make him smile even when he felt like his heart was being pulled out of his chest. "Tessa…" He turned to face her, his hands up in surrender. "I don't want to be free of you. I don't know what I'd do without you. But I'm tired."

"Tired of what?"

He shook his head. He didn't know what it was. He just needed a break. From being the responsible one. The good one. The guy everyone could count on. It felt like his whole identity. It was all he knew about himself and it felt like a suit that didn't fit.

"You're wrong about Dad," she said, her chin edging out to a stubborn line. "He didn't think of you as any different from me and Jamie."

"Then maybe Jamie's right. Maybe he saw that I felt different. Maybe I broke his heart. All I know is that I'm not him, and I can't keep pretending I am. I'm no good at the stuff he was good at, Tessa."

"That's not true, Eric. But if you really feel that way, then do something different. But don't walk away. I won't let you. I swear to God, I won't."

Eric tipped his head back and stared up at the industrial lights above him. He'd meant to walk out, just to get some space and time to breathe. To think. But he'd meant what he said. He didn't want to be free of them. He didn't have anywhere else to go.

"The mechanic will be here this afternoon, and Wallace will be back tomorrow. I'll man the tank room today and the bottling tomorrow. And then maybe I need a few days off."

She threw herself into his arms and hugged him hard. "Yes! Take a vacation. I told you to take a vacation this spring, but you wouldn't. That's all you need."

"Sure," he said, but Eric didn't think a vacation could fix him. He wasn't sure anything could, but he'd give it an honest shot for Tessa, because he didn't want to be that man she couldn't trust. Not again.

EVEN THE TANK ROOM COULDN'T offer comfort today. Eric wanted to rage at someone and that someone was Jamie. After everything they'd been through together, they should've been close. Eric couldn't understand why Jamie seemed to hate him sometimes. Had Eric really screwed things up so badly? Even if he had, why couldn't Jamie give him a break?

He was still fuming an hour later, and when the tank room door opened, Eric looked up with a scowl.

Luke gave a perfunctory wave.

"Oh, it's you." He'd forgotten all about the hearing. Jamie and Tessa would probably be pissed he hadn't said anything. "How'd it go?"

"Pretty well."

"Kendall was ready to deal?"

"Actually, not quite. He came in acting like his usual arrogant self. Monica looked downright smug, as a matter of fact."

"Why?"

Luke cleared his throat, his eyes sliding away.

"What? Is it Jamie? Tell the truth."

"No. Just before I stepped into the meeting, I got a call from Beth Cantrell. She wanted to correct what she'd said in her interview."

"How so?"

"She said she hadn't been telling the truth. That Monica hadn't really said that. I tried to press her on it, but I had to get into the D.A.'s office."

Eric shook his head. "That doesn't make any sense. I know she wasn't lying, so why would she tell you that?"

Luke shrugged. "Kendall's a powerful guy. And he looked pretty damn confident when he came in this morning, considering we were threatening to arrest his daughter."

Eric's mind spun. He couldn't imagine Beth going back on her word like that. It made no sense. She'd come forward voluntarily in the first place. "So you couldn't arrest Monica?"

"We didn't arrest Monica, but not because of that. Kendall didn't realize we already had a statement from the man at the catering company. When you put that with Jamie's statement, and the owner of that construction place, we didn't need Beth's statement, anyway. Kendall was surprised, to say the least. And in the end, he agreed to cut off funding to his son. Not that he admitted sending it to him, anyway."

"Really? It worked?"

"Well, we'll see if we flush that little bastard out. But I don't think he's going to last long in Hong Kong with no money. He's not exactly a scrapper."

Eric nodded and tried to look pleased, but he couldn't quite manage it. "She didn't give you any reason?"

"No."

"What the hell do you think he did to her? Did she sound scared?"

"No, she sounded determined."

Determined? What did that mean? He tugged his phone from his pocket. "Thanks for letting me know. I'll check with her and make sure she's okay. I can't believe she'd…"

Luke's eyebrows rose, and Eric realized that it had just become obvious that he knew Beth pretty damn well. Luke spun on one foot and didn't say another word before walking out.

Eric hit the call button, but the call went straight to voice mail. He was suddenly starkly afraid. Surely Kendall wouldn't have hurt her in any way? He rushed for the door with a curse and headed straight for his car.

Her shop was closer than her apartment, so Eric headed there first. Risking a seriously hefty speeding ticket, he made it in two minutes flat, and breathed a huge sigh of relief when he saw her red car in the lot.

He pulled in, wheels squealing against the blacktop, and jumped out as soon as he hit the brake.

When he burst into the store, everyone looked up, including Beth.

"Beth! Are you all right?"

"Of course," she said, but her eyes slid away, and she looked nervously around.

"But I thought…"

She tipped her head toward the back, and Eric followed her to a small office that was lined with stocking shelves full of merchandise. Beth closed the door and paced away from him, her arms folded tight.

"What happened?" he demanded. "Are you okay?"

"I'm fine. I don't know what you're talking about."

"Luke told me you withdrew your story about Monica. Roland Kendall obviously threatened you in some way. What did he do?"

"Nothing," she said. "I lied about what she said."

"You did not."

"I did. I lied about it because I was always jealous of Monica. But in the end, I couldn't live with it. It's just that simple."

"You're lying to me," he said, hearing the shock in his own voice.

She shook her head and moved carefully to her desk to sit down. Her gaze fell to her hands as she twisted them together.

"You're lying." He couldn't imagine why it hurt, but it did. "Why?"

She shook her head again.

"Wow. You know what? It doesn't matter, anyway."

She blinked, looking startled at the anger in his voice.

Eric was startled, too. He hadn't realized he was furious. "What do you mean?" she whispered.

"You don't know?"

She finally looked up. "Know what?"

"The D.A. had enough evidence to charge Monica regardless. They didn't need your story anymore. So I don't know why you lied, but you could have saved yourself the trouble."

Her face went startlingly pale. "They arrested her?"

"No. When it got to that point, Kendall agreed to deal. He's going to cut off funding to Graham."

"Oh." She looked vaguely ill.

"Beth, what did he do?"

"Nothing," she insisted. "I lied. That's all." Her eyes filled with tears.

"Tell me what happened, damn it!"

"It doesn't matter."

"It matters to me. You lied to me and you did something that might have ruined this case. So it matters to me!"

She shrugged, and the fury inside him broke open and spilled out.

"What was he going to do? Get you fired from this great job? Wait. I know! Maybe he was going to ruin your reputation!"

Her gaze sharpened at the sarcasm in his words. "What's that supposed to mean?"

"Did he pay you off, is that it?"

She stood up. "What did you mean about my reputation?"

"You know what I meant."

Too late, he saw the pain in her eyes. "I'm sorry," he said in a rush. "That was really insensitive. I was pissed and I… With the column and the classes and all this… stuff…" He gestured toward a stack of sex toys on one of the shelves. His fury was receding now, though he was still reeling over what she'd done.

"You meant my reputation is already ruined, so who could possibly care about that."

"I don't think your reputation is *ruined*. What are you talking about? I just meant that you have a reputation for being edgy. Sexual. It wasn't like the guy was going to set you up for a scandal."

She pointed at the door. "Get out."

Eric jumped up. "Beth, I'm sorry I said that."

"You're sorry? Sorry you think I'm so used up and jaded that nobody could possibly insult me?"

"That's not what I said, and this isn't my fault." Tears welled in her eyes and her chin trembled. "God, don't cry, Beth." He started around the desk, but she moved away.

"I'm sorry I said that."

"Just go," she said.

"Come on. I just want to know what happened. I was worried about you. Christ, I don't seem to be doing a good job of explaining myself today. Let's calm down, all right. We can—"

"There is no *we*, Eric. I told you that from the start."

"Things have changed. I care about you."

"You *care* about me?" she bit out. "Oh, yeah? You have a lot of respect for me, too, I bet. The girl you don't want anyone to know about."

"Don't act like you didn't enjoy the secrecy as much as I did. And let's not pretend you had a lot of respect for me at first."

"Because you're a liar," she said.

"You're lying to me right now!"

She pressed her lips together.

"I lied to you when we hardly knew each other. But you're lying to me right now. To my *face.* Beth, please..."

"This is over," she whispered.

"Please don't do this. Not now. You said you were comfortable with me. I know what you meant, because I felt it, too. That's not comfort, it's something more. It's trust and—"

"I don't trust anyone," she reminded him. "Especially a man who'd sneer about my reputation and my job as if it were nothing but trash."

"You know what?" he growled. "If that's what you think of me, then maybe this is over."

"It *is* over!" she yelled. "It was never anything to begin with!"

He slammed her office door when he left, pretending to himself that he was mad. That she'd pissed him off. Infuriated him. But the truth was that he was reeling inside, his brain slowly spinning so that he hardly noticed the people in the store staring wide-eyed as he left.

Eric would have to find a new hobby.

But it felt suspiciously as if he'd have to find a new heart, as well.

CHAPTER TWENTY-ONE

A DAY PASSED WITHOUT any word from Kendall. More importantly, a day passed without word from her father. Beth couldn't relax, though. She couldn't ever relax, because Kendall could call her father at any moment. He could do it today, tomorrow, a year from now. She wouldn't know until it happened.

One day, she'd be walking through her life, happy and unaware, and her phone would ring, and it would be her father telling her he couldn't love her anymore.

The scenario would hang over her like an ax. And Roland Kendall had a long memory.

After work she took a long walk along City Creek, trying to let her mind work. Hoping it would figure something out.

If her dad found out, Beth could just leave. It had worked the first time. She could move anywhere. Get a job in a store that sold nothing but innocent goods. Date men who had no idea she was supposed to be a sexual savant. Send Christmas and birthday cards to her parents and hope that they'd speak to her again someday.

For a moment, the idea fell over her in a wave of relief. She could leave. Start over again. As if she was an eighteen-year-old girl with her whole life ahead of her. An eighteen-year-old girl with no self-esteem who had to run away from everything that hurt her.

She couldn't believe it had happened again. Her sexual desire used like a whip against her. In that moment, Beth hated everyone. Kendall, Monica, Eric. Her mother and father. Christopher. Cairo, with her happy smiles and confidence. And Beth even hated herself. *Especially* herself.

But beneath the hate, she was hollow again, and maybe, in the end, that was the safest way to be.

Beth sighed as she watched kids wade into the shallow, icy water of the creek. It didn't matter what time of year it was, there was always someone challenging themselves to dare that water. She'd done it herself just last spring. Like so many things in life, that first step was an awful, painful shock. It seemed unbearable. But eventually the cold became an ache. And finally, if you stuck it out, you adjusted, you got a little numb, and it was fine.

That was what she should have done. She should have been brave. Instead, she'd panicked and now she had to live with the lie she'd told to protect herself.

"To protect my dad," she murmured, not believing it in the least.

The truth was that she'd buckled to Roland Kendall out of fear, and like any decision made out of fear, it had been a terrible idea.

In that moment of panic, she'd decided that Kendall's threat had been a sign. She'd been unhappy for months, Annabelle was thinking of selling the shop, and she and her father were finally getting to know each other again.

But it had been wrong. So wrong for so many reasons. Dishonest and cowardly and hurtful to Eric, not to mention illegal. Now, in the light of a new day, she couldn't believe she'd let Kendall have that power over her. She had to take it back.

She would have to be honest with her father. Maybe in the end, it would be a good thing. Maybe she'd be happier being honest. Or maybe he'd never speak to her again.

As she walked to her car, Beth tried not to think of that look on his face when the principal had handed her dad the photographs he'd confiscated. Beth had clutched her stomach and breathed carefully through her mouth, trying not to be sick on the principal's floor. Her mother had frowned in confusion when she'd looked at the photos. But her father... Her father's face had fallen into terrible, devastating grief. As if the photos had captured the pale corpse of a beloved daughter, instead of a simple moment of stupid teenage lust. And when he'd turned to Beth, he'd looked at her with hate, as if she'd been the one to kill his sweet little daughter.

He'd eventually forgiven her, or at least they'd reconciled. But this time, the truth might very well be too much for him.

It was a ninety-minute drive to Hillstone, and her knuckles were white the whole way. She couldn't feel her fingers, she didn't care.

She didn't have to call ahead to see if her parents were home. They were always home. Her father had retired as vice president of the local bank years ago. Her mother had long ago devoted most of the hours of her day to her garden and to knitting. They were the perfect retired couple, happy and snug in the house they'd owned for forty years. It was a warm, comforting bubble, and Beth was about to walk up and burst it.

Just as she came over a hill and spotted the first

buildings of town, Beth's phone rang. When she saw Eric's name on the screen, she hit Decline and drove on. She didn't want to talk to him. He knew nothing about her family or her real life. He thought she was nothing more than a walking, talking sexual adventure. The irony of it was like a dull knife to her heart. She'd been real with him. For once, she'd been a real person in bed. Too real, apparently, since it was all he could see about her.

Beth pulled into her parents' driveway just as the last glimmers of twilight faded beyond the trees. She'd only just started to enjoy coming home again, but that was about to change. Another bad memory to add to the pile. The worst part was that there were so many good memories buried underneath. She wished she could get to them without having to wade through the others.

Though she dragged her feet, her parents' sidewalk was only ten feet long. She was at their door within seconds. It felt odd to knock like a stranger, then wait for the sound of her father's footsteps.

He opened the door, and his face broke into such a happy grin that Beth wanted to weep. "Hi, Daddy."

"Beth! What are you doing here? Linda, Beth is here!" He pulled her into a hug, and the familiar scent of his clothing made her put her arms around and squeeze as tight as she could. This could be her last chance to feel his strong arms around her. This could be the last time he'd want to touch her. Eighteen years ago, he hadn't looked at her for months.

Her mom came bustling over to hug Beth, as well. "What are you doing here, sweetheart?"

"Oh, I just wanted to see you," she said, a lie so transparent that even her parents looked uncomfortable.

"Well, come in," her mom said. "We just had ice cream. Would you like a bowl?"

She followed her mom to the kitchen, but shook her head. "No, thank you."

"Coffee, then." She was reaching for the Sanka before Beth answered. "Are you staying over? I'll go put clean sheets on your bed."

"No, I'm not staying, Mom."

She sat down at the table, and her dad sat next to her, immediately taking her hand. "Is everything okay?"

Beth met her mom's wide eyes and looked away. "I need to tell you something."

For a moment, her dad looked a little excited. Maybe he thought she was going to marry Eric. Or maybe he thought she *had* to marry Eric, which wouldn't be the correct order of things, but would still result in Beth being a happily married mother, after all.

"I did something really stupid just because I'm afraid of telling you the truth. Like a scared little girl. It's not even a bad thing, really."

"What is it?" her father asked.

Her heart pounded. "I don't actually work at a bra store. I've wanted to tell you for a while, but I didn't quite know how to say it. I manage a place called the White Orchid."

"I don't understand." He looked toward his wife, but she was staring intently at the cups as she ladled instant coffee into them. "What do you mean?"

"It's a store in Boulder that sells women's clothing and lingerie, but it also sells…marital aids."

She watched her father's mouth form the words. He started to shake his head, but then the confusion in his eyes cleared to understanding.

"It's a nice place," she said quickly. "Ninety percent of our customers are women. It's bright and pretty inside, and—"

He let go of her hand and his spine straightened until he seemed to loom over her. "You're telling me you work at a place that sells pornographic items?"

"It's not…it's not like one of those old places in the city where creepy men hang around, Dad. It's a place where women can feel safe when they—"

He stood up and walked away. "This is outrageous," he said, his voice rising. Her mom stayed with her back to the kitchen, spoon still clutched in her hand. "Did you know about this?" he shouted at his wife.

She didn't answer.

"How long has this been going on?"

"Dad—"

"How many years have you both been lying to me?"

"Dad, listen. I'm sorry. I didn't want to tell you because I knew you'd be upset. But it was wrong to—"

"Upset?" he shouted. "Upset? I'm ashamed. And horrified."

"Dad—" she tried again, but he wasn't interested in a conversation.

"No wonder you don't have a husband. What kind of man would want to marry a woman like you?"

And just like that, she was seventeen again, only this time, she knew how it would turn out. Her dad, a man who rarely raised his voice to anyone, would yell vile things at her. He'd be cruel and cold. And then he'd stop speaking to her entirely.

"Thomas," her mother said, her voice cracking hard in the quiet room.

"I should've known," he muttered. "After what you did—"

"Thomas!"

He stopped his pacing and looked at his wife.

"Stop that. Her generation isn't like ours. I'll bet Beth has plenty of nice young men to date, don't you? Like that Eric, for example."

"Mom, I…I do, but that's not the point. I have friends, and I'm happy, and I'm good at what I do. I'm not hurting anyone. I'm part of the community."

"That whole town is full of hippies," he snapped.

"So what if it is?" Beth demanded. "This town is full of supposedly good people, and they were cruel to me, Dad. They were mean and nasty."

"You made your bed," he said.

"Oh, you made that perfectly clear. Really, you couldn't have made it any clearer. I deserved whatever people threw at me because I was a whore!"

"I never called you that," he said.

Beth could hear the truth in his words. He knew he hadn't called her that, because he'd thought it over and over again but had never let himself say it aloud. But he'd wanted to. And *harlot* and *slut* had been close enough that Beth hadn't been able to feel the difference.

"I'm a good person," Beth said past her tight throat.

"A good person? I raised you to go to church and be modest and save yourself for marriage. And you can look at me like I'm a monster, Beth, but I've loved you for years knowing that you don't go to church and you certainly failed at modesty. But I thought you'd at least learned from your mistakes."

"I did learn," she said, pushing to her feet to face him. "I learned that people are cruel. And that boys can do whatever they want because no one expects them to behave any better than animals. And that my body is made for sex, but I'm supposed to pretend to hate it so a nice man will love me. And you know what else I learned, Dad?"

"Beth," her mother whispered, but Beth ignored her.

"I learned that even my own father will call me names and spit on my heart and leave me broken if I'm not the little girl he wants me to be. I learned that unconditional love comes with lots of conditions. And I learned I couldn't trust anyone with my heart, not even the man who was supposed to always, *always* protect it. That's why I've never gotten married, Dad, if you want to know the truth. That's why I've never even been in love. Because instead of taking care of me when I was hurt, you made me wish I was *dead*."

"Beth," her mom said again, and then Beth felt her mother's arms close around her. She started to pull away, but her mom held tight. Beth stayed stiff for a moment, but the hand slowly rubbing her back only made it harder to hold back her tears. Finally, Beth gave in and put her forehead on her mom's shoulder…and she cried.

She cried for that girl who felt as if she'd lost everything. The girl who'd moved from being Daddy's princess to town pariah.

The crying jag passed quickly. She'd gotten most of those tears out long before. Beth wiped her hands over her cheeks, which sent her mother scurrying out to get Kleenex. Beth was left alone with her father, but she didn't look at him.

"I just wanted to tell you the truth," she said, her voice still catching on her rough throat. "Because I don't want to lie anymore. That's all. You don't have to be happy about it, but at least you know who I am."

"Querida," he said. When he didn't say anything more, Beth looked at him. His head was bowed, one hand rubbing the back of his neck. He looked as if he'd shrunk half a foot in a few seconds.

"I'm sorry, Dad," she whispered. And she was sorry. If she could've chosen, she would've been the daughter he wanted. He was a good man, and she loved him so much.

"Querida, I'm so sorry."

She shook her head, but tears fell from her eyes as if they'd never stopped.

"I'm sorry," he said again. "I didn't...I didn't know what to do. I was so angry. And hurt. And I felt helpless. I didn't know how to make it better for you, and that made me furious."

"You made it worse," she whispered.

"I couldn't believe you'd done that. My little girl. I thought you were still drawing pictures of horses and dreaming of your first kiss. I didn't...I'm sorry. I felt like my heart had been cut out."

"I know."

"I wanted to kill everyone who'd looked at those pictures. I wanted to beat that boy to a pulp. But in the end, I couldn't do anything except take it out on you."

She nodded, and when he took her into his arms, Beth wanted to crawl into his lap and cry for hours. But that little girl was gone, so she only let herself hang on to him for a few heartbeats before she pulled away.

He hugged her one last time. "I love you so much, *querida.* I can't pretend I'm happy about what you've been doing. I can't even pretend to accept it."

"I know."

"But you're my heart, Beth. You always have been."

Her mom stood in the doorway with the box of tissues, but instead of offering them to Beth, she pulled out a bunch and pressed them to her own wet face. "Sit down," she whispered. "Have some coffee."

"There's something else." Beth sighed. "This will take a while to explain."

"What is it?" her mom asked, rushing to take the hot water from the microwave.

Beth grabbed a Kleenex for herself and blew her nose.

Her mom brought the instant coffee over and both her parents sat on the other side of the table, waiting. So she told them. The whole story of the Kendalls and the brewery and Monica calling.

"When Roland Kendall called you, he was trying to figure out a way to control me. He found out you didn't know about the store, and he threatened to tell you."

"He threatened you?" her father asked.

"Yes. And I did what he asked. I took back the story I'd told the police, because I didn't want Roland Kendall to tell you the truth about me."

"Oh, *querida.*"

"I know. I'm ashamed," she whispered. "So I'm trying to make it right."

"Well, you can go to the police. Tell them—"

"It doesn't matter. That's resolved, and despite what I did, it worked out."

"But he threatened you! You should tell the police. If they—"

She shrugged. "He has a team of lawyers, Dad. Nothing is going to happen to him."

Her dad ran a hand over his face.

"I'm sorry," Beth said softly. "I'm sorry I let that bastard make me afraid. But mostly I'm sorry I've been lying to you for so long, because it wasn't fair to either of us."

"Beth." He took her hand. "Please just tell me you're not going to stay at that place. You could get a position anywhere. You could do something amazing with your life."

"You know what? I think I will do something amazing, actually. I just have to figure out what it is."

CHAPTER TWENTY-TWO

ERIC COULDN'T REMEMBER the last time he'd gotten drunk. He squinted down at the bottle of beer and tried to think. In college, maybe? Or just after?

Whenever it had been, he was working damn hard at rectifying it now, and his secluded, sunny patio was the perfect place to do it in privacy.

Wallace had returned to the brewery—sporting a smile beneath his beard that made clear his trip had gone well. Faron was back in Colorado and she was staying at Wallace's house. "And," he'd added with a gleam in his eye, "she's a trained chef. I'm going to have her come in and cook for Jamie."

"Jesus," Eric muttered, taking another swig of beer. That was just what they needed, a volatile couple working side by side in the back of the brewery. It would be a disaster, but Eric was staying out of it. Jamie could hire whoever he wanted. It was none of Eric's business. He stretched out on his patio chair and propped his feet on the railing. It was cool today, but the noon sun was hot on his chest and it felt good. Or maybe that was the beer.

As for the brewery, Eric had no idea what his business was there anymore. If he wasn't a Donovan, who was he? But if he *was* a Donovan, why did he feel so out of place? Maybe he'd find an answer in the bottom of the next bottle. It was a Donovan brew, after all.

He tucked the empty into the six-pack and opened the fourth bottle. But when his phone rang, he set the beer down so hard that it foamed over onto the cement. "Shit." He grabbed the phone, hoping it was Beth, but Tessa's name popped onto the screen.

"Crap," he muttered.

"Hello to you, too," she said.

"I'm not interested in a meeting or group therapy or anything. What do you want?"

"Jeez, you're in a bad mood."

"Obviously."

"Fine," she huffed. "Just listen. It's Mom's birthday today, and I can't get away. Will you buy some flowers and take them to her grave?"

"Are you serious?"

"Yes, I do it every year, but I'm swamped here and I'm afraid I won't get out before dark. Please? For Mom?"

How was he supposed to say no to that? He looked mournfully at the beer bottle. He was only very slightly tipsy, and he really wanted to get drunk enough to stop thinking about Jamie and their dad and the brewery. And Beth. Christ, he'd really screwed that up. Or she had. He had no idea what had happened.

"Fine." He sighed.

"Thank you. There's a little vase at the foot of the grave, so just a few flowers will do."

"Right."

Eric stole one last drink of beer, then headed for the shower. He did his best not to think of Beth, or what they might do in a shower, and how hot it would be. She wasn't returning his calls. It was over. She was done.

Hell, he was done, too. She didn't trust him and she never would. And he couldn't trust her, either. She'd lied to him. About Roland Kendall. And about more than that.

He'd finally read her column about threesomes, and her promise that she never dated more than one guy at a time had flown out the window. Hard not to date two guys at once when you were sleeping with both of them. Together.

Maybe that was why she couldn't trust anyone, because she knew she wasn't trustworthy herself.

Eric leaned his forehead against the cold tile of the bathroom wall and willed himself not to think about it. Beth had been a temporary pleasure in his life. Nothing more. And if he'd let his feelings get a little too deep…

"Fuck," he whispered.

She wasn't the type to settle down, obviously. He'd get over it.

As he got out of the shower and dried his hair, he told himself he definitely wouldn't check her column next week. When he pulled on jeans and a T-shirt, he tried not to remember her in his bed. "It was just sex," he told himself. "Get over it."

At least to her it had been. And if he wanted to play in the big leagues, he'd have to toughen up.

Eric grabbed his wallet and keys and headed out the door. It was only two miles to the cemetery, and he still felt mildly buzzed, so he decided to walk.

There was a flower shop on the way to the cemetery, so he headed that way. Had Tessa really done this every year? How had he not realized that? He visited their graves sometimes, but not often. He couldn't feel them there, not as he did when he was at Tessa's house. There, he could actually see them, in memories like scratchy videos. His mom bringing Jamie home from the hospital. His dad painting a room pink for Tessa before she was born. And that constant feeling of wanting to get things right. To make sure that Michael Donovan never regretted adopting him, not even for a second.

When Eric got to the flower shop, he couldn't bring himself to buy a tiny five-dollar bouquet of flowers, so he bought a huge spray to lay on top of her headstone. She'd been an amazing mom, on her own and with Michael Donovan. Eric should've done this before. He should've brought flowers every month.

Lost in thought, and his vision slightly obscured by baby's breath, Eric didn't realize there was someone else at the grave until he was halfway up the hill.

He lowered the arrangement. Jamie.

"Damn it, Tessa," Eric cursed under his breath. Jamie was there, a bouquet already tucked into the metal vase at the foot of her grave.

Eric was frozen. He wanted to simply turn and leave, but that seemed like an awfully petty thought as he stood in front of his mother's grave. He could already see exactly how Tessa's brain had spit this plot out. *They can't fight on top of Mom's grave. They'll have to talk.*

Eric started forward with a resigned frown.

When Jamie looked up, he didn't even seem surprised. His eyes slid to the big spray of flowers in Eric's hand and his mouth flattened.

"What?" Eric asked.

"Nothing."

Eric laid the flowers on her gravestone, and then

they both just stood looking at it, their hands in their pockets, silence between them.

Eric cleared his throat. "I never seem to know the right thing to say to you," he murmured.

Jamie shot him a look before he went back to staring at the headstone. Silence fell again and dragged out for a full minute. Eric was about to turn and leave when Jamie finally spoke. "You know what I always hated? That you had to be perfect. You had to do everything the right way every single time. It made me feel like shit."

Eric shook his head, trying to clear the shock. "What?"

"You were my big brother, and I wanted to be like you. But I'm not perfect. I'm not even close. It was bad enough before the accident, but then…" He shrugged and looked away.

"I didn't want you to be perfect, Jamie. I just wanted to do the best job I could. For you."

"Maybe after, but you've always been that way. You always set the curve so damn high, I had no chance of meeting it. Straight As. Jobs after school. You did all your chores and then some. You never broke any rules. Never complained."

"I couldn't," Eric said. "Don't you get that? I wasn't competing with you, Jamie. There was no competition. You were his son."

"Oh, come on. Stop with that shit. You—"

"I'm serious. It's not Dad's fault. I know he loved me. But he only adopted me a couple of months before you were born. It was still brand-new, and then there you were, cute and adorable and *his*. The perfect baby. You even looked just like him. I loved you as much as they did, but it seemed impossible that I could compete with that. I had to be the perfect son, because he took me on. He loved me even though I wasn't his. What was I supposed to do with that?"

"He never treated you any different!"

"But I felt different. Jesus, I didn't even look like I belonged in the family! So I made damn sure I did everything right. I wasn't born knowing I belonged. Not like you. So yeah, maybe I did need him to ask me to stay at the brewery, so I could know he really wanted me there."

When Eric looked at Jamie this time, his brother was staring at him. No smirk on his lips, no irritation in his eyes. Eric flushed and shifted a little farther away, but Jamie held his gaze.

"Mom and Dad would talk about you over dinner sometimes," Jamie said. "She didn't want you to go away, but he said you needed to spread your wings. And he thought you'd learn things that would be good for the brewery in the long run. He wanted you there, Eric. Don't doubt that."

For a moment, Eric didn't feel it. They were just words. Nothing more. But then his breath got stuck in his throat. He had to swallow in order to draw air in. "Yeah?" he managed to say.

"Yeah," Jamie answered.

Had it been that simple? Michael Donovan had been trying to set him free, and Eric had only wanted to stay? God, how tragic was that?

He tried to clear the sorrow from his throat. "I'm sorry if I made you feel like I needed you to be perfect," he murmured. "It wasn't what I wanted for you, Jamie."

Jamie nodded, but now he was the one shifting from foot to foot as if he was uncomfortable. "It's not all you. I felt…" Clearing his throat, he dropped his head and stared at his feet. His neck slowly turned red.

"Hey," Eric said. "You okay?"

He shrugged, but didn't look up.

"Jamie. What's wrong?"

His shoulders rose on a deep breath. "I don't know how to tell you this. I felt… Jesus. You were so perfect and I felt like the most worthless piece of shit in the world, and I fucking hated you because of it."

"Whoa. What the hell are you—?"

"The accident," Jamie cut in. "It was my fault."

"The car accident?" Eric asked, his mind reeling. "Jamie, you weren't even there."

When Jamie looked up, there were tears in his eyes. *Tears.* And that scared Eric more than anything had in the past thirteen years. Jamie hadn't even cried at the funeral.

Eric started to reach for his shoulder, but Jamie took a step back. "They were coming to pick me up, because I was drunk. I drove my friends to a party and even though I knew I was supposed to drive them home, I got drunk. I didn't know what to do. My friends needed to get home. So I called Mom."

Eric's jaw had dropped. He couldn't think, much less speak.

"They were at home. They wouldn't have even been in the car, much less on that road, except that I'd fucked up and they had to come bail me out." He swiped an angry hand over his eyes even though no tears had fallen. "It was my fault."

"Jamie," Eric breathed. "Why didn't you tell me? Does Tessa know?"

Jamie shook his head. "I've never told anyone but Olivia. I didn't want anyone to know. Especially not you or Tessa. I killed our parents, Eric."

Eric grabbed both his shoulders before he could back away. "You did not."

Jamie laughed and wiped his eyes again. "I'm the one who doesn't deserve the brewery or the name or the family."

"Jesus Christ," Eric cursed, giving him a little shake before he pulled him in for a hug. Jamie's body was stiff with tension, but Eric just hugged him harder. How the hell had Jamie lived with that? "You were just a fuck-ing kid, Jamie. You should have told me."

He shook his head, and Eric felt Jamie's back shud-der beneath his hands. His own eyes burned with grief. "You should have told me," he repeated, his voice crack-ing.

"I couldn't," Jamie rasped.

"It wasn't your fault. Don't say it again. Ever. It was an accident, damn it. If they'd been on their way to pick Tessa up from school, would you blame her?"

"It's not the same."

"Shut the fuck up," Eric ordered.

Jamie shoved him away, his mouth twisted halfway between a grimace and a pained laugh. "Stop telling me what to do. I didn't even want to tell you. Ever. But Olivia said we'd never have peace if we didn't talk."

"Wait a minute." Eric cocked his head, not believ-ing he was even about to ask this. "Did *you* tell Tessa to call me?"

"Yeah."

"Because you wanted to talk?"

"Yeah."

Now they were back to staring in silence again. Eric's head swam with grief and confusion. And huge, utter relief that he finally understood what had been wrong between them for so long. "I can't tell you what to feel for yourself, Jamie, but I'll never blame you. And neither will Tessa. And Mom and Dad thought you were doing the right thing, or they wouldn't have come for you. It wasn't your fault. And I sure as hell never thought I was perfect. So can we just start from here? Try again?"

"I'd like that," Jamie said. "I'm sick of fighting all the damn time." He glanced up. "Plus, my jaw felt like hell for a while there."

"Consider it payback for all the stress you caused me over the years. I thought you'd never make it out of college with a degree."

"Dude, I serve beer. I would've been okay."

Eric growled, but he left it alone. Considering the burden Jamie had been carrying around, it was a miracle he hadn't lost himself entirely. Eric's heart shook at the thought of how bad it could've gotten if Jamie hadn't been a good person deep down inside.

Jamie rubbed a hand hard over his face. "Okay. Does this mean you'll keep doing all the stuff at the brewery that no one else knows how to do? Much as I hate to admit it, we can't do the things you do."

"Actually…no."

Jamie's hand dropped. "No?" he asked warily.

"I haven't figured it out yet," Eric admitted, "but something's got to change."

"Something like what?"

Eric looked down at his mom's grave, wishing like

hell he had someone to help him puzzle it out. It wasn't just the arguments with his brother that had been slowly tearing him up inside. It was more than that. "I'm not happy doing what I'm doing. I need something else."

"You're not thinking of heading east again, are you?"

"No."

"Well, you can't have my job," Jamie growled.

"I don't want your job. But…maybe somebody else's."

CHAPTER TWENTY-THREE

BETH STRETCHED OUT ON the blanket, pointing her toes and raising her hands as far above her head as she could. The sun beat down on her. The breeze danced over her skin. It felt like the last nice day of the year. She knew it wasn't. There'd be other bright, sunny days, but she felt an urgency to soak up the warmth to see her through the winter.

"They'll be back soon," Cairo said, stretching like a cat on her own blanket. The sandstone beneath them was hard under the thin fabric, but it was nearly as warm as the sun.

"Do you need me to do anything else?" Beth asked, hoping the answer was no. She didn't want to move.

"It's all ready," Cairo answered, her own voice drowsy.

"Good."

The climbers had set off well over an hour before, and Beth was glad she hadn't joined them. She needed this peace right now more than she needed to challenge herself. And she did feel peaceful, despite everything. She felt freer than she had in years. She couldn't change what had happened to her, but she could be free of it. She *was* free of it. No matter what Kendall did.

But nothing was clearer. Because now that she'd been honest with her father, she could see how dishonest she'd been with everyone else. She'd wanted so badly to be everything she'd read about and studied. Everything she'd believed. But she couldn't be *everything*. Nobody could. Cairo had her life with two men, and she was happy with that. She didn't try to fit what other people loved into her life, too. How could there be room for that?

Beth had been trying to be too many people, all at one time. But how was she going to figure out who the real Beth was?

The wind lifted a strand of hair and dragged it over her face. She slipped it back behind her ear. Over the past few months, she'd discovered a few true things. She loved helping people at the White Orchid. She loved putting them at ease and guiding them in the right direction. And she loved the family she'd made for herself at the store. But that was the extent of it. The rest…the rest of it she could do without. And frankly, some of it she was starting to hate.

One more true thing was that she didn't want to be sexually omnivorous. She just wanted to be comfortable. Which led her to the truest thing of all…Eric Donovan. He'd hurt her, badly. But part of that was her fault. If he hadn't known anything about her but sex, it was because she hadn't let him see.

She sighed and stretched again, wishing she could make things different. If they could just go back and start over. If they could both be honest.

"Here they come," Cairo said.

Beth pushed up to her elbows and raised a hand to her eyes to shade them. Sure enough, Harrison and the others were headed back from the rock face. And Davis was with them.

She stood up and greeted them all with a hug, including Davis. She even sat next to him during the picnic lunch. But this time when he put his hand on her knee, Beth didn't feel the least bit tempted.

But one thing did tempt her.

"Beth?" Harrison called. "Did you make a decision? You want to try?"

She looked down at her hands. Did she want to? "I don't want to go too far, okay?"

"You got it," he said with a wink, walking over to pull her to her feet. "Ready?"

"Maybe."

"Come on. It'll be amazing."

"If you say so."

Twenty minutes later, he had her strapped into a safety harness and tied to a rope. Beth put her hand high on the rock and ran it along an edge until she felt a good hold. She put her foot to a crevice and pushed herself up.

"That's it," Harrison said. "Just climb. I've got you."

"I'm a lot heavier than Cairo, you know."

"You're fine," he said with a laugh. "Use your legs. Keep going."

Beth grabbed for a higher hold and fit her other foot onto a narrow step. She pushed again and reached up. With Harrison urging her on and offering direction from below, she was up to the first flat ledge far quicker than she'd expected. As a matter of fact... She boosted herself up and looked down. "Yikes." She hadn't expected to get this high at all.

"How high am I?" she called down to Harrison.

"Thirty-five feet! You want to go higher?"

Beth looked up. And up. "No!" she yelled back, making him laugh. "But can I stay here for a little while?"

"Absolutely! I'll tie you off so you're secure. Take your time!" He tied the end of the safety line to a metal loop in the ground, then gave her a thumbs-up before finding a comfortable rock to sit on.

Beth let her feet dangle over the ledge. She breathed in deeply and closed her eyes, letting the quiet wash over her. She was alone up here, above the world. Well, a *little* above the world. There was plenty of rock still stretching up above her.

The sun felt even stronger here, and it seeped inside her, relaxing everything. Somebody in the group laughed, the sound bouncing between the cliffs. And when Beth opened her eyes again, the red rocks were deeper, the sky a brighter shade of blue. All the colors were more...honest.

In that moment, higher than she'd ever been, all alone on that narrow ledge, Beth knew exactly what she wanted to do.

CHAPTER TWENTY-FOUR

"Well?" Tessa asked before she even made it all the way into Eric's office. "What happened?"

Jamie followed hot on her heels. "Yeah. What happened?"

Eric raised an eyebrow. "Seriously? You guys can't give me one second to get settled in?"

Tessa dropped into a chair. "Nope."

Jamie followed her lead. "Come on, man. Tell us what he said."

Eric's monitor finally blazed to life, and he tried his best not to be distracted by it. It was Wednesday. He'd checked for Beth's column first thing this morning, but it hadn't been up yet. He shouldn't look. God only knew what it would be about. Whatever it was, it wouldn't help him feel better.

Tessa kicked his desk, making him jump. "Focus, Eric. Jeez."

"All right." He leaned back with a smile. "Wallace has agreed on one condition."

Jamie frowned. "What's that?"

"He wants Faron in as chef."

"I was going to hire her anyway," Jamie said.

Eric laughed. "Yeah, I know. But I didn't tell Wallace that."

"Seriously," Tessa interrupted. "He agreed to everything?"

"I'm going to apprentice to him for a year. After that, we'll pay for him to attend a three-month brewing course in Germany that he's always wanted to take. He's never been able to be away that long, obviously."

Jamie shook his head. "He's really okay with it? Sharing the tank room with you?"

"I told him he'll have the title of brewmaster as long as he wants it, but that I need to be in there, too. We can split some duties and expand others. But I can't stay behind that desk anymore. This is what I want to do. I don't need the title. I just need the work."

"Awesome," Tessa breathed.

"Frankly, I think Wallace is excited to have an indentured servant for the next year. I'll start interviewing someone for a dedicated sales and marketing position next week. Someone who can take over trade show and distribution responsibilities."

Tessa held up a finger. "*We'll* start interviewing. I've got to get along with this person more than you do."

"You got it," he said with a grin. He couldn't believe this was really happening. He was going to get out of this box of an office and into the tank room. "You'll call Faron?" he asked Jamie.

"I'll make an offer right now."

Eric wanted to get started with Wallace today. Hell, yesterday. But he had to get everything in place. He needed to put out the call for a new employee, but first things first....

As soon as Tessa left and closed the door behind her, Eric clicked on his bookmarked link to *The Rail* and held his breath. He didn't know what he thought it would say. Would it be about privacy? Betrayal? Breakups? Or would it just be one of her normal columns, leaving him to wonder if she was talking about a past relationship or a current one? If she'd moved on already and—

The page finally loaded, and Eric's breath hissed between his teeth. Sex & Lies, the title read. Would the whole thing be a shot at him?

He braced himself and started reading, but halfway through he was already reaching for his phone.

Last week, I got an email from a woman who wanted to know whether she should tell her husband the truth about her past. She'd had nearly twenty sex partners, and she knew he wouldn't like that, so wouldn't it be better to lie?

My initial thought was, "No, of course not! You have nothing to be ashamed of!" But it's not so simple, is it? Life is complicated. And frankly, I'm not really qualified to answer the question because my entire sex life has been a lie.

Most of us lie a little. We fudge the numbers. We pretend to like something for our partner, or not to like something that our spouse isn't into.

It's usually about shame. And embarrassment. Sometimes it's just about privacy. For me, it was all those things and more. So here's my confession: I am not Sexuality Personified. I do not know everything about sex. I don't know anything about threesomes. Or domination. Or bisexuality. Or fetishes. That's why I write this column with three other women, because none of us is sexuality personified on her own.

Still, I've tried to be all things to all people.

*Because of that, I've never been me. The real me
is shy, private and not very sexually adventurous.
I've spent so many years trying to hide that from
people that I've hidden myself. And who can love
someone they can't really see?*

*So my advice to the reader is to tell the truth.
But my truth is that I understand why she might
not be able to. It's scary. You might tell him and
he might walk away. I might tell him and he might
walk away. But if he does—*

A soft knock drew Eric's head up. When the door
opened, he stood so quickly that his chair fell over.

"*Beth?* What are you doing here?"

She smiled uncertainly, hanging back in the hallway
as if she wasn't sure he'd want to see her.

"I was just…" He looked from the computer back to
her.

She nodded, still wearing that nervous smile. "Can
we talk?"

"Yes. Of course."

When her smile fell away, he noticed that her hands
were clenched into fists.

"Do you want to go somewhere else?"

"Maybe we could go for a walk? Are you busy?"

Eric walked around and took her hand in answer. He
couldn't talk because she'd curled her fingers into his
and she hadn't pulled away, and that had to be a good
sign, right?

He led her through the back door, trying to ignore
the wide-eyed stares of his brother and sister as they
left. He kept his pace slow, even though he wanted to
race, and Beth held her silence until they reached the

blacktop trail that disappeared into a grove of golden aspen.

He squeezed her hand. "I need to apologize again. For what I said and the way I said it."

"No, it's fine. I've been thinking about it a lot. You were angry, and you had a right to be. I'm so sorry about lying. I called Luke this morning to apologize and try to explain."

"Did you tell him what happened?"

She looked at him, but then her eyes fell to her shoes and she pulled her hand away. "Roland Kendall threatened to tell my dad about the store."

"Oh." He tried to summon up some understanding, but he didn't get it. She was a grown woman.

"I know it must seem silly to you, that I'd panic about that, but there's more to it than you know."

"Okay." He waited, his whole body straining with the need to stop and hurry her up. To make her explain so he could forgive her.

It seemed hours before she spoke. "When I was seventeen, my boyfriend took pictures of me. Nude photos. Some of them were more than that."

"Did you know?"

"Yes. I let him. But what I didn't know was that he would take them to school and show everyone."

"Jesus, Beth. I'm sorry."

"It was bad. Terrible. The worst thing that's ever happened to me. When the principal discovered the pictures, he called my father."

Eric thought of that elegant, old-fashioned man and cringed.

"I'd been Daddy's little girl my whole life. I loved him more than anything in the world. And when he saw those pictures, he didn't love me anymore. That was what it felt like. He said I'd shamed him and my mother and our name. He couldn't even look at me for months."

"Oh, Christ. Beth..."

"School was torture, and when I couldn't take it a moment longer, I asked my dad if I could homeschool for the last two months of my senior year. Do you know what he said?"

Eric shook his head.

"He said, 'If you didn't want to be treated like a slut, you shouldn't have acted like one.' He made me go to school every single day until I graduated, because that was what I deserved."

"I don't know what to say," he whispered. "I know you love your dad, but that's terrible."

"It's why I never told him the truth about working at the White Orchid, but it's also the reason I work there. I wanted to prove something to myself. That sex wasn't bad. That I shouldn't be ashamed. But the truth is every single partner was just a potential betrayal. I could never stop worrying, until I met you."

"Me? Why?"

"I don't know. I can't explain it."

"I read your column," he said, hoping she would keep talking.

She nodded. "I'm glad. I've been lying for a long time. I'm not that experienced. I'm not very good at sex, and I never have been. I can't relax. I can't enjoy myself no matter how hard I try, or maybe because of how hard I try."

"Um..." He didn't get it. Was she just an amazing

actress? "I thought you were pretty good at it," he ventured.

She flashed a quick smile. "It's different with you, Eric."

He stopped so quickly that she had to turn and take a step back. "Is it?"

"Yes. I'm comfortable with you, and you can't know what that means. I..." She reached up to smooth his hair off his brow. Eric took her hand and pressed it to his mouth.

"What are you saying?"

"I'm saying that I want to be honest. And I want to trust. And I want to do that with you, if you're willing to try. No lying about anything. No sneaking around. Just...us."

"Us."

"When you said those things to me, I realized that I was closer to you than I'd been to anyone in years, but you didn't know anything about me except sex. I—"

"That's not true," he cut in, angry now. "That's not true at all. I said that because I was pissed. But I know a lot about you. I know that you laugh at terrible jokes in movies. I know you're generous. I know that when you sleep you tuck your hand under your chin like a little kid and it makes my heart melt. And I know you don't trust anyone, but you're going to trust me."

She ducked her head. "Am I?"

"Yes." He pulled her closer and she slid her arm around his waist. "I'm making changes, too. I've been living my life for other people for thirty-seven years. I'm done with that. I don't want to be perfect anymore. I just want to be me. With you."

"With me?" she whispered. "Does that mean you forgive me?"

"There's nothing to forgive. I know what it's like to be scared."

She tucked her head against his neck, and the scent of her hair set off an ache in his chest that nearly brought tears to his eyes. It hadn't just been sex with her for a while now. In fact, it hadn't ever just been sex. They'd just used that as an excuse to feel this connection.

"I told my dad," she whispered. "I told him the truth. And I'm buying the White Orchid."

"What?" He pulled back, and when Beth looked up she was smiling.

"I'm going to make some changes, and it's going to be exactly what I want it to be, instead of being everything to all people."

"Yeah?" He touched her chin, brushing his thumb against her bottom lip.

"I'm going to make it a little calmer. Fewer novelty items. More lingerie, especially for larger sizes. And the classes will be run by a real therapist, not just me pretending I know what I'm talking about."

"More lingerie? I like that."

"But just the higher-end stuff. Really pretty things that compliment women's bodies."

"Wait. You're not getting rid of that black leather number I saw on the wall, are you?"

Her eyebrows rose. "Leather, huh?"

"I just thought it would look great on you." He pressed a kiss to her mouth while she was still laughing, but he pulled back when a startling thought hit him. "That whole toy thing in your column?"

She grinned. "Yeah?"

"Was that you?"

"No."

"Oh." Eric felt the blush begin at his throat and work its way up in a slow path of scalding heat. "I see."

"It wasn't my column, but I definitely had fun pretending it was."

"You were *pretending?*"

She laughed and pressed her mouth to his again. "Not with you," she said into his kiss. "Never with you. But I have one more confession," Beth whispered.

Eric felt more than a little nervous. "What?"

She leaned closer, her lips brushing his ear. "I stole a pair of your underwear and keep them in my sock drawer."

"You're lying."

"I'm not. I wanted a memento."

"Wait a minute. You just wrote a whole column declaring that you weren't a pervert!"

Her lips touched his ear, then trailed down his neck until Eric shivered. "I lied," she breathed. And he really, truly hoped she had.

CHAPTER TWENTY-FIVE

"Are you nervous?" Beth asked, giving his hand a re-assuring squeeze.

Eric turned his head and breathed in the scent of her hair. "No," he answered. Any minute now, people would start to show up for the grand reopening of Donovan Brothers. The front room looked perfect.

"A little?" she pressed.

"A little. I'm nervous for Jamie. I want everything to be perfect."

"It will be," she assured him, and Eric felt better, even though she couldn't have any idea. He glanced back, through the small windows in the double doors. It was strange to look back and see the kitchen so busy. They'd only used it for prep work in the past.

"Maybe I should go check on the—"

"It's fine," Beth assured him. "Jamie's got it under control. Leave him alone."

"Right. Okay. Leave him alone."

"Good boy," she said with a smile that immediately made him think of sex.

Eric raised an eyebrow. "Good boy? Is this something new you're into?"

Laughing, she tried to swing away from him, but Eric caught her and tugged her close again. "Tell the truth.

You've dreamed of getting me in a dog collar, haven't you?"

When she threw her head back with a loud laugh, Eric took the opportunity to taste her neck. "Mmm."

"Stop!"

"Why?"

"Because there are people…"

"Maybe that's what I'm into."

She clutched his hair and tugged him back. Did she think that would make him less interested? But her wide smile finally distracted him. The sight of her so happy unleashed a frighteningly warm feeling in his chest.

"I have an idea," she said. "If you really want to try something new."

"Oh, yeah?" He leaned a little closer.

"Have you ever thought about…waxing?"

"Waxing? Who?"

"You."

He drew back so quickly that he nearly stumbled. "Are you *insane?*"

"Come on. I hear it's amazing."

"Amazingly painful!"

When she started giggling, Eric managed to calm down, though his skin still crawled with terror. "Are you serious?"

She shrugged. "Rex and Harrison do it for Cairo."

"I don't want to know that!"

"Sorry," she said with a shrug that said she wasn't sorry at all.

"You're a monster," he muttered just before the doors flew open.

Jamie's mouth was grim as he faced the front door. "It's time."

"Are you ready?" Eric asked.

"Maybe."

He slapped his brother on the back. "You'll be great, Jamie. You need any help?"

"We're good."

An hour later, the place was packed with people. Like any normal night, the brewery rang with laughter and music. But the differences were strange and surreal. There were plates and silverware crowded on the tables, the air smelled like spice and tomatoes, and every single face in the crowd was a good friend.

Luke was there, helping out with the occasional spilled glass or dropped utensil. And he'd brought along Simone, who cradled her baby girl in her arms.

Jamie's girlfriend, Olivia, had brought a few of her friends from the university, and she looked more relaxed than Eric had ever seen her, her face aglow with triumph for Jamie.

The other three dozen people were all friends they'd made over the years. Former servers and employees. Women who worked at the White Orchid. Allies from the local business community.

Smiling, Eric loaded a tray with dirty plates and took it to the kitchen.

If the front room looked subtly different, the kitchen was a different place entirely. Between the oven and the new fridge and the freezer and racks of flatware...he wouldn't have recognized it if he hadn't seen the transformation himself. And Faron ruled over it all like a tiny, peaceful dictator. Her word was law in the kitchen, even if her voice was soft and gentle. No one wanted to disappoint her, certainly not Wallace. The man was as lovesick as ever, though much happier now that he'd convinced Faron to love him back. What Eric hadn't expected was a kinder, gentler Wallace. He didn't like to yell, because that always drew a disappointed frown from Faron's direction. Hiring Faron may, in fact, have saved Eric's sanity. It had certainly saved his eardrums.

"Hey," Luke said as he pushed through the double doors with two beers in his hands. "You look like you need a drink."

"Thanks." Eric took the lager that Luke offered and clinked it against Luke's beer. *"Sláinte."*

"It's a good night," Luke said. "The pizzas are all great. Hell, I even liked the one with marinated eggplant on it."

"It is a good night. I'm glad you brought Simone. I haven't seen the baby since September."

"She's big now, huh? Smiles and everything."

"Is it true you babysat this weekend?"

Luke cringed. "With Tessa's help."

"Are you in training?"

Luke gave him a sidelong glance. "We haven't discussed that yet."

"Yeah," Eric said with a grin. "I bet that conversation will happen soon. I mean, I can only assume you're thinking of proposing, since you're living with her."

Luke shifted, clearly trying to keep a secret, but Eric just stared.

"Yeah," he finally admitted. "I'm thinking about it."

"Good. Don't think too long."

Luke cleared his throat. "Anyway, I wanted to tell you that I think Graham Kendall is coming back to the States. The D.A.'s working out a deal."

"Really?"

"Yep. His dad cut him off, but he's still paying for

the lawyers. Graham will get some jail time and some hefty fines. And I'm sure he's going to face quite a few civil cases."

"Good. And Monica?" Eric pressed.

Luke just shook his head. "We had to give that up."

Eric wanted to tell Luke about Roland Kendall and what he'd done, but Beth had been adamant. She didn't want any more trouble.

"Thank you," he said to Luke. "I know a lot of cops wouldn't have pushed as hard as you did."

"I had my reasons," he said with a wink. He tapped his beer against Eric's one more time, then headed back out to the front.

Beer in hand, Eric watched Faron work with her line cook for a few minutes, but his head was buzzing. Everything was so new. So happy. Needing peace for just a moment, he wandered toward the tank room, using the excuse that one of the bright tanks had been having cooling problems. It took only a moment to check the temperature and pressure gauges, but the faint hum of the machinery was as relaxing as ocean waves for him. Eric pulled up a stool, leaned against a tank and closed his eyes, feeling more at home than he ever had before.

"MOM! DAD!" BETH CALLED, rushing forward to give her parents a hug. "You made it!"

"We wouldn't have missed it, sweetheart," her mom said. Beth squeezed her hard, then let herself be folded into her father's arms. He'd worn the same cologne for fifty years, and the smell of it tightened her throat with happy tears.

"*Querida,* we've missed you."

"I'm sorry, Dad. I've been so busy, trying to get

Cairo fully trained as manager before the end of the year."

"I'm happy, so happy you're changing that place."

Beth shook her head. "I'm not changing it that much. There will still be plenty of things for you to be embarrassed about, Dad."

"I'm sure," he said, though he was clearly telling himself that she really was turning it into a bra store. If that made it easier for him, she was fine with it. He'd been surprisingly silent on the issue, and she could let him have that.

Financially, it wouldn't be easy for Beth, but every single morning, Beth woke up excited. She was going to be helping women every day. She'd contracted a sex therapist to give classes and seminars every single week. Cairo was running the column and helping to narrow down the toy selection. They were turning half of the back room into a fitting and dressing area, complete with gorgeous pearl satin on the walls. The other half would still showcase toys, but only the best of the best. None of the novelty items that had always made Beth uncomfortable. No more blow-up dolls or two-foot-tall phalluses.

Hiding a smile, Beth turned away to look around the crowded room for Eric, but her dad touched her arm. "What's that?" he asked, pointing to a sign that had just been hung the day before. Beth nearly groaned at the Devil's Cock logo.

"A new beer," she explained.

"Ah. I might have to try it."

Beth cleared her throat. "Let me find you a—"

"Just a moment. I wanted to tell you something." He drew her to the side.

"What?"

He glanced around. "I went to see Roland Kendall."

"You *what?*"

"I've been trying to contact him for weeks, actually. I finally caught him on his way into work yesterday morning."

"Dad… *Why?* Why would you do that?"

"I wanted to make this right for you, Beth."

His quiet words cut through her worry, and she shut her mouth so quickly that her teeth clicked. He didn't say more, but she heard the meaning behind that simple sentence. The things he couldn't say. And she loved him for it. "But there's nothing to make right. I told you about the store."

"I spoke to him father-to-father. I told him he should be ashamed of himself."

"I don't think that kind of thing works on a man like him, Dad."

Her father smiled. "Regardless, I let him know I was proud of you, *querida.* And that he could never change that. Nothing ever will."

"Aw, Dad." She let herself fall into his arms, but she wasn't the least bit tempted to cry. He was trying. A little late, but better late than never. Much better.

"Thank you," she whispered.

"Don't thank me, Beth. It's what I should have done a long time ago."

"Come on. Let's find you a table. I know you miss the amazing Italian restaurants in Argentina, but I think you're going to love this pizza."

After seeing her parents seated and waving a server over, Beth stopped at Luke's table and leaned close to Simone Parker. "How did it go?" she whispered.

"The date?" She transferred her tiny daughter to her other shoulder and patted her back. "It was a dud, but at least I tried it. Next time it won't be so scary."

"Come into the shop next week. I've got a great new line."

"I will."

Beth was still smiling when she slipped into the back to find Eric. She hadn't seen him for a while, and she worried he was getting in Jamie's way. But Eric wasn't in the kitchen, and he wasn't in his office. She finally wandered farther back and spotted him in the tank room. She stopped in her tracks to watch him, his private moment framed behind glass.

A pint of beer in hand, he sat in a pose of complete relaxation…his head resting on the steel tank behind him, eyes closed, a small smile turning his lips up. He seemed to relax a little more every day. He was just… happier.

Beth didn't want to intrude on his space, so she backed up a few feet and turned away to give him a few more minutes alone. But once those minutes were up, she sent a text. *Can you meet me in your office? I want to show you something.*

His office door opened more quickly than she'd expected it to. He shut it behind him.

"Hey," she said.

She was perched on his desk, and his eyes slid down her legs. "Hey, yourself. Is there something I can do for you?"

Beth laughed, happy that her carefully worded text had done the job. She uncrossed her legs and watched his eyes widen for a moment. "I actually just wanted to check on you," she said, laughing. "And my parents are here. I thought you might want to say hi. You know how much they love you."

"I'm a pretty great guy." He stepped closer and spread his hand over the part of her thigh exposed when her skirt had hitched up.

"Everybody thinks you're so upstanding and reserved," she said.

"Well, I don't know how to tell you this, but I think my family suspects we're having sex."

"No." She edged her legs farther apart, sighing when his thumb snuck higher up her inner thigh.

"It's just a hunch. Plus, haven't you noticed the way Jamie has blushed every time he saw you this week?"

"Actually, now that you mention it, he has seemed nervous. I thought it was grand-opening jitters."

"Wrong. It was your last column."

Beth frowned, trying to remember. Then she slapped a hand over her mouth to stifle her horrified laugh. "Oh, my God. Didn't you tell him I didn't write that one?"

"I thought I'd let him squirm for a little while. And he's finally starting to treat me with the respect and awe I deserve."

She slapped his arm, but Eric caught her wrist and drew it around his waist as he slipped between her knees. "Was there anything else you wanted to show me?"

"We need to get back to the party," she murmured, already distracted by the heat of his body.

"Do we? You're always telling me to give Jamie his space."

"Yes, but…" His hand slid up, pushing her skirt higher.

"Jesus, you feel good," he whispered.

"Eric, we can't. Not now."

"Aren't you supposed to be the kind of woman who'll do anything, anywhere?"

She smiled as his mouth brushed hers. "You know I'm not."

"Funny." His breath chased across her cheek as he kissed toward her neck. "You always are with me."

Beth felt a proud grin stretch across her face. "That's true. I think—" His thumb dragged along her panties, and she gasped when he touched her clit. "Oh." His mouth sucked at the perfect spot on her neck, and she sighed as his thumb pressed again. She was immediately, unbearably aroused.

"Eric," she whispered, meaning to say something and forgetting what it was. Instead, she brushed her knuckles along his pants, just to know that he was already hard for her. She touched him again, tracing her fingertips along the zipper.

"Do it," he ordered.

Her breath hitched at the hardness of the words. Over the past few weeks, he'd picked up on the way she reacted when he got assertive. Every day, he pushed a little further. And every day, she yielded a little more. Funny, she'd always thought that as a strong, educated woman she needed to be strong in bed. But now she was brave enough to give more than strength.

Beth unbuttoned him and eased the zipper down. He shoved her skirt up with both hands and reached for her panties.

"Eric, we can't. Someone might look in and…" Still she tipped her hips up to help him slip the underwear off.

"I think you like that," he murmured, pulling a condom out. "I think that might actually be something you *are* into. The danger of being caught."

Breathing fast, she watched him roll the condom on, but her eyes flickered past his shoulder to the small window in the door. "But they might... Your family. They already think I'm a freak."

"Mmm," he said, a murmur of agreement, but he tugged her hips forward and slid himself along her. Her fingernails dug into his shoulders as he pushed inside, slowly sinking himself deep.

"Oh, God. Eric. We can't." But her thighs were already shaking as her heart thundered with hot danger.

He pumped slowly in and out, then in and out once more before glancing over his shoulder. "I guess you're right."

"Oh," she sighed, nearly heartbroken at his agreement. "Okay," she whispered. "But just...just a few more seconds?"

"Seconds, huh?"

"Please," she begged, loving the taste of it on her tongue. He surged deep, and she moaned.

Eric held himself very still for a moment, his breathing finally racing to catch up to hers. He looked over his shoulder one more time and cursed. "I blame you for this," he growled.

"Me?"

"I can't stop thinking about you. About this. Us."

She laughed, but when he shifted, her laugh broke into a sigh. "Please," she begged again, opening her thighs wider to bring him just a little deeper. "You're in control," she whispered. "It's all your fault."

"You're right. Put your arms around my neck."

She did as he asked, shocked when he slid his hands under her ass and lifted her. "Eric!"

He turned and took a few steps toward the door, then pressed her to the wall right next to it. "No one can see us now," he said. She put one foot to the floor, but Eric curved his arm under her left knee to open her wide, and he began to drive himself into her.

"Oh, God," she breathed, reaching toward a filing cabinet to brace herself. His body ground hard against hers, the position pushing her pelvis into him. She could hear people in the kitchen talking, laughing, shouting for orders. They were right there, just a few feet away. Someone could open the door at any minute.

"Eric," she whispered as he filled her, his thick shaft stretching her body, forcing his way in. Her fingers twisted in his hair. "Oh, God, Eric. I'm…"

"Shh," he warned, but that only made it worse, the reminder that if she screamed, someone would hear. When she moaned again, Eric curved his free hand over her mouth and held her head tight to the wall as he took her harder. Harder.

It was too much. All her pleasure gathered into a center of hot weight that pulled all her nerves tight. Twisting them until…Beth screamed against his hold as her body spasmed around him. Eric's fingers pressed hard against her mouth. He kept up his rhythm for just a few more strokes before he stiffened and quietly moaned against her neck.

Beth was shaking, but it wasn't just her legs or arms or hands. Her heart was shaking, too. They couldn't keep going like this. They couldn't keep getting more serious, more intense. It was too much. Too close to…

"I love you, Beth," he panted against her neck.

Her eyes popped open. She clutched his hair tighter in her hand as his fingers slid off her mouth.

"I love you," he said again as her heart shook harder. "You, your body, your secrets, your fears. And I love who I am with you."

He let her leg slide slowly down, but Beth wasn't sure she could support herself. She wasn't sure. She wasn't…

He kissed her, soft and sweet, and her heart shook so hard she thought it might fly away. His thumb brushed a tear from her cheek, but he didn't tell her not to cry. He didn't ask anything from her at all, he just pressed his lips to the next cool tear that slid down.

"I won't let you down," he said.

"Don't say that." Her voice was just a rough ghost of a whisper. "You can make mistakes. You don't owe me perfection."

"No," he murmured. "But you deserve it."

She shook her head and tugged him back to her mouth so she could kiss him. "I love you," she said, amazed at the way her heart slowed at her own words. "Just the way you are. And just the way I am, too."

He smiled against her mouth, kissing her one more time before he stepped back to try to fix his appearance. Beth found her underwear on the floor and pulled them on, but the wrinkled state of her skirt worried her.

"Do I look like I just had sex?" she asked, patting down her hair.

"Yes," Eric answered.

"Eric," she scolded, still searching for the perfect curse when he reached to run his fingers through her tangled strands. He smoothed a hand over her crown, then pulled her shirt straight before tugging her skirt an inch to the right.

His eyes glowed with a warm smile. "There. Perfect."

She started to fix his hair, then stopped herself. It looked good mussed. He looked sexy. And his brother would probably tease him about it, and they'd all laugh, and she loved to see Eric happy.

"Are you ready to do this?" he asked.

She was. She finally was.

* * * * *

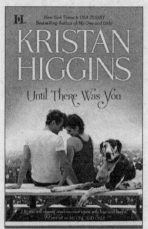

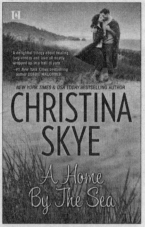

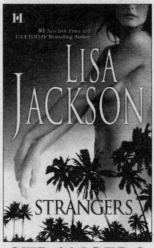

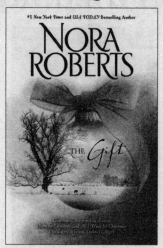

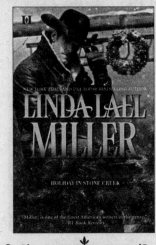

REQUEST YOUR FREE BOOKS!

2 FREE NOVELS
FROM THE ROMANCE COLLECTION
PLUS 2 FREE GIFTS!

YES! Please send me 2 FREE novels from the Romance Collection and my 2 FREE gifts (gifts are worth about $10). After receiving them, if I don't wish to receive any more books, I can return the shipping statement marked "cancel." If I don't cancel, I will receive 4 brand-new novels every month and be billed just $5.99 per book in the U.S. or $6.49 per book in Canada. That's a saving of at least 25% off the cover price. It's quite a bargain! Shipping and handling is just 50¢ per book in the U.S. and 75¢ per book in Canada.* I understand that accepting the 2 free books and gifts places me under no obligation to buy anything. I can always return a shipment and cancel at any time. Even if I never buy another book, the two free books and gifts are mine to keep forever.

194/394 MDN FELQ

Name	(PLEASE PRINT)
Address	Apt. #
City	State/Prov.	Zip/Postal Code

Signature (if under 18, a parent or guardian must sign)

Mail to the **Reader Service:**
IN U.S.A.: P.O. Box 1867, Buffalo, NY 14240-1867
IN CANADA: P.O. Box 609, Fort Erie, Ontario L2A 5X3

**Not valid for current subscribers to the Romance Collection
or the Romance/Suspense Collection.**

**Want to try two free books from another line?
Call 1-800-873-8635 or visit www.ReaderService.com.**

* Terms and prices subject to change without notice. Prices do not include applicable taxes. Sales tax applicable in N.Y. Canadian residents will be charged applicable taxes. Offer not valid in Quebec. This offer is limited to one order per household. All orders subject to credit approval. Credit or debit balances in a customer's account(s) may be offset by any other outstanding balance owed by or to the customer. Please allow 4 to 6 weeks for delivery. Offer available while quantities last.

Your Privacy—The Reader Service is committed to protecting your privacy. Our Privacy Policy is available online at www.ReaderService.com or upon request from the Reader Service.

We make a portion of our mailing list available to reputable third parties that offer products we believe may interest you. If you prefer that we not exchange your name with third parties, or if you wish to clarify or modify your communication preferences, please visit us at www.ReaderService.com/consumerschoice or write to us at Reader Service Preference Service, P.O. Box 9062, Buffalo, NY 14269. Include your complete name and address.

ROM11

PS
KO

VICTORIA DAHL

77602 BAD BOYS DO	___ $7.99 U.S.	___ $9.99 CAN.
77595 GOOD GIRLS DON'T	___ $7.99 U.S.	___ $9.99 CAN.
77462 CRAZY FOR LOVE	___ $7.99 U.S.	___ $9.99 CAN.
77434 LEAD ME ON	___ $7.99 U.S.	___ $9.99 CAN.
77390 START ME UP	___ $7.99 U.S.	___ $8.99 CAN.
77356 TALK ME DOWN	___ $6.99 U.S.	___ $6.99 CAN.

(limited quantities available)

TOTAL AMOUNT	$ _____
POSTAGE & HANDLING	$ _____
($1.00 FOR 1 BOOK, 50¢ for each additional)	
APPLICABLE TAXES*	$ _____
TOTAL PAYABLE	$ _____

(check or money order—please do not send cash)

To order, complete this form and send it, along with a check or money order for the total above, payable to HQN Books, to: **In the U.S.:** 3010 Walden Avenue, P.O. Box 9077, Buffalo, NY 14269-9077; **In Canada:** P.O. Box 636, Fort Erie, Ontario, L2A 5X3.

Name: _____
Address: _____ City: _____
State/Prov.: _____ Zip/Postal Code: _____
Account Number (if applicable): _____

075 CSAS

*New York residents remit applicable sales taxes.
*Canadian residents remit applicable GST and provincial taxes.

HQN | **HARLEQUIN®**
www.Harlequin.com

PHVD1111BL